SYNTHETIC STORM
EVOLUTION UNLEASHED

BOOK 7 IN THE ETHAN REEVE'S WEREWOLF DETECTIVE SERIES

RAE STONEHOUSE

LIVE FOR EXCELLENCE PRODUCTIONS

PROLOGUE: ECHOES OF TOMORROW

2:17 AM - Daybridge Corporate Research District

Breach Alert: Lab 7, Quantum Enhancement Division

Sarah Chen's fingers flew across holographic displays as emergency protocols flashed red across the laboratory walls. "They're breaking through the quantum barriers," she warned, watching reality itself fracture around the containment field. "The artifacts are destabilizing."

Fifteen ancient relics, each humming with supernatural resonance, pulsed with increasing power. They had been inert museum pieces until three months ago, when corporate scientists discovered their quantum enhancement potential. Now they threatened to tear reality apart.

"Security teams are eight minutes out," Alice Chen's voice came through the quantum-encrypted channel. Unlike her older sister Sarah, she had chosen government service over corporate research. "Just hold the containment field."

Sarah watched probability waves ripple through supposedly solid matter. The artifacts were reaching out, calling to something buried deep in human genetic code. "This isn't just enhancement anymore, Alice. The artifacts... they're awakening something. Something that's been dormant in us."

Through the observation window, she could see the test subjects changing. Corporate executives who had volunteered for "controlled enhancement" were manifesting abilities that defied traditional physics. One woman phased through quantum states while a man's consciousness expanded across multiple probability streams.

"Ma'am," Lieutenant Foster's tactical team reached the outer security perimeter. "We're detecting massive supernatural energy signatures. Traditional containment protocols aren't designed for this."

"Because it's not just supernatural," Sarah realized, watching ancient symbols materialize in the quantum foam. "The artifacts aren't creating something new - they're remembering something old. A time when reality was more... flexible."

The building's enhancement dampeners whined under increasing strain. In secure labs across the city, other artifacts began resonating in response. Centuries of accumulated supernatural energy sought release through quantum channels that corporate science had inadvertently reopened.

"Sarah, get out of there," Alice's voice carried rare urgency. "The probability models are cascading. This isn't just a containment breach - it's a catalyst event."

But Sarah couldn't move, transfixed by the patterns emerging in the quantum field. Ancient magic merging with modern science. Supernatural potential awakening through enhancement protocols. Reality itself remembering older, deeper patterns.

"It was always going to happen," she whispered, watching probability waves expand beyond containment. "The synthetic formula, the corporate enhancement programs - they just accelerated what was already coming. We're remembering what we used to be."

The artifacts pulsed in perfect resonance as reality's quantum framework began to shift. In that moment, Sarah understood - this wasn't an ending, but a beginning. Humanity's long-dormant supernatural potential was awakening, and nothing would ever be the same.

"Sarah!" Alice's voice crackled through failing quantum channels. "The containment field is..."

The artifacts released their accumulated power in a quantum cascade that rippled through every probability stream. As reality fractured around her, Sarah smiled. The bridge between what was and what could be had finally opened.

The Daybridge Evolution had begun.

COPYRIGHT

Published by Live For Excellence Productions

ISBN:

Ebook: 978-1-998591-58-9

Paperback: 978-1-998591-59-6

Audiobook: 978-1-998591-60-2

∼

CHAPTER ONE

RETURN TO NORMAL

ALICE CHEN STARED at the churning storm above Daybridge, its unnatural triple helix pattern defying meteorological explanation. Three months after Kane Industries' 'incident,' and nothing was returning to normal.

Her quantum scanner hummed, recording energy signatures that shouldn't exist. Enhanced humans moved through the city streets below, their hybrid abilities creating ripples in reality itself. A teenager phased through a wall while maintaining werewolf strength. A business executive manipulated blood magic without being a vampire.

"Beautiful, isn't it?" Dr. Nash's voice carried across the rooftop observation deck. The Kane Industries lead researcher approached with calculated steps; her lab coat pristine despite the wind. "Reality adapting to new possibilities."

Alice pocketed her scanner. "You mean reality breaking down. Pure supernatural beings are losing control of their powers. Territory boundaries fail. Vampire sanctums collapse. Even the Fae courts report reality distortions in their realm."

"Evolution is rarely comfortable," Nash smiled, watching an enhanced human demonstrate impossible abilities below. "But tell me, Ms. Chen – did you ever wonder why supernatural species remained separate? Why vampire abilities never merged with werewolf genetics? Why Fae magic remained distinct?"

The storm's energy intensified, making nearby instruments spark and fail. Alice felt reality thin around them as another enhanced human passed nearby, their hybrid powers creating localized physics violations.

"My father's research," Alice said. "The quantum-supernatural interface theory. You found his hidden files."

"James was brilliant," Nash nodded. "He understood something fundamental about supernatural abilities. They're not magical – they're quantum mechanical. The barriers between species weren't natural. They were imposed."

Below, enhanced humans gathered in increasing numbers. Each one demonstrated power combinations that violated every known supernatural law. Werewolf healing merged with vampire speed. Fae reality manipulation enhanced by blood magic.

"You're breaking down the barriers," Alice realized. "Not just enhancing humans – you're removing the limitations between supernatural abilities."

Nash's smile widened as reality rippled around them. "Your father discovered the truth. Supernatural beings didn't evolve separately. They were separated. Something, long ago, imposed artificial limitations on what was naturally possible."

The storm's triple helix pattern pulsed with increasing intensity. Alice's backup scanner showed quantum fluctuations that matched her father's theoretical models perfectly. Not theoretical, she realized. Remembered.

"Pure supernatural beings are becoming unstable," Alice argued. "Their powers fluctuate. Reality itself warps around them."

"Because reality remembers," Nash explained. "It remembers when vampire blood magic could merge with werewolf genetics. When Fae abilities could enhance supernatural healing. The barriers between species were never natural – they were a prison."

Enhanced humans demonstrated their hybrid abilities below, each impossible combination creating cascading reality effects. The storm responded to their presence, its pattern growing more complex.

"Your father's last message," Nash continued. "Reality remembers what was possible." He wasn't theorizing – he was rediscovering something that had been locked away. Something that existed before the barriers were created."

Alice watched as reality bent around another enhanced human. Their quantum signature showed power combinations that shouldn't be stable yet somehow were. As if reality itself was adapting, remembering how to accommodate possibilities that had been forbidden.

"It's too late to stop it," Nash said softly. "The barriers are breaking down. Pure supernatural beings will evolve or become obsolete. Reality itself is changing, remembering what it used to allow."

The storm's energy reached even their shielded observation deck. Alice's instruments recorded quantum signatures that matched her father's final calculations. The truth he had discovered, the secret that had led to his disappearance, was finally becoming clear.

Supernatural abilities weren't separate forces to be controlled. They were expressions of the same quantum framework, artificially divided long ago. And now, thanks to Nash's work, reality itself was remembering how to be more flexible.

As enhanced humans gathered below, their hybrid powers creating ripples in the fabric of existence, Alice understood what her father had tried to warn them about. This wasn't just about creating enhanced humans or breaking supernatural laws.

This was about reality itself waking up from a very long sleep. And it remembered being far more interesting than anyone had imagined possible.

BREAKING NEWS TICKER:

GLOBAL NEWS NETWORK FEED - LIVE UPDATES

FINANCIAL MARKETS

NYSE Halts Trading After Enhanced Traders Display Precognitive Abilities

- Multiple traders reported seeing "probability streams" of market movements
- SEC launching emergency investigation into "supernatural insider trading"
- Global markets in turmoil as enhanced analysts predict shifts before they occur

CORPORATE NEWS

KANE INDUSTRIES STOCK SURGES 500%

- Enhanced employees reported in multiple global offices
- Competing corporations scrambling to develop similar programs
- Tech sector in upheaval as enhanced programmers rewrite reality protocols

INTERNATIONAL DEVELOPMENTS

BEIJING: Chinese State Council Announces "Controlled Enhancement Initiative"

- Government-supervised enhancement programs launching in major cities
- Ancient dragon clans appointed as program supervisors

- Hong Kong markets chaos as enhanced traders clash with traditional supernatural entities

EUROPEAN UNION

BRUSSELS: EU Parliament Declares Enhancement Emergency

- Enhanced human rights legislation fast-tracked
- Traditional vampire houses threatening withdrawal from supernatural accords
- London financial district under supernatural quarantine after mass enhancement event

TECHNOLOGY SECTOR

TOKYO: Silicon Valley-Yokai Partnership Announces Breakthrough

- Tech giants merging with traditional supernatural entities
- Enhanced AI developers creating quantum-aware systems
- Digital-supernatural hybrid networks emerging globally

ENVIRONMENTAL IMPACT

Enhanced Activity Affecting Weather Patterns

- Meteorologists report probability storms in major cities
- Environmental agencies tracking supernatural ecosystem changes
- Climate models adapting to include enhancement variables

LOCAL ALERTS

- Enhanced traffic controllers causing highway probability shifts
- Public transportation adapting to quantum tunnel phenomena
- Emergency services overwhelmed with enhancement incidents
- Reality stabilization centers opening in major cities

MARKET DATA

Kane Industries: +500%

Quantum Tech: +300%

Supernatural Index: +250%

Traditional Magic: -150%

Vampire Holdings: -200%

WEATHER

Probability of rain: Currently existing in multiple quantum states

Please carry both umbrella and sunscreen until reality stabilizes

TRAFFIC

Multiple probability lanes open on major highways

Quantum-aware GPS systems recommended for enhanced zones

Alice Chen muted the news feed but couldn't ignore the quantum ripples affecting her own office. Her coffee existed in three different temperature states simultaneously, a side effect of the building's enhanced maintenance staff.

"Four hundred and seventy-two enhancement incidents reported in the last hour alone," Dana reported, dropping a quantum-secured tablet on Alice's desk. "And those are just the ones people are willing to admit to."

"Pattern analysis?" Alice asked, trying to focus on just one version of reality.

"Moira from Data Analytics sent this up - before she apparently turned her entire department into a probability cloud." Dana pulled up a holographic display showing enhancement spread patterns. "It's not just random anymore. The Quantum Framework is adapting to existing corporate and social networks. Traditional supernatural power structures are collapsing."

Through her office window, Alice watched enhanced employees manipulating quantum probabilities in the parking lot, their cars existing in multiple parking spaces simultaneously. A group of junior executives had accidentally created a temporary time loop in the coffee shop across the street.

"Dr. Nash needs to see this," she said, gathering her quantum-stabilized research materials. "The enhancement process isn't just changing individuals anymore. It's rewriting the basic rules of reality itself."

~

CHAPTER TWO

IMPOSSIBLE ABILITIES

ALICE CHEN CROUCHED behind the dumpster, watching the enhanced human move through Kane Industries' security perimeter. The woman – barely twenty, according to stolen files – phased through solid walls while maintaining a werewolf's enhanced senses. An impossible combination that defied everything Alice knew about supernatural genetics.

Her scanner hummed, recording quantum fluctuations that shouldn't exist. The enhanced human's presence created ripples in reality itself, distorting the natural laws that kept supernatural species separate.

"Getting some interesting readings?" Sarah Chen materialized beside her, causing Alice's instruments to spark and fail. Her sister's enhanced form flickered between states of existence, a living testament to Kane Industries' experiments.

Alice pocketed the useless scanner. "Three months ago, you were human. Now you can phase through reality, use blood magic, and tap into Fae energy. Want to explain how that's possible?"

Sarah's smile held secrets. "You've seen Dr. Nash's research. Supernatural abilities aren't magical – they're quantum mechanical. The barriers between species were never natural. They were imposed."

Above them, the strange storm pattern intensified. Triple helix lightning illuminated Sarah's shifting form as she demonstrated her hybrid abilities. Vampire speed merged with werewolf strength. Fae magic enhanced by blood rituals that shouldn't work for a former human.

"Nash isn't just breaking supernatural laws," Sarah explained. "She's proving they were artificial to begin with. Reality itself is more fluid than anyone imagined."

Another enhanced human emerged from Kane Industries, this one combining Fae glamour with vampire blood manipulation. Reality distorted around them, creating localized zones where normal physics failed.

Alice's backup scanner recorded impossible energy signatures. "These combinations shouldn't be stable. Supernatural genetics aren't compatible. The quantum interference alone should—"

"Should tear reality apart?" Sarah finished. "That's what everyone thought. But Nash discovered something in Dr. Winters' original research. Something about how supernatural abilities actually work at the quantum level."

The mention of their father's work made Alice pause. James Chen had vanished three years ago, his quantum-supernatural research declared theoretical and dangerous. Now Kane Industries was achieving what he'd only hypothesized.

"Dad knew," Alice realized. "The quantum bridges between supernatural genetics. He wasn't theorizing – he was remembering something that used to be possible."

Sarah nodded as reality rippled around them. "Nash found his hidden files. The barriers between species aren't evolution – they're imprisonment. Something, long ago, separated supernatural beings into distinct species. Limited their natural ability to combine powers."

The enhanced humans gathered near the facility's quantum research lab, their hybrid abilities creating cascading reality effects. Alice's scanner showed power combinations that violated every known supernatural law.

"Nash isn't enhancing humans," Sarah continued. "She's removing artificial limitations. Restoring possibilities that were locked away. The storm above Daybridge? It's reality itself responding to the change."

A security alarm blared as more enhanced humans emerged. Each one demonstrated impossible abilities – werewolf healing merged with Fae reality manipulation; vampire blood magic enhanced by supernatural strength.

"How many?" Alice asked, watching reality bend around the gathering hybrids.

"More every day. The quantum-supernatural interface works perfectly. Pure supernatural beings are starting to experience power fluctuations as the old barriers break down."

The storm's triple helix pattern pulsed with increasing intensity. Alice's scanner showed reality itself growing thin around the enhanced humans, as if natural law was becoming more suggestion than rule.

"Dad's last message," Alice remembered. "'Reality remembers what was possible.' I never understood what he meant until now."

Sarah's form stabilized momentarily. "Nash's work isn't just about creating enhanced humans. It's about understanding why supernatural abilities were separated to begin with. What existed before the barriers. What reality itself remembers is possible."

Above them, the storm responded to each new demonstration of hybrid powers. Reality rippled and bent, adapting to possibilities that had been locked away for millennia.

"It's too late to stop it," Sarah said softly. "The barriers are breaking down. Pure supernatural beings will have to adapt or become obsolete. Reality itself is changing, remembering what it used to allow."

Alice watched as another enhanced human phased through solid matter while manipulating blood magic. Her scanner recorded quantum signatures that matched their father's theoretical models perfectly. Not theoretical, she realized. Remembered.

Whatever Nash had discovered in James Chen's' research, whatever truth lay behind the artificial barriers between supernatural species, one thing was becoming clear: reality itself was waking up from a very long sleep. And it remembered being far more flexible than anyone had imagined possible.

CHAPTER THREE
CORPORATE CONSIDERATIONS

Kane Industries Internal **Memo - Classified**

Priority Level: ALPHA

Distribution: Executive Board Only

Timestamp: 22:45 EST

Victoria Kane's quantum-enhanced vision traced the classified report floating in her private office. Enhancement rates surged across global operations: Shanghai showing a 47% activation spike, London climbing to 35%, Dubai accelerating to 29%. New data streams from Tokyo, Moscow, and São Paulo painted an undeniable pattern of supernatural awakening spreading through corporate networks.

The quantum-shielded boardroom thrummed with dampening fields as twelve executives gathered around the probability-stabilized table. Their forms occasionally flickered between quantum states – a visible reminder of their own transformations. Victoria studied the holographic data streams, her enhanced perception simultaneously processing every possible outcome.

"Ladies and gentlemen," she began, her voice resonating across multiple probability frequencies, "we're facing an unprecedented situation. Moira, share your analysis."

Moira Rodgers rose, her enhanced abilities transforming the boardroom's display into an intricate web of corporate-supernatural interactions. "The quantum framework isn't just affecting our employees – it's integrating with our entire global network. Every transaction, decision, and market movement creates new enhancement vectors."

The display revealed Shanghai's dragon clans merging with tech divisions as ancient chi networks adapted to quantum frameworks. London's financial district experienced reality fluctuations as Fae courts established corporate treaties. In Dubai, djinn energy powered enhancement processes while desert ley lines connected to corporate networks.

Chief Financial Officer Abe Doubleday, calculating quantum probabilities instantaneously through his enhancement, interrupted. "The profit potential is astronomical, but so are the risks. We're witnessing complete displacement of traditional supernatural power structures."

"The vampires threaten investment withdrawal," Liz from Supernatural Relations added, her form shifting between quantum states. "Werewolf unions demand enhancement protection clauses-"

"The Fae courts are irrelevant," Victoria cut in. "Show them the projection, Moira."

The holographic display shifted to reveal future probability streams. Current phase showed spontaneous enhancement spreading amid traditional supernatural resistance and market disruptions. The three-to-six-month projection displayed controlled enhancement programs and corporate-supernatural mergers. The six-to-twelve-month outlook predicted full integration and global quantum network establishment.

Risk Assessment Director James Porter's enhanced probability sense flared as he reported competitor status. GlobalTech Industries, Supernatural Solutions Inc, Quantum Dynamics Corp, and Ancient Magic LLC all showed increasing activation rates, though none matched Kane Industries' integration stability.

Victoria stood, her enhanced presence filling the room with quantum potential. "We make our move now. Authorization for full enhancement integration across all global operations. Moira, establish quantum framework protocols with Dr. Nash. Abe, prepare supernatural markets. Dana, negotiate with adaptable traditional powers."

She paused, watching probability streams shift around her decision. "The world is changing. Kane Industries will either lead that change or be consumed by it."

Outside, the night sky above Kane Industries Tower rippled with probability storms as reality adjusted to their decisions. Victoria's enhanced perception revealed one final crucial detail from Dr. Nash's latest report – whatever started this change was still evolving.

The memo and meeting marked Kane Industries' full commitment to the new supernatural-corporate paradigm. As executives accessed their enhanced abilities to process multiple futures, reality itself pulsed with approval in the building's lower levels, beginning another subtle shift in the fabric of existence.

CHAPTER FOUR

CORPORATE SECRETS

I

Iron Heights Correctional **Facility**

Supernatural Containment Wing - Sublevel 5

2:15 AM

Dr. Nash stood at the window of her top-floor Kane Industries office, watching the strange storm gather above Daybridge. The triple helix pattern in the clouds matched her quantum predictions perfectly. Phase one was proceeding exactly as planned.

Behind her, screens displayed the latest test results from Lab 7. Enhanced humans demonstrated increasingly stable hybrid powers – werewolf strength combined with vampire speed, Fae magic merged with supernatural healing. But it was the quantum signatures that truly mattered. Each successful combination created tiny reality distortions, weakening the barriers between species.

Sarah Chen entered without knocking, her enhanced form causing nearby instruments to spark. "Security breach in Lab 4. Someone accessed Dr. Winters' original research files."

Nash smiled, not turning from the window. "Your sister, I assume? Alice always was too clever for her own good."

The storm's energy intensified, making Sarah's form flicker between states of existence. Three months of enhancement procedures had transformed her into something unprecedented – a being capable of channeling multiple supernatural energies simultaneously.

"The underground market is growing," Sarah reported. "More pure supernatural beings experiencing power fluctuations. They're desperate for answers."

"Let them come," Nash replied. "Each failure of pure supernatural power proves my theory. The barriers between species were never natural. They were imposed. Artificial limitations meant to prevent exactly what we're achieving."

Alarms flashed as reality distortions spread from Lab 7. Another enhanced human had achieved stable hybrid status, their quantum signature resonating with the storm above. Nash's instruments recorded every fluctuation, every breach in reality's normal laws.

Sarah moved to the quantum monitoring station, her presence causing temporary reality warps. "Alice accessed the files on quantum-supernatural interface theory. She'll figure it out soon."

"Good." Nash finally turned from the window. "We need her to understand. The quantum nature of supernatural power isn't just a discovery – it's the key to everything. Reality itself is mutable, if you know how to manipulate the underlying quantum framework."

The storm's pattern grew more complex as Nash activated her primary research systems. Quantum calculations merged with supernatural energy readings, revealing patterns that shouldn't exist. Reality itself seemed to bend around certain mathematical constants.

"Dr. Winters saw it too, didn't she?" Sarah asked. "Before she disappeared. The quantum bridges between supernatural genetics weren't theoretical. They were remembered."

Nash nodded, studying the storm's evolving pattern. "Supernatural beings didn't evolve separately. They diverged. The species barriers were created to prevent power combinations. To maintain reality's stability. But stability isn't the same as truth."

Security alerts indicated more breaches across Kane Industries facilities. Werewolf packs testing boundaries. Vampire elders seeking answers. Fae nobles attempting to understand why their ancient magic was failing.

"Phase two is ready," Sarah confirmed. "Enhanced human numbers are reaching critical mass. Reality distortions are self-sustaining. The old limitations are breaking down exactly as predicted."

Nash's instruments recorded increasing quantum fluctuations across Daybridge. Pure supernatural beings struggled to maintain their forms while enhanced humans grew stronger. Evolution was accelerating beyond even her calculations.

"Your sister will try to stop us," Nash mused. "The supernatural councils will resist. They'll see this as an attack on their power structures."

"They don't understand," Sarah's form stabilized momentarily. "This isn't about power. It's about truth. About remembering what was possible before the barriers were created."

The storm's triple helix pattern pulsed with increasing intensity. Nash's quantum calculations showed reality itself responding to the changes, adapting to possibilities that had been locked away for millennia.

"Winters called it 'remembered potential,'" Nash explained. "Supernatural powers aren't separate forces. They're expressions of the same quantum framework. We didn't create hybrid abilities – we removed the blocks preventing natural power combinations."

Security feeds showed more enhanced humans gathering near Lab 7. Their hybrid powers created cascading reality effects that matched Nash's theoretical models perfectly. The barriers between species weren't just failing – they were being remembered as the artificial constructs they always were.

"Phase three?" Sarah asked, watching reality ripple around the enhanced humans.

Nash smiled as her instruments recorded the next quantum shift beginning. "Reality isn't fixed, Sarah. It's mutable. Fluid. What we think of as natural law is just the current configuration. And configurations can be changed."

The storm above Daybridge intensified, its pattern now visible even through the quantum shielding. Nash watched as reality itself seemed to shiver, remembering possibilities that had been locked away since the first supernatural beings were confined to their separate species.

What came next would rewrite everything they thought they knew about reality itself. And somewhere in Kane Industries' labs, Dr. Winters' final research notes held the key to understanding why these changes felt less like evolution and more like remembering.

CHAPTER FIVE

PATTERNS AND PORTENTS

ALICE PAUSED outside Ethan's office, her enhanced senses picking up the subtle shift in his quantum signature. Full moon was three days away, and his control always got a bit shakier during these periods. She entered without knocking - six years of partnership and two years of navigating their post-Daybridge relationship had eliminated such formalities.

The air shimmered with temporal distortions as she found him surrounded by crime scene photos, his coffee long cold. His eyes had that amber tinge that preceded a shift, but his breathing exercises were keeping him centered.

"You should have called earlier," she said softly, settling into her usual spot on the floor. The space was already cleared - he'd arranged the files in her preferred pattern, just as she'd brought the specially formulated tea Dr. Nash had developed to help manage his transformations.

"Wanted to be sure first," Ethan managed, accepting the tea with a grateful look. The amber in his eyes faded slightly. "But this one... it feels like the Chandler case from two years ago. The same precision. And the quantum signatures..."

Just as Alice reached for his hand, the quantum stabilizers flickered. Purple smoke swirled through the room, coalescing into the form of Lila Darkmagic. Her dramatic entrance was somewhat undermined by the steaming coffee cup clutched in her perfectly manicured hands - a triple shot espresso laced with reality stabilization compounds.

"I was wondering how long it would take you two to notice," Lila said, her dark robes shimmering with both ancient runes and modern quantum interfaces. Digital displays flickered across the fabric, monitoring enhancement fields and reality anchor points.

Ethan's posture shifted, his werewolf instincts responding to the surge of magical energy. "Lila. We haven't even called you yet."

"Please." She perched on the edge of his desk, reality rippling slightly around her. "Three bodies with quantum distortion patterns, all found during lunar convergence points? This has my name written all over it." Her gaze settled on Alice. "And your enhanced perception must have picked up the magical residue by now."

Alice nodded, finally completing her reach for Ethan's hand. Since Daybridge, their connection allowed her to share her enhanced perception with him, while his werewolf senses helped ground her when the temporal echoes became overwhelming. "The temporal signatures are... wrong. Like they've been rewritten multiple times."

"Precisely." Lila's fingers traced one of the glowing symbols on her sleeve, and holographic data streams materialized around them. "Someone's trying to recreate an ancient enhancement ritual, but they're using corporate quantum technology to amplify it. Very messy. Very dangerous."

"The weather patterns caught my attention first," Ethan said, his thumb tracing circles on Alice's wrist - another grounding technique they'd developed. "Just like you taught me. But there's something else. Something in the lunar cycles."

"The weather patterns aren't natural," Lila confirmed, studying the crime scene photos. "They're part of the ritual matrix. And these positioning marks?" She pointed to details they'd overlooked. "Classic necromantic geometry but modified with quantum algorithms."

"Reminds me of Portland," Ethan said, shifting closer to Alice. His body heat had increased - another pre-moon symptom - but she leaned into it. They'd learned that proximity helped stabilize both their abilities.

"Similar principle, different application." Lila manipulated the holographic display, showing overlay patterns. "The cult was trying to punch through reality. This is more... subtle. Like they're trying to rewrite it from within."

"The corporate connection - it's not just about location, is it?" Alice asked, her free hand moving through the quantum distortions.

"Smart girl." Lila smiled approvingly. "Corporate structures create their own kind of reality - hierarchies, beliefs, shared purposes. Perfect framework for reality manipulation, if you know what you're doing." She glanced at Ethan. "Your wolf senses must be going crazy trying to track all the overlapping territories."

"Hence the meditation mat," he admitted, pulling it closer. "But there's something else. Something you're not telling us."

Lila's expression turned enigmatic. "Let's just say I've seen this pattern before. Long before Daybridge, before modern corporations even existed. And if I'm right about what's happening..." She stood, her robes settling into new configurations of arcane symbols and quantum interfaces. "Well, let's hope I'm not right."

"Lila," Alice said quietly, "we need to know what we're dealing with."

"What you're dealing with," Lila replied, "is someone trying to merge ancient magic with modern quantum enhancement on a corporate scale. And they're using murder to calibrate their calculations." She turned to the evidence wall. "I'll help you track them, but we need to move fast. The next lunar convergence is in three days."

"The full moon," Ethan said grimly, his eyes flickering amber again despite the tea.

"Exactly." Lila's fingers danced through the air, adding new layers of magical analysis to their evidence. "Hope you didn't have plans for the weekend. We've got rituals to disrupt, quantum patterns to unravel, and corporate conspiracies to expose."

Alice and Ethan exchanged glances, their unique bond humming with shared purpose. "Where do we start?" Alice asked, already reaching for the first box of files.

Lila's smile was both mysterious and predatory. "First, we need to visit an old friend of mine in the Kane Industries archives. I think you'll find their collection of ancient grimoires quite... illuminating." She paused, eyeing the meditation mat. "And Ethan, dear? You might want to bring that along. The archive's reality anchors can be... temperamental during lunar convergences."

The night ahead would test all their abilities and connections, but they'd face it together - detective, werewolf, and witch, each bringing their own unique perspective to the mystery unfolding before them.

CHAPTER SIX

THE DEVIL IN THE DETAILS

THE DRIVE back to the precinct was quiet, both of them processing what they'd learned. The sun was setting, painting the city in shades of orange and purple that reminded Alice of other cases, other drives, other breakthroughs. The quantum field was always more visible at twilight, enhancement signatures easier to track.

"We should check the victim's social media history," she said finally, breaking the comfortable silence. Her fingers traced patterns in the air, following probability threads only she could see. "If our suspect was studying the witness's posts..."

"They might have been studying the victim too," Ethan finished, already reaching for his phone to call the tech team. His enhancement picked up the echo of her excitement, the familiar rush of a case starting to break. "Looking for patterns, preferences, vulnerabilities."

"Just like the Riverside case last year," Alice added, her mind already racing ahead to the implications. The quantum connections were becoming clearer, forming a web of causality in her enhanced perception. "Remember how the killer used social media to..."

She stopped mid-sentence, sitting up straighter. Ethan recognized that sudden tension - it usually preceded one of her most brilliant insights. He could feel the spike in her emotional energy, the way her enhancement surged with revelation.

"What is it?" he asked, already looking for a place to pull over. Some of their best breaks in cases had happened during moments like this, parked on random street corners while Alice's mind made connections nobody else could see. The car's reality stabilizers hummed as her enhancement activated fully.

"The posts weren't just surveillance," she said, quantum patterns dancing around her hands as she gestured. "They were calibration. Each interaction, each response – they were measuring the victim's and witness's enhancement signatures. Learning their quantum frequencies."

Ethan pulled into an empty parking lot, turning to face her fully. His own enhancement let him feel the weight of her realization, the dark implications. "You think they're targeting enhanced individuals specifically?"

"Not just targeting," Alice's eyes tracked invisible patterns. "Hunting. These aren't random kills – they're studying how enhancement manifests, how it can be..." She paused, a chill running through her despite the warm evening. "How it can be harvested."

Their enhanced perceptions merged for a moment, years of partnership creating a temporary quantum link. They both saw it then – the larger pattern, the true nature of what they were hunting. This wasn't just a killer. This was something else entirely, something that understood enhancement in ways they were only beginning to grasp.

Ethan started the car, quantum energy rippling around his hands on the steering wheel. "We need to talk to Dr. Goddard."

"And warn the others," Alice added, already sending quantum-encrypted messages to their enhanced colleagues. "Whatever this is, it's not going to stop with these victims."

The city's evening traffic flowed around them, most people unaware of the quantum energies pulsing beneath everyday reality. But Alice and Ethan could see it now – the pattern of a predator moving through their enhanced world, leaving disturbed quantum wakes in its path.

The case had just become much bigger than a simple homicide. And somewhere in the city, someone was watching, learning, harvesting – and waiting.

～

CHAPTER SEVEN

QUIET MOMENTS

ALICE FOUND Ethan on the roof of the precinct; his familiar silhouette outlined against the city's quantum-distorted skyline. The protection wards hummed as she stepped through them, recognizing her enhanced signature. Up here, away from the dampeners, the full spectrum of enhancement signatures painted the air in waves of possibility.

"Brought your tea," she said, settling beside him on their usual spot. The concrete still held warmth from the day, though reality rippled strangely around them – a common occurrence since Daybridge. That case had torn holes in the fabric of their world, letting ancient magics seep through. Some nights, like tonight, you could still see quantum echoes of the breach in the sky.

"Remember the first time we came up here?" Ethan accepted the tea, his fingers brushing hers. The contact sent subtle waves through the quantum field, their enhancement signatures harmonizing like they always did now. "Right after that shapeshifter case?"

"When you were still pretending the wolf wasn't part of you?" Alice smiled, leaning into his warmth. She could feel the wolf's presence through their bond, a deep current of wild energy beneath his human facade. "And I was trying to hide my quantum sensitivity because I thought it would get me removed from field duty?"

The memory was clear – her growing awareness of quantum patterns, the fear of being seen as unstable, unreliable. She'd hidden her enhancement until that case forced her hand, when seeing the quantum distortions had saved both their lives.

"We were both so careful then." His arm slipped around her waist, their energies harmonizing naturally now. The rooftop wards shifted in response, adapting to their combined signature. "Keeping our distances, maintaining boundaries..."

"Professional detectives," Alice agreed. "Until Daybridge changed everything." She traced the scar on his forearm – the one he'd gotten protecting her during the reality breach. The tissue still held traces of quantum disruption, visible to her enhanced senses. "Sometimes I wonder if we would have ever..."

"We would have," Ethan said quietly. "Maybe not as quickly, but we were always heading here." His wolf stirred beneath the surface, a presence she'd learned to sense through their bond. The animal aspect of him had recognized her from the start, even before his human side admitted what was growing between them. "Though I never imagined we'd end up quantum-linked."

That had been unexpected – the way the Daybridge incident had fused their enhancement signatures, creating a connection deeper than either of them had thought possible. Now they could sense each other's emotions, share perceptions, even draw on each other's abilities in moments of crisis.

"Quantum-linked werewolf and enhanced detective." Alice watched reality shimmer around their joined hands, their combined energy creating patterns that reminded her of starlight on water. "Not exactly the partnership they teach about at the Academy."

"Better." He pressed a kiss to her temple, their combined energy making the rooftop wards flutter. Outside the wards, the city's quantum field responded to their resonance, creating ripples of possibility that spread outward like rings in a pond. "Even with all the complications."

And there were complications. The department's enhanced oversight board was still struggling to classify their partnership. Traditional protocols hadn't been designed for their level of connection. Some cases had to be reassigned due to concerns about their "compromised objectivity." But up here, watching enhancement signatures dance across the skyline, none of that seemed to matter.

Alice felt the wolf's contentment through their bond, matched by Ethan's human emotions – love, protectiveness, and a deep certainty that this was right. Her own enhancement responded, quantum patterns aligning with his in a display that would have fascinated the department's researchers if they could see it.

"The new case," she said finally, reluctant to break the moment but knowing they needed to discuss it. "The quantum harvesting... it's going to be dangerous."

"We're stronger together," Ethan reminded her, his enhancement signature wrapping protectively around hers. "Whatever's out there hunting enhanced individuals, they'll have to deal with both of us."

The wolf stirred again, ready to defend what it considered pack. Alice let her quantum sensitivity expand, scanning the city below for any threatening patterns. For now, though, there was just this – the warm night, their harmonized energies, and the quiet understanding that had grown between them since that first rooftop conversation.

Later, they would return to the case. But for now, they allowed themselves this moment of peace, watching their combined enhancement signatures paint impossible colors across the quantum-touched sky.

CHAPTER EIGHT

UNDERGROUND MARKET

DAYBRIDGE UNDERCITYABANDONED SUBWAY Level B3

11:45 PM

The abandoned subway tunnel hummed with supernatural energy as Marcus Kane navigated through crowds of desperate beings. Werewolves with partial transformations bartered with vampires suffering blood magic disruptions. Fae creatures, their glamours failing, sought answers from anyone who might understand what was happening to their powers.

Marcus passed a makeshift testing station where a former Kane Industries scientist examined a young werewolf. The wolf's partial transformation had stuck – fur and claws permanent yet somehow merged with vampire speed. The scientist's instruments sparked and failed as they tried to measure the impossible hybrid energy.

"Market's busier than usual," Sarah Chen materialized beside him, her presence distorting reality slightly. "More coming every night as their powers destabilize."

The underground market had sprung up three months ago, when the first enhanced humans appeared. Now it served as a gathering point

31

for supernatural beings experiencing power fluctuations. Black market Kane Industries tech traded hands alongside ancient supernatural artifacts.

A vampire elder Marcus recognized from the European courts huddled with a Fae noble, both examining a quantum measurement device stolen from Kane Labs. Their powers visibly warped around each other, creating small reality distortions that nobody seemed to notice anymore.

"Four more territory breaches last night," Sarah reported, leading him deeper into the market. "Werewolf pack boundaries don't hold. Vampire sanctums fail. Fae realms bleed into our reality."

They passed a group of enhanced humans demonstrating their hybrid abilities. One phased through solid matter while maintaining a werewolf's strength. Another combined vampire blood magic with Fae reality manipulation, creating localized time distortions.

At the market's heart, a makeshift lab had been established. Dr. Rivera, another Kane Industries deserter, worked frantically to understand the changes affecting supernatural beings. Her instruments measured quantum fluctuations alongside supernatural energy signatures.

"The barriers between species are quantum in nature," Rivera explained, showing them her latest findings. "When they fail, powers don't just combine – they evolve into something new. Something that shouldn't be possible."

A commotion near the tunnel's entrance drew their attention. A young vampire stumbled in, his form flickering between states of existence. Market guards rushed to contain the reality distortions spreading from him.

"Third one tonight," Sarah noted. "Pure supernatural beings are becoming unstable. As if reality itself is rejecting the old limitations."

Marcus watched as Dr. Rivera attempted to stabilize the vampire. Her instruments showed impossible readings – vampire blood magic interacting with quantum fields, creating cascading reality effects.

"Nash's work," Rivera muttered. "The quantum-supernatural interface wasn't meant to enhance humans. It was meant to break down the barriers between species. Between realities."

The storm above Daybridge pulsed, its energy reaching even this deep underground. The market's makeshift reality shields flickered as enhanced humans gathered, their hybrid powers resonating with the storm's pattern.

A werewolf alpha approached Marcus, her form shifting between human and wolf without conscious control. "Kane Industries promised answers," she growled. "Instead, they've broken something fundamental. Reality itself bleeds."

Sarah's presence caused nearby reality meters to spike. "Nash understood something we didn't. Supernatural powers aren't magical – they're quantum mechanical. And quantum mechanics allows for possibilities we never imagined."

The market grew more crowded as midnight approached. Supernatural beings sought answers, enhancement, or stability. Black market tech promised control over hybrid powers. Ancient artifacts offered temporary relief from reality distortions.

Marcus observed it all, noting how the old supernatural hierarchies meant nothing here. Power now came from successful enhancement, from stability amid chaos, from understanding the new rules of reality.

A Fae noble's glamour failed completely, revealing their true form as reality fluctuated. "The courts remember something like this," they whispered. "Long ago, before the barriers. Before reality settled."

The storm's triple helix pattern became visible through the tunnel's ceiling, reality growing thin. Enhanced humans moved with increasing confidence while pure supernatural beings struggled to maintain their forms.

Sarah Chen watched the chaos with knowing eyes. "Nash isn't destroying supernatural powers," she said. "She's removing artificial limitations. The question is: what existed before those limitations were put in place?"

As midnight struck, reality rippled through the market. The enhanced humans gathered, their hybrid powers creating cascading effects that bent space and time. The underground market had become more than a black market – it was a preview of what was coming.

The age of pure supernatural beings was ending. And in this makeshift market, beneath a reality-bending storm, the future was already taking shape. One where the boundaries between species, between possibilities, between realities themselves, no longer held meaning.

Marcus Kane left the market knowing one thing with certainty: Nash hadn't started this evolution. She had simply discovered something that had always been possible, if only someone was willing to break down the walls between what was and what could be.

CHAPTER NINE

SUBTLE CHANGES

MOIRA RODGERS STARED at her computer screen as numbers began floating off the display, transforming into three-dimensional data structures she could manipulate with her thoughts. The quarterly reports she'd been analyzing had become more than just data - she could see patterns in probability itself, corporate futures branching into quantum possibilities.

"Hey Moira, you okay?" Trevor from Marketing leaned against her cubicle wall, his usual confident demeanor showing cracks. "You're doing that thing with your eyes again."

She blinked, realizing her vision had shifted to quantum perception mode. The office around her was a maze of probability streams, each person trailing possible futures like cosmic contrails.

"I'm fine," she lied, then noticed how Trevor's hand trembled as he held his coffee cup. Quantum ripples disturbed the liquid's surface, matching his agitated emotional state. "Actually... have you been experiencing anything strange lately?"

Trevor glanced around before sliding into her cubicle. "You mean like seeing things that shouldn't be there? Lisa in Accounting swears her spreadsheets started predicting market changes before they happened. And James in IT..." he lowered his voice, "I saw him teleport between floors yesterday. He played it off as taking the stairs, but I know what I saw."

Moira pulled up the confidential enhancement reporting form on her screen, the text now swimming with quantum possibilities. From two floors below, she could sense other enhanced employees hiding similar abilities, their quantum signatures pulsing with familiar fear.

Across town, Alice stood in Ethan's office, staring at a wall of reports about unexplained incidents at various corporations. Her fingers traced patterns in the air that only she could see.

"Three more reports from Kane Industries this week," Ethan said, adding another file to their growing collection. "Employees experiencing... unusual perceptions. HR is writing them off as stress-related incidents."

"They're connected," Alice murmured, her unique abilities letting her see patterns others missed. "Not just at Kane. Look at these timing sequences." She pointed to a timeline they'd constructed. "The incidents are clustering. Like ripples spreading outward."

"There's a support group," whispered Diane from the next cubicle over, joining their hushed conversation. The plants on her desk had been growing at impossible rates lately, responding to her emotional states. "We meet in Conference Room C after hours. Dr. Nash from Research comes sometimes - she's studying what's happening to us."

Moira's enhanced perception picked up the quantum connections forming between affected employees - subtle networks of shared experience and mutual support. She could see similar patterns spreading through other floors, other buildings, creating a web of enhanced individuals trying to understand their changing reality.

"Yesterday in the break room," Trevor admitted, "I accidentally accessed everyone's probability streams at once. Saw every possible conversation happening simultaneously. Nearly drove me crazy until Lisa helped me focus on just one timeline."

"The headaches are the worst," Diane added, absentmindedly causing her succulent to bloom instantly. "Every decision point creates these quantum echoes..."

In the precinct's conference room, Alice and Ethan reviewed security footage from Kane Industries' lobby. Alice repeatedly paused on frames showing employees entering the building.

"Their movements are... different," she said, rewinding a sequence showing Trevor from Marketing. "Watch his coffee cup. The liquid's behavior defies physics."

"Like our witness last month," Ethan noted, pulling out an older file. "The one whose statement didn't match the physical evidence until..."

"Until we factored in impossible variables," Alice finished. She turned to their evidence board, where photos of various corporate employees were linked by red string. "We're not looking for traditional corporate espionage anymore, are we?"

Moira watched their quantum signatures interact, each enhanced individual unconsciously adapting to others nearby. The corporate environment itself seemed to be shifting, accepting and integrating these changes into its basic structure.

"We should go to the support group together," she suggested, her data visualization abilities showing her the most probable positive outcomes of this decision. "There's strength in numbers, and maybe together we can figure out what's really happening."

Through her enhanced perception, she could see similar conversations happening throughout Kane Industries - small groups of affected employees finding each other, forming support networks, learning to adapt. The Quantum Framework wasn't just changing individuals; it was transforming the entire corporate culture from within.

As if to emphasize this point, her computer screen suddenly projected a complete three-dimensional model of corporate probability streams, showing how their small group's decision to attend the support meeting would ripple through the company's future.

"Did... did everyone else see that?" Trevor asked, staring at the fading quantum projection.

"Welcome to the new normal," Moira replied, saving another enhancement incident report. "I think things are going to get a lot stranger before they start making sense again."

After Moira's meeting, Alice and Ethan sat in their unmarked car outside Kane Industries, watching employees leave for the day. Alice's hand trembled slightly as she tracked quantum signatures only she could perceive.

"Whatever's happening in there," she said quietly, "it's spreading. And it's bigger than anything we've investigated before."

"Think we should bring in the corporate crime division?" Ethan asked, already knowing her answer.

"Not yet. We need to understand what we're dealing with first." Alice watched as Moira and her colleagues exited the building, their quantum signatures leaving traces only she could detect. "These people aren't perpetrators, Ethan. They're witnesses to something transformative."

CHAPTER TEN

QUANTUM BONDS

ALICE STOOD in Nadia's archive, watching the quantum distortion patterns shift around her hands. The recent case work had intensified her sensitivity, making it harder to maintain normal reality perception. Behind her, Ethan's steady presence anchored her, his werewolf energy a familiar counterpoint to the archive's swirling temporal fields.

"The resonance patterns are getting stronger," Nadia said, her archive-enhanced perception tracking multiple data streams. "Your connection is affecting how you both process the quantum framework."

Lila materialized from a swirl of purple smoke, coffee cup in hand. "That's what happens when a quantum-enhanced detective bonds with a werewolf during a reality breach." She studied them with ancient eyes. "Fascinating, really. I've never seen anything quite like it."

"We're not here for a research project," Ethan growled softly, his hand finding Alice's shoulder. The contact sent ripples through the surrounding quantum field.

"No," Lila agreed, "but understanding what's happening between you two might help us solve our corporate enhancement problem." She gestured, and holographic displays materialized showing their intertwined energy patterns. "Your quantum signatures are harmonizing in ways that shouldn't be possible."

Alice watched their combined pattern flow across the displays. "It's been getting more intense since the last full moon. The shared perceptions, the energy transfers..."

"The dreams," Ethan added quietly. His thumb traced circles on her shoulder - their usual grounding technique, though lately it seemed to affect the surrounding reality more than calm their abilities.

Nadia's fingers danced through data streams. "The archive records show similar patterns in ancient bonding rituals. But those were deliberate workings, not spontaneous quantum evolution."

"Which is why our corporate friends are so interested," Lila mused. "They're trying to recreate artificially what happened to you two naturally during Daybridge." She paused, sipping her enhancement-laced coffee. "Of course, they're missing the key ingredient."

"Which is?" Alice asked, though part of her already knew.

"Choice," Lila said simply. "You two chose each other, before and after your enhancements. The Quantum Framework responded to that choice, creating something new." She gestured at the displays. "Something they can't replicate with all their technology and ancient magic."

Ethan's grip tightened slightly. "The victims in our case..."

"Were forced," Nadia confirmed, pulling up new data. "Their quantum signatures show trauma patterns. Whatever the corporations are trying to achieve, they're forcing incompatible energies together."

"It's killing them," Alice realized, her enhanced perception catching the pattern. "And destabilizing reality around their corporate centers."

"Hence the weather anomalies and temporal distortions we've been tracking," Lila nodded. "But you two..." She studied them thoughtfully. "Your natural bond might be the key to understanding how to stabilize artificial enhancements without destroying the subjects."

"We're not becoming lab specimens," Ethan said, a hint of wolf in his voice.

"No," Lila agreed, "but we do need to understand what's happening between you. Especially with the lunar convergence approaching." She glanced at Nadia. "Show them."

Nadia hesitated, then brought up a new display. "Your combined energy signature is affecting local reality stability. During the convergence, with the corporate enhancement experiments already straining the quantum framework..."

"We could make things worse," Alice finished. She turned to face Ethan, their proximity sending new ripples through the archive's reality anchors. "Or better, if we understand how to control it."

"I can help with that," Lila offered. "Traditional bonding rituals combined with modern quantum stabilization techniques. Help you channel the connection constructively." Her smile turned slightly wicked. "Unless you'd rather keep accidentally rewriting reality every time you touch."

Ethan's eyes flickered amber. "And this would help stop the corporations from killing more people?"

"Understanding your bond could help us develop safe enhancement protocols," Nadia said. "Save lives, stabilize reality..."

"While keeping your connection intact," Lila added. "And possibly making it stronger, if you're interested in that possibility."

Alice met Ethan's gaze, their unique connection humming between them. "Together?" she asked softly.

He nodded, pressing his forehead to hers. The gesture sent cascading waves of quantum energy through the archive, making the reality anchors sing. "Together."

"Well then," Lila said, her robes shifting with new patterns of ancient and modern power. "Shall we begin?"

CHAPTER ELEVEN

PACK POLITICS - BLOOD AND STORM

THUNDER CRACKED over Daybridge as Alpha Rachel Blackmane stalked through the Northern Pack's territory boundaries. The air crackled with supernatural tension – not just werewolf energy, but something else. Something wrong. Her pack members prowled behind her, fur bristling at the approaching vampire delegation.

Lord Viktor emerged from the shadows, his ancient presence distorting reality itself. Behind him, three vampire elders moved with predatory grace, their pale skin reflecting the storm's unnatural lightning. "The blood tells us things are changing, Alpha Blackmane," Viktor's voice carried centuries of authority. "Your wolves feel it too."

Rachel's enhanced senses detected the wrongness in the air. Werewolf and vampire energies were bleeding together at territory boundaries, creating impossible hybrid zones where neither species' powers worked quite right. The storm above pulsed in response to each supernatural surge, its pattern unlike anything she'd seen in three decades as Alpha.

"Four enhanced humans detected in neutral territory this morning," Rachel reported, watching Viktor's reaction carefully. "Two showing combined wolf-vampire traits. One with Fae abilities. And one..." she hesitated, "One showing all three."

Viktor's ancient composure cracked slightly. "Impossible. The species barriers are absolute. They've held since the first supernatural beings emerged."

But they both knew that wasn't true anymore. The evidence was in the storm above, in the shifting territory boundaries, in the way reality itself seemed to bend around certain individuals. Something was systematically dismantling the natural order.

A Fae noble materialized between them, her form shimmering with otherworldly power. Lady Seren of the Summer Court didn't bother with pleasantries. "The walls between courts are failing. Reality bleeds. And Kane Industries grows stronger."

Rachel shared a knowing look with Viktor. Kane Industries had been pushing boundaries for years, researching supernatural genetics, and developing new technologies. But lately, their experiments had become more aggressive. More dangerous.

"Dr. Nash's latest project," Viktor mused. "The quantum-supernatural interface. She claims it's meant to help us understand our powers better."

"She lies," Lady Seren's voice carried the weight of Fae truth-magic. "The quantum research is a key. The enhanced humans are not accidents. They are proof of concept."

Rachel's enhanced senses picked up approaching figures – more enhanced humans, their mixed supernatural energies distorting the air around them. Among them was someone familiar. Someone impossible.

Sarah Chen stepped into view, her form flickering between states of existence. Alice's sister, once purely human, now radiated power signatures from all three supernatural species. But there was something else, something quantum and wrong about her presence.

"The territories aren't just failing," Sarah's voice echoed strangely. "They were never real to begin with. Species barriers, supernatural limitations – all artificial constructs. Nash proved it. Reality itself is mutable."

The storm intensified; its triple helix pattern now clearly visible. Rachel felt her wolf form trying to emerge, but the power flow felt wrong. Around them, vampire elders struggled to maintain their forms while Fae magic sparked unpredictably.

"Kane Industries isn't causing this," Sarah continued, her form stabilizing. "They're just opening the door. What comes through... that's up to forces far older than any of us."

Lady Seren's power flared. "The Fae courts have seen this before. Reality inversions. Timeline corruptions. But never at this scale."

Viktor's ancient eyes tracked the storm's pattern. "Blood magic shows ripples in time itself. Enhanced humans aren't just breaking species barriers – they're breaking reality barriers."

Rachel watched Sarah carefully, noting how her presence seemed to distort the very air around her. "How many others like you are there?"

Sarah's smile was both familiar and alien. "More every day. Nash's work is accelerating. The storm is just the beginning. Soon, every supernatural being will face a choice – evolve or become obsolete."

The territory boundaries flickered as reality shuddered. Enhanced humans were appearing across Daybridge, each one a living proof that supernatural limitations could be broken. The ancient balance between species was crumbling.

As thunder cracked overhead, Rachel Blackmane faced the terrible truth: this wasn't just a supernatural crisis. It was the end of reality as they knew it. And somewhere in Kane Industries' labs, Dr. Nash was orchestrating every moment of it.

The storm's triple helix pattern

spelled out their future in lightning: adapt or perish. The age of pure supernatural beings was ending. What would replace it remained to be seen – if reality itself survived what Nash had set in motion.

Sarah Chen vanished through a reality distortion, leaving the supernatural leaders to face a world where their ancient laws meant nothing. Above them, the storm continued its transformation, and reality itself held its breath, waiting to see what would emerge from the chaos of evolution.

CHAPTER TWELVE

WHEN OLD MAGIC BREAKS

THE ANCIENT VAMPIRE lords gathered in their underground sanctum beneath Daybridge's financial district, while Fae nobles shimmered into existence around them. The storm's energy penetrated even here, making the reality-enforced walls flicker.

Lord Viktor's voice carried across the chamber. "Our containment efforts have failed. Three more vampire houses reported enhanced humans breaching their defenses. Pure blood magic no longer holds them."

Lady Seren's form shifted between summer and winter aspects as reality fluctuated. "The Winter Court lost contact with their north-eastern stronghold. When our scouts reached it, they found reality had... rearranged itself. The entire structure exists in multiple dimensions simultaneously."

The chamber erupted in chaos as younger vampires argued with elders. Lord Manley, barely three centuries old, stepped forward. "We've already lost House Blackthorn to this evolution. Their entire bloodline chose enhancement. They can walk in daylight now, merge with shadows, bend time itself."

"Abominations," spat Lord Viktor, but uncertainty tinged his voice.

Lady Seren's power flared, silencing the chamber. "You mistake this for a war you can win through resistance. The Fae courts remember. Reality shifts like this have happened before, long before your kind walked the earth. We do not stop such changes. We survive them."

Through the chamber's ceiling, the storm's triple helix pattern became visible, reality growing thin enough to see through solid rock. Several vampire elders instinctively stepped back as enhanced humans passed overhead, their hybrid powers leaving reality distortions in their wake.

"The Winter Court has already begun negotiations," a frost-covered Fae noble announced. "Enhanced humans seek our ancient knowledge. They offer power combinations we thought impossible."

Lord Viktor's composure cracked. "House Blackthorn breached our deepest sanctum yesterday. They moved through pure darkness as if it were daylight, commanded blood magic without the ancient rites. If they can do this..."

"Then your choice becomes survival or extinction," Lady Seren completed. "The Twilight Court discovered something interesting. These reality breaches Nash created? They follow patterns. Ancient patterns. She hasn't invented something new. She's rediscovered something that existed before reality settled into its current form."

The storm's energy intensified, making vampire and Fae powers fluctuate wildly. Through the reality distortions, they glimpsed other versions of their chamber. In one, enhanced vampires conducted blood rituals that bent space itself. In another, Fae nobles wove quantum enchantments that transcended traditional magic.

"House Constantin will adapt," a young vampire lord declared, others quickly joining his stance. "Better to evolve than fade into extinction."

Lord Viktor watched his power structure crumbling. Centuries of absolute authority meant nothing against the tide of evolution. "The old ways protected us," he whispered, but the words sounded hollow even to him.

"The old ways were never meant to be permanent," Lady Seren corrected. "Reality itself grows, changes, evolves. Nash simply found the catalyst. Now we all face the same choice: adapt to the new reality or be erased by it."

Above them, Sarah Chen passed through solid rock as if reality's laws were mere suggestions, the storm responding to her presence. Enhanced humans weren't just breaking supernatural barriers – they were rewriting the rules of existence itself.

The chamber divided along invisible lines – those who would embrace evolution versus those who would resist it. But as reality continued to fracture around them, as the storm's pattern grew more complex, both vampire and Fae leaders faced an uncomfortable truth: their ancient power structures were already obsolete.

The age of pure supernatural beings was ending. What emerged from this metamorphosis would depend not on their resistance, but on their ability to adapt to a reality that had finally remembered how to change.

CHAPTER THIRTEEN

ARCHIVE ECHOES

THE QUANTUM ANCHORS hummed as Alice passed through the archive's security field, her enhanced perception catching the subtle changes in Nadia's reality stabilizers. Since Daybridge, they'd all developed their own unique signatures – Alice's quantum enhancement, Ethan's werewolf energy, Lila's arcane frequencies, and Nadia's archive-attuned perception.

"Your temporal signature's unstable again," Nadia said without looking up from her holographic displays. "Full moon's affecting both of you more intensely this cycle."

"That obvious?" Alice settled into her usual spot, surrounded by floating data streams. "Ethan noticed it too. His wolf's been more reactive to the quantum fluctuations."

"Your signatures are becoming more synchronized." Nadia's fingers danced through the archive interface, pulling up their combined pattern analysis. "Remember when you first started working together? His werewolf energy would disrupt your enhancement field every time you got close."

Alice smiled, touching the quantum-scarred bracelet Ethan had given her last anniversary – spelled by Lila to help stabilize their shared resonance. "Now we can't maintain stable patterns unless we're connected. Lila says it's unprecedented."

"Lila says a lot of things," Nadia remarked dryly, but her expression was fond. "Though she was right about the bonding rituals helping control your joint abilities. The archive records show significant improvement in your reality anchor stability since you started her training program."

"When she's not being deliberately cryptic," Alice agreed. "But we wouldn't have made it through that first year without her guidance. Or your research."

Nadia's hands paused over the data streams. "Speaking of research..." She brought up a new display showing familiar energy patterns. "These corporate enhancement signatures you're tracking? They're trying to artificially recreate what happened between you and Ethan during Daybridge."

"That's impossible," Alice said, but her enhanced perception was already catching the similarities. "The Quantum Framework only responded to us because..."

"Because you were already connected," Nadia finished. "Partners in every sense, even before the enhancement. Your professional trust, your personal bond – it created a foundation the quantum energy could build on."

Alice watched their past case data flow across the screens. "Like that shifter case, right before Daybridge. When Ethan's wolf first started responding to my presence."

"And you could sense his transformations before they happened," Nadia nodded. "The archive records show your quantum sensitivity increasing in sync with his lunar cycles, months before the incident. Your connection was evolving naturally."

"Unlike these corporate test subjects," Alice realized, studying the new data. "They're forcing incompatible energies together, trying to shortcut the bonding process."

"With predictably disastrous results." Nadia expanded the display. "But that's not what really concerns me. Look at these temporal echoes."

Alice leaned forward, her enhanced perception catching the pattern. "They're similar to..."

"Your shared dreamspace," Nadia confirmed. "The quantum realm you and Ethan access during full moons. The corporations aren't just trying to recreate enhancement bonds – they're trying to breach the barriers between realities."

"Like Daybridge." Alice's hand went to her quantum scars, remembering. "But controlled, directed..."

"And potentially catastrophic." Nadia's archive-enhanced eyes showed complicated data patterns. "You need to tell Ethan. And probably Lila, though she likely already knows."

"She usually does," Alice agreed, standing. "Speaking of Ethan, he's probably finished that protection ritual by now. Want to join us for dinner? He's making that quantum-stabilized pasta you like."

"The one Lila spelled to maintain normal physics even during reality fluctuations?" Nadia smiled. "Count me in. Just let me finish updating these archive records."

As Alice waited, she watched their combined temporal signatures flow across the displays – detective, werewolf, witch, and archivist, each bringing their own unique perspective to the mystery. They'd grown from reluctant allies into something closer to family, bound together by shared experiences and supernatural evolution.

The ancient texts in their quantum-sealed cases seemed to whisper with accumulated wisdom, while modern data streams pulsed with new possibilities. Whatever the corporations were planning, whatever challenges lay ahead, they'd face them together – just as they had since Daybridge changed everything.

"Ready?" Nadia asked, securing the archive's reality anchors.

"Always," Alice replied, thinking of Ethan waiting at home, of Lila who would probably materialize uninvited with exotic wine and cryptic warnings, of their strange but functional supernatural family. "Let's go home."

CHAPTER FOURTEEN

GLOBAL RIPPLES

United Nations Security Council

Emergency Session #247-A

Classification: ULTRA BLACK

Location: Quantum-Shielded Chamber, Sublevel 5

Time: 0300 GMT

The session commenced with Permanent Security Council Members (Enhanced-Certified), International Supernatural Monitoring Agency (ISMA) Leadership, Corporate Oversight Committee Representatives, and Traditional Supernatural Delegates in attendance.

The global reality stability status painted a dire picture: North America showed CRITICAL conditions, Europe faced SEVERE disruption, Asia was DESTABILIZING, the Middle East remained FLUCTUATING, Africa displayed EMERGING PATTERNS, and South America was ACCELERATING.

Ambassador **Li Wei** manipulated the probability streams through the quantum display, revealing the Daybridge Incident's 'Cascade Effect.'

"Ladies and gentlemen, I would like to draw your attention to the global reality stability status, which paints a dire picture in the wake of the Daybridge Incident."

"As you can see from the quantum display, the "Cascade Effect" has triggered widespread quantum framework manifestations across Asia. In Shanghai, our monitoring stations have detected significant reality breaches in the financial district, leading to the destabilization of dragon court territories. We are also witnessing the emergence of corporate-supernatural hybrids and the activation of ancient ley lines at an alarming rate of 78%."

"Moving on to Hong Kong, the situation is equally concerning. Enhanced trading algorithms are directly affecting probability, resulting in the dissolution of traditional spirit boundaries. The Quantum Framework integration has reached 65%, while the corporate enhancement rate stands at a staggering 89%."

"In Tokyo, we face a unique set of challenges. Digital yokai are merging with the city's network infrastructure, while enhanced salary workers are accessing ancestral memories, leading to critical reality stability issues. Our projections indicate an imminent failure of traditional barriers."

"The implications of these developments cannot be overstated. The rapid proliferation of quantum framework manifestations and corporate-supernatural hybridization poses a significant threat to the stability of our reality. It is crucial that we take immediate action to address these issues and develop comprehensive strategies to mitigate the risks associated with the Daybridge Incident's Cascade Effect."

"I urge the council to prioritize the allocation of resources toward further research and containment efforts. We must work together to prevent the collapse of our reality and ensure the safety of our citizens in the face of this unprecedented crisis."

"Thank you for your attention."

Ambassador Sarah Collins, flickering between quantum states, addressed the council regarding London's equally critical situation.

"Good morning, everyone. I would like to bring your attention to the alarming situation unfolding in London's Financial District and Underground Network."

"In the Financial District, we have observed a disturbing trend of Fae courts merging with trading systems. This unprecedented integration has led to significant reality fluctuations, which are directly impacting market stability. Furthermore, enhanced traders are actively manipulating probability streams, causing a breakdown in traditional warranties and safeguards."

"The situation in the Underground Network is equally concerning. Our reports indicate that enhanced transport systems are breaching the fabric of reality, while ancient tunnels are now accessing quantum pathways. This has led to a sharp increase in supernatural territory disputes and the rapid expansion of human-supernatural hybrid zones."

"Moreover, our monitoring points have detected off-scale quantum readings at the Thames barrier, suggesting a severe destabilization of the city's protective wards. The Tower of London, a critical focal point for London's supernatural defenses, is experiencing a similar destabilization of its wards."

"In addition to these localized issues, we have recorded an unprecedented surge in ley line activity throughout the city. This, combined with the exponential growth of the enhanced population, poses a significant risk to the overall stability of London's supernatural and human communities."

The implications of these developments cannot be overstated. If left unchecked, the merging of Fae courts with trading systems, the manipulation of probability streams, and the breaching of reality by enhanced transport systems could lead to a complete collapse of London's financial and social infrastructure.

"It is imperative that we take immediate action to address these issues. I recommend the formation of a specialized task force to investigate and contain the situation in the Financial District and Underground

Network. We must also prioritize the reinforcement of the city's protective wards and the stabilization of ley line activity."

"Time is of the essence, and we must act now to prevent further deterioration of the situation. I urge the council to allocate the necessary resources and personnel to tackle this crisis head-on."

"Thank you for your attention, and I look forward to working with you all to ensure the safety and stability of our great city."

Director George Blake's enhanced perception revealed global enhancement patterns across major financial centers. He adjusts his papers at the podium.

"Q4 2024 Reality Integration Status Report - Major Hub Analysis"

"Our latest monitoring data reveals significant developments across our primary observation zones. In Moscow, we're tracking a reality stability index of just 45%, with ancient oligarch families reasserting control over three major nexus points. The local vampire councils have lost jurisdiction in four districts since September, though our corporate-supernatural merger rate exceeds projections at 67%."

"The Dubai situation demands immediate attention. Our breach containment systems are showing critical failures, even as djinn energy signatures have successfully merged with the local quantum framework. While this has led to enhanced extraction efficiency in oil operations through metaphysical optimization, the desert ley line network has reached 89% activation."

"Moving to São Paulo, we're observing rapid dissolution of traditional boundaries between corporate and spiritual zones. The ancient pathway reactivation program has reached 73% completion, with corporate enhancement protocols spreading beyond designated containment zones. The Quantum Framework integration stands at 56% and continues to rise."

"The Singapore hub presents unique challenges. Trading algorithm anomalies are directly affecting the local reality fabric, while spirit courts demonstrate unprecedented adaptation to corporate protocols.

Hybrid zones are expanding beyond projected parameters, and the quantum stability metrics indicate a need for immediate intervention."

Director Blake looked up from his notes.

"These findings suggest accelerating integration rates across all monitored zones. I'm prepared to address any questions regarding specific metrics or containment proposals."

Dr. Helena Schmidt presented the crisis timeline, outlining three phases and immediate concerns across security, economic, and social sectors. The council proposed emergency measures including a Global Enhancement Protocol, Reality Stabilization Initiative, and International Response Framework.

As reality fluctuations intensified, the quantum-shielded chamber flickered, offering glimpses of alternate versions of their meeting. Director Blake's final report emphasized that the Daybridge Incident was fundamentally altering reality's evolution, with adaptation to this new paradigm being crucial for survival.

"You're avoiding me," Ethan said, his wolf form rippling as he paced Alice's quantum-shielded apartment. "Ever since the enhanced perception bond deepened."

Alice kept her eyes on her research tablet, trying to ignore how his emotions created visible patterns in the air between them. "I'm working. Kane's enhancement program is accelerating."

"And our connection lets me know that's not the whole truth." The wolf shifted back to human form, quantum energy settling around him. "You're scared of how much I can sense now."

"Wouldn't you be?" Alice finally met his gaze. "Every thought, every feeling... it's too much exposure."

"Yet you let Lila help stabilize your enhancement without hesitation."

"That's different. Lila's..."

"Not as emotionally complicated?" Ethan stepped closer, reality shimmering around him. "Or just safer because you don't feel the same way about her?"

Before Alice could respond, Lila materialized in the apartment, her ancient magic clashing with the quantum field. "If you two are done with your relationship drama, we have a situation. Dr. Goddard's clinic just reported three new cases of forced corporate enhancement."

"I'll grab my gear," Alice moved toward her room, but Ethan caught her arm.

"We need to talk about this eventually," he said softly. "The bond only amplifies what's already there."

"Which is exactly what worries me," Alice pulled away. "We can't afford distractions right now."

Lila watched the exchange with centuries-old eyes. "Your connection is stronger together. Even an ancient being like myself can see that. But force it, and you'll create the kind of instability Kane's counting on."

"Stay out of it," Alice and Ethan said simultaneously, their quantum patterns synchronizing for a moment before they both looked away.

"Children," Lila sighed, creating a portal to the clinic. "The world's transforming, reality itself is in flux, and you're both still fighting basic human emotions. At least some things never change."

～

CHAPTER FIFTEEN
SCIENTIFIC MAGIC

ALICE CHEN STOOD ALONE in Kane Industry's restricted laboratory section at 4:15 AM, watching genetic sequences pulse across her holographic display. Each pattern radiated an energy signature that defied conventional science – supernatural genetics intertwined with quantum mechanics in ways that shouldn't be possible.

Her hands trembled as she studied the latest results from enhanced human testing. Subject #274 showed active werewolf markers merged with partial vampire genetics, all underlaid with unstable Fae resonance. But it was the quantum binding that made her blood run cold – supernatural energy tethered directly to DNA through particle entanglement.

Dr. Winters' final research notes lay scattered across her desk, the pages filled with increasingly frantic observations. Her last entry, dated just 72 hours ago, broke off mid-sentence: "The quantum bridge between supernatural genetics isn't theoretical anymore. Each species' power has a unique quantum signature that..." The rest was illegible, as if reality itself had rejected the words.

Through her monitoring systems, Alice tracked the growing crisis. Enhanced humans across Daybridge were experiencing critical failures

– spontaneous combustion, reality fractures, power cascade failures. The pattern was clear: their abilities weren't just combining; they were becoming dangerously unstable.

The thermal imaging of the old industrial district revealed the truth behind its abandoned facade. Two hundred meters below ground, a massive facility sprawled across 3.2 kilometers, its power usage off the charts. Quantum containment fields hummed alongside supernatural energy signatures, while multiple test subjects registered on her scanners.

Her breakthrough in understanding supernatural genetics now seemed like a curse. The powers weren't magical at all – they were quantum mechanical manifestations, capable of being artificially replicated. And someone was using that knowledge to break down the barriers between species.

Movement on the security feed caught her attention. Dr. Winters stumbled into view, clutching her research notebook. Her form flickered between states, multiple power signatures warping reality around her. "Alice," her voice crackled through the feed, "Nash... she's not creating hybrids. It's worse. The quantum binding... it's breaking down the walls between—" The feed exploded in light, and Winters vanished.

A message flashed across her screen, heavily encrypted: "Your sister understood. The quantum nature of supernatural power isn't a discovery, Detective Chen. It's a key. Reality is just another barrier to break. Come to Lab 7. -N"

In the underground facility, enhanced humans were gathering. Their unstable powers created cascading effects – werewolf strength combined with vampire speed produced time distortions. Fae magic merged with wolf pack bonds resulted in mass consciousness. But most terrifying were the combinations that defied analysis, their results too reality-bending to measure.

Alice's research now painted a horrifying picture. All supernatural powers were quantum phenomena. Species barriers were artificial constructs. Power combinations followed quantum rules. And reality

itself was mutable. Nash wasn't just breaking supernatural barriers –
she was breaking reality itself.

The storm above Daybridge pulsed in response, its triple helix pattern
mirroring the quantum readings from the underground lab. Enhanced
humans converged on Lab 7, their power signatures approaching critical mass. Timeline stability was failing. And within the chaos, Alice's
instruments detected two impossible things: Dr. Winters' quantum
signature, somehow still present, and Sarah Chen's energy pattern,
unlike anything she'd seen before.

Alice gathered her research tablets and drew her service weapon.
Reality itself seemed to shiver as she headed for the door. The choice
was clear: reach Lab 7 before Nash's experiments tore reality apart. But
her quantum scanner's final reading suggested it might already be too
late. Multiple timelines were converging, reality breaches expanding
from Lab 7 like cracks in a mirror.

The Nash Protocol was already in motion. Stage one was complete.
Stage two was progressing. And stage three remained encrypted, its
purpose hidden but its threat clear in the way reality itself seemed to
bend around the very idea of it.

This wasn't just about evolution anymore. It wasn't even about supernatural power. Nash was pursuing something far more dangerous –
the ability to rewrite reality itself. And as Alice Chen stepped into the
night, she knew she was walking into something far worse than a
simple supernatural war.

The storm's triple helix pattern danced above Daybridge, a key turning
in reality's lock. And somewhere below, in Lab 7, Nash waited with
answers that might destroy everything they thought they knew about
the nature of existence itself.

CHAPTER SIXTEEN

PATTERN RECOGNITION

KANE INDUSTRIES RESEARCH Division - Assessment Room

In the assessment room, Detective Alice Chen examined Moira Rodgers while a quantum stabilization field remained active, facilitating enhanced data analysis in progress.

Moira demonstrated her abilities through manipulation of probability lattices, transforming financial projections into quantum matrices. She showcased enhanced decision point visualization with crystal-like structures displaying economic outcomes.

The enhancement observations revealed unprecedented quantum information processing and adaptation to natural analytical abilities. A notable break room incident involving simultaneous probability simulations had required security intervention.

During surveillance analysis of global Kane Industries facilities footage, enhanced perception revealed hidden patterns correlating with corporate communication networks and underlying supernatural elements.

Moira's Pattern Analysis, classified under Enhanced Quantum access level, revealed three distinct layers. The first layer of Corporate

Communications showed enhancement spreading via digital networks, following email and video conference pathways with social connection acceleration. The second layer exposed Supernatural Ley Lines, displaying ancient power network activation, corporate infrastructure alignment, and hybrid energy channel formation. The third layer of Quantum Framework contained base reality protocols, probability manipulation matrices, and reality stability indicators.

Global Network Patterns emerged across continents. North America displayed tech hub primary nodes, corporate channel secondary spread, and social network tertiary enhancement. Asia revealed dragon ley line activation, ancient wisdom network emergence, and corporate-supernatural fusion points. Europe showed old world magic integration, financial district enhancement clusters, and historical power site activation.

The Quantum Signal Discovery yielded several components: geographic coordinates, temporal markers, reality protocols, and activation sequences.

Key findings indicated enhancement following corporate networks, a hidden quantum framework signal, coordinates to an ancient waiting entity, patterns suggesting a larger purpose, and warnings of an awakening force.

Immediate actions included securing data on a protected terminal, notifying Dana Somers, integrating Moira into the investigation team, pending further pattern analysis, and enhanced security protocols.

The implications proved far-reaching: enhancement spread appeared purposeful, an ancient connection was discovered, global awakening seemed imminent, the investigation scope expanded, and reality framework showed signs of shifting.

CHAPTER SEVENTEEN

ANCHORS

The meditation room in their apartment hummed with quantum stabilizers and reality anchors – a necessity for nights like this, when their enhanced abilities threatened to overwhelm normal space-time. The walls were lined with Lila's ancient runes interwoven with Dr. Nash's cutting-edge tech, creating a space where they could safely let their guards down.

Alice sat cross-legged on their reinforced mat, watching Ethan pace. His wolf form shimmered beneath his skin, quantum energy making the air ripple with each step. Three years ago, his pre-moon restlessness would have worried her. Now she just adjusted the quantum field, creating a pocket of stable reality around them. Their combined enhancement signatures had become a familiar dance – his primal energy contained and directed by her quantum manipulation.

"You're getting better at that," he noted, finally settling beside her. The wolf's restlessness eased as their energy fields synchronized. "Remember when you first started manifesting? How the whole block would flicker?"

"Like you were any better," she teased, reaching out to trace the quantum patterns that always appeared around him before a full moon. "That first full moon after Daybridge? You howled and every reality anchor in the district went offline. The Enhancement Response Team thought we were under attack."

"We were a mess," he agreed, taking her hand. Their fingers interlaced automatically, energy patterns aligning with a familiar warmth. The quantum field stabilized further, responding to their harmonized frequencies. "Scared of our own abilities, scared of losing control..."

"Scared of losing each other," Alice added softly. The confession hung between them, weighted with shared memories. "After seeing what happened to other enhanced individuals..." She didn't need to finish – they both remembered the early days after Daybridge, when enhanced partnerships often ended in tragedy. Unstable quantum signatures, incompatible transformations, minds burned out by too much power too quickly.

"But we figured it out." Ethan's thumb traced familiar patterns on her wrist, their personal grounding ritual. Each movement sent small ripples through the quantum field, creating a stabilizing rhythm they'd discovered through months of trial and error. "Together."

"With help," Alice reminded him. "Lila's enhancement training, Nadia's research, Dr. Nash's protocols..." She paused, feeling their bond pulse with shared emotion. The names carried weight – friends who'd helped them navigate their changing reality when everything seemed impossible. "But mostly because we stopped fighting it. Stopped trying to be what we were before."

The quantum field shimmered with memories – their first successful transformation together, when Alice's enhancement had helped Ethan maintain consciousness through the change. The night they'd discovered they could share perceptions, her quantum sensitivity merging with his wolf senses to create something entirely new. The careful experiments that had led to their current balance, where his primal energy amplified her quantum manipulation instead of disrupting it.

"Partners," Ethan said, the word carrying layers of meaning now. Through their bond, she felt the depth of it – partners in work, in life, in this new enhanced reality they were helping to shape. The wolf stirred contentedly, accepting her as pack in a way that went beyond human understanding.

"Even when it means accidentally rewriting local reality?" She smiled, watching quantum patterns dance around them. Last week's incident with the temporal fluctuations had required some creative explanations to their non-enhanced neighbors. "I still think we should send Mrs. Henderson a gift basket for not reporting the floating furniture."

"Especially then." He pulled her closer, their enhanced perceptions merging naturally. The room's reality anchors adjusted, compensating for the surge in quantum energy that always accompanied their closeness. "Though maybe we should work on that part. The neighbors are getting suspicious about the temporal fluctuations."

Through their bond, she felt his amusement mixed with genuine concern. They were still learning the limits of their combined abilities, still discovering new ways their enhancements could interact. Each full moon brought fresh challenges and discoveries.

"Let them wonder," Alice murmured, settling into their shared space. The quantum field wrapped around them like a cocoon, their signatures perfectly aligned. "We've earned this."

Around them, reality hummed with possibility. Tomorrow would bring new cases, new challenges, new attempts to balance their enhanced lives with their roles as protectors of this transformed world. But for now, there was just this – their shared sanctuary, their hard-won harmony, and the quiet certainty that whatever came next, they would face it together.

The moon rose outside, its light creating strange patterns through the quantum-touched windows. Ethan's wolf stirred again, but there was no anxiety now, no fear of losing control. Alice's enhancement responded automatically, their frequencies finding that perfect resonance that had once seemed impossible.

～

CHAPTER EIGHTEEN

GLOBAL CURRENTS

THE UN ENHANCEMENT OVERSIGHT COMMITTEE's secure briefing room hummed with quantum dampeners, designed to prevent both techno-logical and supernatural surveillance. Alice studied the holographic display showing global enhancement spread patterns, her quantum perception catching details others might miss.

"The Chinese Supernatural Integration Bureau has officially denied involvement in the Mumbai incident," Director Blake said, his quan-tum-enhanced prosthetic arm displaying real-time data streams. "Though our analysts confirm their enhancement signatures were present."

"Of course they deny it," Lila remarked from her position near the window, where reality shimmered slightly around her. "Just like the Russians denied their enhancement program caused the Baltic anom-alies." She sipped her ever-present coffee, though Alice's enhanced senses detected more than just reality stabilization compounds in it today.

"The situation is deteriorating faster than predicted," Nadia Marsh added, her archive-linked tablets showing historical trend analysis.

"Enhancement technology is spreading beyond controlled channels. We're seeing underground labs in Lagos, Buenos Aires, Jakarta..."

"Everybody wants their own enhanced agents," Ethan growled softly. His wolf was restless – these high-level meetings always set him on edge, especially with representatives from multiple agencies present. "Their own supernatural weapons."

"Which is exactly what we've been trying to prevent since Daybridge," Alice said, remembering the chaos of those early days. Her hand found Ethan's under the table, their combined energy signatures making the room's quantum dampeners work harder.

The Russian representative, Colonel Volkov, leaned forward. His own enhancement was subtle but distinctive – military-grade quantum integration. "Perhaps it is time to acknowledge reality. Enhancement is here to stay. The question is how we manage it."

"Manage it?" Lila's laugh carried centuries of magical knowledge. "Like you managed it in St. Petersburg? Those temporal tears are still causing problems, by the way."

"At least we are transparent about our program," the Chinese delegate, Dr. Zhang, countered. Her quantum signature showed signs of experimental enhancement – corporate-derived, if Alice's perception was correct. "Unlike certain Western nations who hide their enhanced assets behind private contractors."

"Speaking of corporate involvement," Director Blake interrupted, bringing up new data, "our investigation into Kane Industries has revealed concerning patterns. They're not just experimenting with enhancement – they're actively selling stabilization protocols to multiple governments."

Alice exchanged glances with Ethan. Their current case suddenly took on new dimensions.

"The corporations are playing both sides," Nadia Marsh observed, her archive-enhanced perception analyzing patterns. "Selling different pieces of enhancement technology to different nations, creating artificial scarcity..."

"While keeping the full integration protocols for themselves," Lila finished. "Clever. Dangerous, but clever."

"We're seeing increased enhancement activity in traditionally neutral countries," a Swiss representative added. "Singapore, Switzerland, New Zealand – they're positioning themselves as safe havens for enhancement research."

"Creating sovereign enhancement zones," Alice realized, the pattern becoming clear. "Outside traditional power structures."

"Which makes our current case more significant," Ethan said quietly. "If Kane Industries has found a way to stabilize forced enhancement..."

"Then every government and corporation will want it," Director Blake concluded. "Regardless of the human cost."

The room fell silent as implications sank in. Alice's enhanced perception caught the subtle shifts in quantum signatures as each representative considered their nation's position.

"There's something else," Nadia Marsh said, bringing up archived data. "The pattern of enhancement spread... it's following old ley lines, ancient power networks. The Quantum Framework isn't just enabling new abilities – it's remembering old ones."

"Which is why corporate enhancement experiments keep triggering supernatural phenomena," Lila added. "They're accidentally tapping into systems that existed long before modern nations."

"Systems that don't care about borders," Ethan noted, his wolf senses picking up underlying patterns.

"Or sovereignty," Colonel Volkov agreed grimly. "If we cannot control enhancement spread..."

"Then we need to focus on stabilization," Alice said firmly. "Working together to establish safe protocols, instead of competing for advantage."

"A noble sentiment," Dr. Zhang smiled thinly. "But how many nations will actually commit to it?"

"That's why this case matters," Director Blake said. "What we uncover about Kane Industries' experiments could determine whether enhancement becomes a tool for cooperation or a weapon of war."

As the meeting continued, Alice felt the weight of global implications settling over their investigation. What had started as a series of corporate murders was expanding into something that could reshape international power structures.

She squeezed Ethan's hand, their quantum bond providing mutual support. Whatever they uncovered, whatever they faced, they'd handle it together – just as they had since Daybridge changed everything.

CHAPTER NINETEEN
EVERYDAY MIRACLES

Dr. Sylvia Goddard's enhancement support clinic occupied a converted warehouse in downtown Daybridge, its walls lined with quantum stabilizers disguised as modern art. She adjusted her reality-anchored glasses and checked the day's schedule on her augmented tablet.

8:15 AM - Teen Enhancement Support Group

Stephanie Simpson, sixteen, sat cross-legged in the circle, quantum patterns flickering around her hands. "I sneezed during math class and turned my textbook into butterflies," she said, voice trembling. "Real ones. They flew around for twenty minutes before dissolving."

"My parents want me to suppress it," Thomas Rodriguez added, his newly-emerged ability to see quantum probabilities making his eyes shift color. "They say colleges won't accept enhanced students. But how do you suppress seeing every possible future when someone asks you a question?"

Sylvia noted how the other teens nodded. Enhanced or not, some parental fears were universal.

10:30 AM - Professional Integration Counseling

"I'm an accountant," James Wheeler explained, his quantum signature carefully dampened by corporate-approved stabilizers. "Was an accountant. Now I can see the mathematical patterns underlying reality. Do you know how hard it is to balance books when you can literally see the flow of economic energy?"

"My law firm put me on leave," Rebecca Martinez said, reality rippling subtly around her. "Said my new 'truth perception' ability might violate client confidentiality. Even with dampeners, I can tell when someone's lying. How do I not know?"

1:00 PM - Family Adjustment Session

"We just want our daughter back," Mrs. Peterson wiped tears while her husband squeezed her hand. Their enhanced daughter Amy, twelve, floated several inches above her chair, quantum energy making her pigtails defy gravity.

"I'm still me, Mom," Amy insisted, her voice echoing slightly across quantum frequencies. "I just... see more now. Feel more. Why is that scary?"

3:30 PM - Emergency Walk-in

"It happened at the grocery store," Michael Sullivan, retired bus driver, demonstrated how reality warped around his shopping bags. "Was thinking about how I needed to make the food last till pension day, and suddenly everything started multiplying. Like Jesus with the loaves and fishes, except I can't control it. What do I tell my pastor?"

5:00 PM - Corporate Enhancement Recovery

"Kane Industries said the enhancement would be subtle," Susan Chang showed her quantum scans, corporate enhancement patterns clearly forced into natural energy flows. "Just enough to improve productivity. They didn't mention the dreams. Or that I'd start affecting electronic devices. Or that I'd feel everyone's emotions within fifty feet."

7:15 PM - Support Staff Debrief

"Reality stabilizers are holding," Maya Patel reported, checking the clinic's quantum readings. "Though we had some fluctuation during the teen group. Their emotions tend to amplify enhancement effects."

"Referral requests are up 300%," Lisa from intake added. "Especially since the corporate enhancement programs expanded. People need help integrating these changes."

Sylvia rubbed her temples, her own modest enhancement letting her see the patterns of need spreading through the city. Every day brought new cases, new manifestations, new challenges.

Her phone buzzed – Alice requesting data on corporate enhancement trauma patterns. Sylvia typed a quick response, remembering the agent's last visit to the clinic. At least someone was investigating the bigger picture.

8:30 PM - Personal Log Entry

Sylvia recorded her daily observations, trying to capture the human side of enhancement for future researchers:

"Enhancement continues spreading through ordinary channels: stress, emotion, necessity. A mother lifts a car off her child. A teacher suddenly understands every language her ESL students speak. A homeless man manifests quantum shelter during a freezing night.

Corporate programs attempt to standardize and control enhancement, but human consciousness proves stubbornly individual. Each person's abilities reflect their needs, fears, and deepest beliefs.

Most challenging are the children - their natural acceptance of enhancement clashing with adult fears. They adapt quickly, seeing new abilities as natural as smartphones, while their parents struggle with fundamental questions about human identity.

Religious communities remain divided. Some see enhancement as miraculous, others as dangerous. Many enhanced individuals report deepened spiritual experiences, while others struggle with how their abilities affect their faith.

The Quantum Framework responds to human consciousness in increasingly complex ways. Each enhanced individual affects local reality, creating overlapping fields of influence that require active management in populated areas.

Integration of enhanced individuals into existing social structures grows more complex daily. Corporate attempts to standardize naturally occurring abilities create as many problems as they solve. Religious and cultural adaptation to new human capabilities varies widely by community. Educational systems struggle to accommodate enhanced students while maintaining fair standards. Family dynamics shift dramatically when enhancement manifests unexpectedly. Workplace policies regarding enhanced employees remain inconsistent. Mental health support for rapid consciousness expansion barely keeps pace with demand.

Tomorrow brings another day of helping people navigate their new reality. Enhanced or not, they're all human, all trying to understand their place in a rapidly changing world."

9:00 PM - Clinic Closing

Sylvia locked up, checking the quantum stabilizers one last time. Outside, reality rippled subtly around evening commuters, enhancement becoming as common as cellphones. A street musician's songs carried emotional resonance that made colors dance in the air. A food cart vendor's belief in his cooking created actual golden halos around his tacos.

Just another day in the enhanced world.

～

CHAPTER TWENTY
ESCALATION

THE KANE INDUSTRIES boardroom dissolved into chaos as reality fractures splintered across its quantum-reinforced windows. Through each breach, Alice glimpsed different versions of the same room – timelines where things had gone differently. In one, Kane Industries had never existed. In another, it dominated global supernatural research. In a third, most haunting of all, she saw Nash as she must have once been: younger, desperate, standing over someone's hospital bed in a timeline that no longer existed.

The truth of Nash's motivation hit Alice as hard as the reality waves pulsing through the building. Nash hadn't infiltrated Kane Industries – she had created it, or rather, guided its creation across multiple time-lines until she found the version that would serve her purpose. Every board member she'd turned, every scientist she'd recruited, every security protocol she'd implemented had been carefully selected from different realities and brought together in this one.

Sarah Chen materialized through a reality breach, her form shifting between states of existence. "You're starting to understand, aren't you, sister?" Her voice echoed across multiple frequencies of reality. "Nash didn't corrupt Kane Industries. She built it, piece by piece, person by person, choosing the versions of each that would help her reach this moment."

The enhanced humans attacking the board weren't random mutations – they were carefully selected iterations of people Nash had identified across thousands of timelines. Each one chosen for their potential to survive the quantum-supernatural merger.

Through the fractured windows, Alice watched supernatural forces converging on the tower. Werewolves, vampires, and Fae united too late against a threat they barely understood. Nash had played them too, using their ancient rivalries to blind them to her true purpose.

"The storm isn't meant to transform reality," Alice realized aloud. "It's meant to find one specific reality. The original timeline – the one Nash came from. The one she's been searching for across countless dimensional variations."

Sarah's form flickered as she approached the quantum core. "Nash lost someone," she said, her voice carrying echoes of other Sarahs from other timelines. "Someone who only lived in one specific reality. She's been breaking down the walls between dimensions, searching every possible version of history to find the one where that person survived."

The quantum core pulsed with impossible energy as enhanced humans positioned themselves around it. Each one a carefully chosen piece of Nash's multidimensional puzzle, each one necessary for what came next.

"Can you stop her?" Marcus Kane asked, his quantum shield failing against the reality distortions. "Is there still time?"

Alice watched as her sister initiated the core's final sequence. Reality itself began to unravel around them, showing glimpses of countless Daybridges, countless histories, countless possibilities. Nash hadn't just built Kane Industries – she had engineered this exact moment across multiple timelines, ensuring that no matter what choices anyone made, all paths led here.

"It was never about stopping her," Alice said as the storm above reached its crescendo. "Nash made sure of that. Every possible way this could play out, every potential intervention – she's seen them all, planned for them all. We're not just fighting one version of Nash. We're fighting every version that succeeded, every timeline where her plan worked."

The quantum core's energy reached critical mass. Through the reality breaches, Alice saw Nash in her lab, surrounded by temporal equations and dimensional maps. She wasn't trying to evolve supernatural beings or merge realities. She was trying to find one specific moment in one specific timeline – the last moment before she lost everything that mattered to her.

As reality began to collapse around them, Alice realized the terrible truth: they weren't watching the end of their world. They were watching Nash tear apart every version of reality until she found the one she'd lost. And in her grief, in her desperate search across dimensions, she'd become something far more dangerous than any supernatural being – she'd become someone willing to destroy every reality to save just one.

The storm's triple helix pattern wasn't random. It was a key, designed to unlock the barriers between all possible timelines. And as it reached its final form, Alice understood that stopping Nash was impossible – because Nash had already succeeded, countless times, across countless realities. This moment wasn't the end of her plan.

It was just one more step in a journey that had already destroyed countless versions of reality in Nash's relentless search for the one timeline she could call home.

~

CHAPTER TWENTY-ONE

GHOST IN THE MACHINE

KANE INDUSTRIES RESEARCH Lab - Quantum Analysis Chamber

Time: 2:47 AM

Security Level: Maximum

Reality Stability: Fluctuating

In the Quantum Analysis Chamber, with active scanners, reality anchors engaged, supernatural containment online, and enhancement detection showing critical alert, Alice Chen faced an impossible reading on her quantum scanner. Her enhanced perception confirmed a quantum pattern matching her sister's autopsy from fifteen years ago, with a 99.97% pattern match.

Sarah Chen materialized from the Quantum Framework, her form shifting between states of existence, appearing exactly as she had on her last day - lab coat, precision-cut hair, and determined expression, now flickering with enhanced energy that distorted local reality.

"Hello, sister," Sarah spoke with quantum harmonics that resonated with Alice's enhanced senses. "We need to talk about what's really happening at Kane Industries."

The reality distortion log showed local quantum field destabilization, converging probability streams, manifesting memory patterns, and detected timeline anomalies. Alice accessed her secure files, confirming Sarah's official status as deceased from a laboratory accident at Kane Industries Supernatural Research Division fifteen years prior, with full quantum dissolution and no residual energy signature.

Sarah explained her false death was necessary due to changing supernatural world circumstances, requiring someone to work from the shadows. Her quantum state remained fluid, without reality anchor, showing unknown enhancement levels and multiple timeline signatures.

The security system blared alerts of quantum containment breach, compromised reality stability, enhancement detection overload, and pattern recognition failure. Sarah revealed that during the past fifteen years, she had conducted underground enhancement research, reality manipulation studies, and corporate-supernatural integration.

The classified research, dubbed Project EVOLUTION, encompassed enhancement formula development, reality manipulation protocols, supernatural integration studies, and quantum framework access. Hidden memories flickered through Sarah's quantum state, showing secret laboratories, underground networks, enhanced operatives, and reality manipulation experiments.

Sarah warned that the Daybridge incidents - the storm, enhancements, and reality breaches - were part of Victoria Kane's decades-old plan reaching critical mass. As her form began to destabilize, she delivered a crucial message: the enhancement formulas weren't creating something new but helping humans remember something they used to be.

Before dissolving into quantum streams, Sarah left coordinates, access codes, and timeline markers, all heavily classified and encrypted. Her final warning suggested the enhancement revolution wasn't random evolution, but an orchestrated awakening of reality itself.

Alice's enhanced perception caught one final pattern in the probability matrix, confirming her sister's warning about the true nature of the enhancement phenomenon - a carefully orchestrated awakening rather than random evolution.

CHAPTER TWENTY-TWO
POWER PLAYS

Strategic Analysis Room - Pentagon

Time: 0600 EST

Classification: ULTRA BLACK

Operation Code: QUANTUM SHIFT

The meeting convened with high-ranking military officials including General James Harrison from Joint Chiefs, Colonel Sarah Martinez from Enhanced Operations, Admiral David Chen from Pacific Command, and General Michael Stone serving as NATO Liaison. Supernatural representatives included Lord Arawn from the Fae High Council, Viktor Konstantin of the Vampire Authority, Dr. Wei Zhang as Dragon Court Envoy, and Sheik Hassan Al-Rashid from the Djinn Collective. Corporate observers from Kane Industries Security Division, Global Enhancement Monitoring Team, and Quantum Framework Analysis Group were also present.

General Harrison activated the quantum-hardened display system, revealing the global enhancement proliferation status. Russia showed critical status with Oligarch-Vampire Alliance Program, Siberian Enhancement Facilities, and Ancient Power Site Activation, maintaining 34% reality stability. Their enhancement vectors included blood magic integration, corporate-supernatural fusion, quantum framework exploitation, and traditional power adaptation.

China's status was accelerating, implementing State-Dragon Partnership Initiative, Quantum Enhancement Research, and Ancient Site Reactivation, with 45% reality control. Their program focused on dragon court knowledge access, corporate enhancement development, traditional power integration, and reality manipulation research.

The Middle East showed emerging status, featuring Djinn Energy Exploitation, Desert Power Site Activation, and Enhanced Oil Production, maintaining 56% reality stability. Development areas included ancient power access, corporate-supernatural merger, reality framework manipulation, and traditional boundary dissolution.

Europe reached critical status with Fae-Corporate Integration, Ancient Site Reactivation, and Enhanced Population Growth, showing 39% reality control. Their program emphasized traditional power adaptation, corporate enhancement spread, reality manipulation research, and supernatural integration.

Satellite surveillance detected enhancement facilities in the Ural Mountains Complex, Gobi Desert Installation, Black Forest Center, and Dubai Underground Facility. Energy signature analysis showed declining traditional supernatural presence, rising enhanced human signatures, emerging hybrid patterns, and increasing reality distortions.

Colonel Martinez's enhanced perception revealed shifting power structures among traditional supernatural entities, enhanced humans, corporate influences, and hybrid developments. Lord Arawn provided supernatural perspective on failing traditional boundaries and emerging power distributions. Admiral Chen outlined global security concerns, while Dr. Zhang offered historical context from ancient records.

The briefing concluded with immediate recommendations for enhanced military response, supernatural cooperation, corporate oversight, and international coordination. General Harrison emphasized they faced more than a new arms race or power shift - they witnessed the emergence of a new world order where traditional military power, supernatural authority, and corporate influence underwent quantum-level transformation.

As the meeting concluded, reality anchors fluctuated with passing enhanced humans, offering glimpses through quantum interference of alternate briefings and different outcomes in parallel realities.

CHAPTER TWENTY-THREE

GLOBAL SUPERNATURAL SITUATION REPORT

Classification: ULTRA BLACK

Source: International Supernatural Monitoring Agency (ISMA)

Time: 1200 GMT

The Tokyo Sector reports critical transformation throughout the Greater Tokyo Metropolitan Area. The Sony-Inari Alliance Program demonstrates digital fox-fire manifestation, quantum computing enhancement, and reality-warped production facilities, with enhanced employee transformation reaching 67%. The Mitsubishi-Nine Tails Partnership focuses on ancient knowledge digitization and enhanced manufacturing processes. Tech integration patterns show AI systems absorbing kitsune wisdom, while digital illusions become reality. Salary workers manifest fox abilities as subway systems breach reality, with digital yokai emerging in networks. Risk assessment indicates 45% reality stability with exponential enhancement spread.

In the London Sector, chaotic evolution manifests through the Enhanced Hooligan Phenomenon. Premier League impacts include Chelsea Firm developing weather control and West Ham ICF manifesting strength enhancement. Stadium incidents feature reality breaches during matches and spontaneous Fae portal formation. Fae integration patterns show Summer Court magic in victory celebrations and Winter Court power in rival confrontations. Public safety concerns include enhanced pub brawls breaching reality and football chants affecting probability.

Dubai Sector undergoes rapid transformation across UAE Economic Zones. The Financial District exhibits wish-enhanced trading algorithms and reality-warped skyscrapers. The Emirates-Djinn Trading Partnership combines ancient power with modern commerce through reality-bent luxury developments. Desert operations involve sand spirit merger programs and enhanced construction projects. Power integration shows traditional djinn adapting to corporate structure while enhanced executives gain wish powers.

Moscow Sector reveals underground expansion as a Global Network Nexus. Black market operations trade vampire blood enhancement formulas and Fae power extraction methods through Siberian enhancement labs and Ural Mountain power sites. Product lines include DIY enhancement kits and bootleg supernatural powers, distributed via dark web supernatural trading and enhanced smuggling routes.

Global impact analysis shows economic effects through destabilizing traditional markets and emerging enhanced trading systems. Security concerns encompass enhanced criminal organizations and supernatural weapon proliferation. Social changes indicate breaking traditional boundaries and forming new power hierarchies.

Immediate trends point toward corporate-supernatural fusion, underground evolution, social transformation, and global integration. Traditional powers modernize as corporate entities gain supernatural abilities, while black market enhancement spreads and enhanced populations grow.

The report recommends enhanced surveillance through reality breach detection and power manifestation tracking, alongside response protocols for reality stabilization and enhanced incident management.

Adaptation strategies suggest power integration frameworks and reality management systems.

The conclusion warns of accelerating changes rendering traditional monitoring methods obsolete as reality continues to evolve, emphasizing urgent need for new frameworks in understanding and managing these transformations.

CHAPTER TWENTY-FOUR
SACRED AND PROFANE

THE INTERFAITH ENHANCEMENT symposium at St. Michael's Cathedral created an interesting visual contrast: quantum stabilizers mounted beside ancient stained glass; reality anchors nestled among gothic arches. Alice sat in the back row with Ethan, their combined energy signature carefully dampened to avoid disrupting the proceedings.

"The very existence of enhancement technology challenges fundamental beliefs about human nature," Cardinal Ramsey was saying, his traditional robes incorporated with modern quantum shielding. "Are we not altering God's design when we deliberately modify human consciousness?"

"With respect," Dr. Joyce Cohen from the Progressive Rabbinical Council responded, "Jewish tradition has long held that humans are meant to be co-creators with the divine. Enhancement could be seen as an extension of our obligation to improve ourselves and the world."

Imam Hassan nodded thoughtfully, his prayer beads containing subtle reality stabilizers. "The Quran speaks of signs in the universe for those who understand. Perhaps enhancement is simply revealing aspects of creation that were always present?"

Alice felt Ethan shift beside her, his wolf responding to the charged atmosphere. Through their bond, she sensed his unease with being discussed as a theological case study.

"The indigenous perspective," Dr. Marie Blackfoot added, her quantum signature harmonizing naturally with the cathedral's ancient stones, "is that the boundaries between human and supernatural were never as rigid as Western thought assumed. Enhancement may be simply remembering what we once knew."

"That aligns with certain Buddhist concepts," Venerable Chen noted, her robes shimmering with both traditional symbols and modern quantum interfaces. "The illusion of separate self, the interconnectedness of all things..."

"Pretty words," a new voice cut in. Reverend James Marshal stood, his anti-enhancement collar gleaming. "But we're talking about corporations playing God, about werewolves and witches walking among us. About so-called 'quantum enhancement' that looks suspiciously like what scripture would call possession."

Alice felt Ethan tense. Lila, materializing silently beside them in a swirl of purple smoke, placed a calming hand on his shoulder.

"The Theological Preservation Movement's position is clear," Marshal continued. "Enhancement is an abomination. These abilities – if they truly exist and aren't elaborate technological tricks – come with a price we can't yet see."

"We've already seen the price of fear and rejection," Dr. Goddard spoke up from her place near the quantum stabilizers. "My clinic treats enhanced individuals who've been cast out by their communities, denied basic rights because they're considered 'unnatural.'"

"Nature itself is being rewritten," Professor Williams from the Secular Humanist Alliance added. "We need to move beyond traditional frameworks entirely. Enhancement isn't just changing individuals – it's forcing us to reconsider what it means to be human."

"Assuming we were ever purely human to begin with," Lila murmured, just loud enough for Alice and Ethan to hear. "The archives tell a different story."

The debate continued, touching on free will, divine purpose, and the ethics of corporate enhancement programs. Alice watched reality ripple subtly around the gathered speakers, their varying beliefs affecting the local quantum framework.

During a break, Dr. Goddard approached their corner. "Thought you two might be interested in our latest support group findings. We're seeing interesting patterns in how different faith backgrounds affect enhancement integration."

"Let me guess," Ethan said dryly. "Those who believe it's possible have better control?"

"Essentially," she confirmed. "Belief shapes reality, especially now that the Quantum Framework is more accessible. Which makes these discussions more than theoretical."

"The corporations understand that," Lila added, her ancient eyes tracking patterns others couldn't see. "Why do you think they're funding religious opposition groups while simultaneously running enhancement programs? They're studying how belief affects quantum stability."

Alice's enhanced perception caught the subtle shift in the cathedral's energy field. "The philosophical debate is part of the experiment."

"Always has been," Lila agreed. "Humanity's belief shapes what's possible. Change the beliefs..."

"Change reality itself," Ethan finished, understanding dawning. "That's what the corporate ritual murders are really about. They're not just forcing enhancement – they're trying to change humanity's funda-mental beliefs about what's possible."

"Which makes our case more complex," Alice said, watching the various religious leaders resume their debate. "We're not just dealing with corporate crime or enhancement ethics. We're dealing with an attempt to rewrite humanity's relationship with reality itself."

The symposium was reconvened but with their new understanding, Alice heard the underlying currents in every argument. Behind the theological and philosophical debates lay the real question: who would control humanity's evolution into whatever came next?

As the quantum stabilizers hummed and reality flickered around ancient stones, Alice realized their investigation had to expand beyond physical evidence. To stop the corporations, they needed to understand not just what was happening, but what it meant – for faith, for humanity, for the future itself.

CHAPTER TWENTY-FIVE

CORPORATE WOLVES

THE ABANDONED Kane Industries research facility's quantum shielding sparked against the triple helix storm. In the facility's deepest vault, ancient clay tablets covered in pre-Sumerian script lay scattered across monitoring stations. Quantum sensors recorded energy patterns from the artifacts that matched the enhanced wolves' signatures perfectly.

"The Codex Primordia," James Porter traced the tablets' symbols. "Kane Industries found them beneath a forgotten temple in Turkey. They describe a time before the Great Sundering, when supernatural beings could freely combine abilities."

Ethan Reeves studied the artifacts while Alice's scanner hummed. The tablets depicted werewolves channeling blood magic, vampires merging with Fae energy, and hybrid beings that defied modern supernatural categories.

"Nash cracked the quantum resonance pattern," Marcus Kane explained, his enhanced form shifting between states. "The tablets weren't just historical records – they're quantum keys. Each symbol contains encoded energy signatures from before the barriers were created."

The storm intensified as James revealed more artifacts: crystalline structures that pulsed with remembered power, metallic fragments that bent reality around them, ancient scrolls whose ink shifted between phases of existence.

"Fifteen artifacts in total," James continued. "Kane Industries found them at sites across the world – places where reality feels thin. Each one contained part of the quantum framework that existed before supernatural abilities were artificially separated."

Alice's scanner recorded impossible energy patterns from the artifacts. "The enhancement process – you're using these to unlock the combined abilities?"

Marcus nodded, demonstrating how his werewolf strength now merged seamlessly with vampire speed. "The artifacts remember what was possible. Kane Industries developed quantum resonance chambers that sync enhanced humans to these ancient patterns. We're not creating new abilities – we're remembering what was natural."

Ethan watched as more enhanced wolves gathered around the artifacts. Each tablet, crystal, and scroll pulsed in harmony with their hybrid powers. Reality itself seemed to bend more easily in the artifacts' presence.

"The Mesopotamian tablets describe the ritual," James indicated specific symbols. "The Norse runestones contain the energy patterns. The Chinese oracle bones show how abilities naturally merged. But it was the crystalline keys from Antarctica that held the Quantum Framework itself."

The artifacts' combined energy made nearby instruments spark and fail. Alice's enhanced scanner showed reality growing increasingly fluid around them, natural laws adapting to remembered possibilities.

"Kane Industries spent years learning to replicate the artifacts' quantum signatures," Marcus explained. "The enhancement chambers expose subjects to specific combinations of these ancient patterns. But the process only works because these abilities were always possible – just locked away."

Ethan felt the artifacts' power call to his wolf nature. Their energy resonated with something deep in his supernatural genetics, like a key recognizing its lock.

"You feel it," Marcus observed. "The artifacts remember what wolves truly were. What all supernatural beings could be before the barriers. The choice isn't about becoming something artificial – it's about remembering what's natural."

James revealed the final artifact: a black opal that seemed to exist in multiple phases simultaneously. "This showed us how to stabilize the combined abilities. The quantum framework wasn't just separated – it was fragmented. Each supernatural species received only part of what was once whole."

The storm's pattern matched the opal's shifting energy as reality rippled around them. Enhanced wolves demonstrated increasingly impossible ability combinations yet remained perfectly stable.

"Fifteen artifacts," Alice mused, studying her scanner readings. "Fifteen pieces of a quantum framework that existed before supernatural abilities were artificially divided. Kane Industries didn't just unlock combined abilities – they're reconstructing something ancient."

Ethan approached the artifacts, feeling their power call to abilities locked within his genes. The tablets showed wolves wielding powers he'd been taught were impossible, yet his enhanced former packmates proved otherwise.

"The choice is yours," Marcus said softly. "But understand what you're choosing between. These artifacts prove the barriers between species were imposed. Reality itself remembers when supernatural beings were whole."

The storm's energy intensified as Ethan faced his decision. The artifacts pulsed with ancient power, offering to unlock abilities that had been his birthright before the Great Sundering. Evolution or obsolescence. Artificial limitation or remembered potential.

Around them, reality bent and shifted as the artifacts resonated with the enhanced wolves' hybrid powers. Each impossible combination created cascading effects that felt increasingly natural, as if reality itself was remembering how to accommodate these ancient possibilities.

The truth hidden in Kane Industries' discovered artifacts was becoming clear: supernatural beings hadn't evolved separately – they had been deliberately divided. And now, as the barriers broke down, each species faced a choice between holding onto artificial limitations or remembering what they truly were.

As Ethan stood before the quantum resonance chamber, watching reality ripple around his enhanced former packmates, he understood the real meaning of Kane Industries' discovery. The artifacts hadn't given them new abilities – they had reminded supernatural beings of what they'd lost.

The storm above Daybridge pulsed in harmony with the ancient quantum framework as another wolf stepped forward to remember what they used to be.

CHAPTER TWENTY-SIX

ARCHIVE INSIGHTS

THE QUANTUM ANCHORS hummed as Alice passed through the archive's security field. Her enhanced perception registered the familiar sensation of reality stabilizing - a necessary precaution since Daybridge had weakened the barriers between dimensions. The late hour meant most researchers had left, but Alice knew Nadia would still be here. The archivist's dedication had only intensified since the Incident.

Location: Daybridge Historical Research Center

Section: Quantum-Secured Special Collections

Time: 11:27 PM

Reality Stability: FLUCTUATING

She found Nadia surrounded by hovering holographic displays, her hands moving through data streams with practiced grace. Since Daybridge, Nadia's natural talent for pattern recognition had evolved into something more - an almost symbiotic relationship with the archive itself.

"Your temporal signature's unstable," Nadia said without looking up, her fingers still dancing through data. "Rough case?"

"Kane Industries," Alice replied, settling into the chair Nadia had already positioned for her. Their post-Daybridge abilities complemented each other - Alice's enhanced detective skills and Nadia's archive-augmented perception had solved more than one impossible case. "But you knew that, didn't you?"

"I've been tracking probability threads since you called." Nadia finally turned, her eyes showing the peculiar iridescence that marked deep archive integration. "The corporate enhancement programs? They're not as new as everyone thinks. And they're connected to what happened to you and Ethan during Daybridge."

In the archive environment with active holographic displays, flowing quantum data streams, engaged reality anchors, and online ancient text preservation fields, Nadia's enhanced workspace merged old and new, displaying traditional archives alongside quantum data analysis.

The research summary materialized around them, covering historical analysis from 1800 to present, focusing on the Daybridge Financial District. Nadia revealed layered historical records showing a progression through different eras.

"I started with the 1850s land purchases," Nadia explained, expanding a section of the display. "The patterns seemed random until I overlaid the ley line data from your werewolf case last month."

Initial corporate land purchases showed unusual property patterns and supernatural incident clusters. The 1900s witnessed strategic building placement and underground construction at power convergence points. By the 1950s, corporate-supernatural research and secret enhancement trials emerged, leading to the 2000s' advanced enhancement programs and reality manipulation technology.

"Wait," Alice said, her detective instincts firing as she spotted a familiar pattern. "Can you highlight the 1950s enhancement trials? Something about those energy signatures..."

"Matches the quantum residue from your latest crime scene?" Nadia was already pulling up the comparison data. "The corporate experiments back then were crude, but the basic framework... it's the same one that affected you during Daybridge. They've been working toward this for over a century."

The ley line analysis revealed major convergence points at Kane Industries HQ, Global Financial Center, Technology Park, and Research District. Energy signatures showed ancient power flows merged with corporate enhancement patterns. Every major corporate headquarters was strategically built on ley line convergence points, suggesting deliberate planning.

"That's why their employees are showing controlled enhancement," Alice realized, her hand unconsciously touching the scar on her neck that still pulsed with quantum energy. "They're using modified versions of century-old technology, refined through decades of secret research."

The historical timeline display traced through various periods - from the Ancient Period's original power sites, through the Colonial Era's strategic land purchases, to the Industrial Age's corporate power centers, culminating in the Modern Period's advanced enhancement patterns.

"There's more," Nadia said, her voice dropping lower though they were alone. "Those architectural anomalies you and Ethan investigated? They were actually early enhancement attempts." Her fingers traced complex patterns, bringing up archived records of reality-warped architecture and enhancement equipment traces.

The investigation findings presented physical evidence of reality-warped architecture and enhancement equipment traces, while historical records revealed secret research programs and corporate-supernatural studies. Pattern analysis showed deliberate placement and strategic timing with global connections.

"I need everything you have on the Global Financial Center's original construction," Alice said, feeling the familiar tingle of quantum insight. "And... thank you, Nadia. For always being here, for understanding what we're dealing with."

"That's what archives are for," Nadia smiled, but her expression turned serious. "Just be careful, Alice. These corporate entities - they've had a century to perfect what Daybridge did to you by accident. And they're not going to want their secrets exposed."

"That's why I have you watching my back," Alice said, already diving into the new data streams Nadia was generating. "And speaking of watching backs - how's the protection spell Ethan helped you set up last month?"

"Holding strong," Nadia replied, her hands never stopping their dance through the archive's quantum interface. "Though we might need to reinforce it after what I'm about to show you..."

The deeper implications suggested long-term corporate planning with supernatural knowledge, historical context involving ancient power access, and a coordinated global pattern leading toward enhancement evolution and reality transformation. As Alice absorbed the full scope of what they'd uncovered, she realized their investigation had just become far more complex - and far more dangerous - than anyone had imagined.

~

CHAPTER TWENTY-SEVEN

LATE NIGHT ANALYSIS

Research Lab 7 - Kane Industries

Time: 0247

Security Level: Maximum

Reality Stability: Variable

In Lab 7, with quantum analysis active, reality monitoring online, enhancement detection running, and pattern recognition processing, Alice rubbed her tired eyes as quantum data streams blurred into iridescent rivers. Her enhanced perception frayed at the edges from exhaustion while she monitored multiple displays showing enhancement pattern analysis, field incident reports, and historical comparisons.

A coffee cup appeared at her elbow, the rich aroma carrying subtle notes her enhanced senses could dissect: Brazilian dark roast, trace enhancement formula, reality stabilization compound, and quantum framework harmonics.

"You missed dinner again," Ethan's voice carried the gravelly undertone of someone who'd spent the day shouting orders. His tactical gear bore marks of field operations, showing reality breach residue and enhancement energy traces. His own enhancement signatures revealed elevated awareness state and reality anchor stability.

"I keep seeing patterns in the enhancement data," she gestured at the holographic display, where reality itself seemed to ripple. The pattern analysis revealed quantum level framework stretching and reality membrane thinning, while the macro scale showed global pattern formation and reality structure evolution.

Instead of dismissing her concerns, Ethan leaned forward, his enhanced perception immediately syncing with the data flow. "Show me." His presence stabilized her fraying enhancement, their signatures harmonizing automatically after years of partnership. The lab's reality anchors adjusted to accommodate their combined energy field.

Their joint analysis session merged Alice's scientific perspective of quantum mechanics and enhancement theory with Ethan's security viewpoint of field experience and tactical implications. They worked through the night, their enhanced perceptions complementing each other. Where she saw theoretical patterns, he recognized practical applications. When his tactical experience identified threats, her scientific insight provided potential solutions.

At 0300, they focused on reality stretching, examining framework stress points and enhancement pressure. The holographic models showed alarming patterns of reality degradation, concentrated around areas of high enhancement activity. Alice's fingers danced through the data streams, highlighting quantum signatures that matched incidents from their field operations.

By 0400, they addressed security implications and containment strategies. Ethan's tactical overlay mapped vulnerable locations against known enhancement hotspots, while Alice's quantum analysis predicted potential breach points. Their enhanced perceptions worked in tandem, creating a more complete picture of the threats they faced.

At 0500, pattern recognition revealed global connections and historical parallels. The data showed an acceleration in enhancement manifestations worldwide, following patterns that reminded Alice of the Daybridge incident. Through their bond, she felt Ethan's recognition of the similarities – and his concern about what it might mean.

When Alice's hands started trembling from exhaustion, her enhancement flickering with depleted power levels and weakening reality anchor, Ethan wordlessly handed her his jacket. The garment carried residual enhancement energy and a reality stabilization field, its quantum-infused fabric designed to support enhanced individuals during extended operations. The warmth of his energy signature wrapped around her like a protective shield.

The gesture felt natural despite its novelty, their enhanced perceptions recognizing deeper patterns in their interpersonal dynamics. Professional research collaboration merged with growing personal trust and mutual understanding. The lab's reality anchors hummed softly as dawn approached, their combined enhancement signatures creating unique patterns of complementary frequencies and stable enhancement fields.

Through their quantum link, they shared more than just data analysis. Concern for each other mixed with determination to solve the puzzle before them. Their enhanced awareness revealed layers of meaning in every shared glance, every finished sentence, every moment of synchronized movement through the lab's holographic displays.

Their interaction balanced professional respect with growing connection, enhanced awareness with natural trust, as their research progressed through pattern recognition toward strategic planning. The night's work demonstrated both their professional capabilities and their deepening personal dynamic, all underscored by their unique enhancement harmonics.

As the first hints of sunrise filtered through the lab's quantum-shielded windows, they had compiled a comprehensive analysis of the growing enhancement crisis. But more than that, they had reinforced what they both already knew – that their partnership, both professional and personal, represented a new kind of enhancement symbiosis, one that might prove crucial in the challenges ahead.

CHAPTER TWENTY-EIGHT

ENHANCED EMPLOYEE SUPPORT GROUP

Research Lab 7 - Kane Industries

Time: 0247

Security Level: Maximum

Reality Stability: Variable

The converted conference room hummed with reality stabilizers, the air shimmering with dozens of unique enhancement signatures. Around the quantum-reinforced table, Kane Industries' enhanced employees gathered for their weekly support session. Dr. Nash's protocols mandated these meetings, though most had come to value them beyond mere requirement.

Alice watched the others settle in, her enhanced perception noting the various states of their quantum signatures. Lisa from Accounting, still struggling to control her probability manipulation. John from Security, his molecular density shifting causing subtle ripples in local reality. Dr. Williams from R&D, whose temporal perception sometimes left ghostly afterimages in the air.

"Let's begin," Dr. Sylvia Goddard said, her own enhancement creating a calming resonance in the room's quantum field. As both therapist and enhanced individual, she understood their challenges uniquely. "I see some new faces tonight. Remember, this is a safe space – quantum-shielded and reality-anchored."

"And what happens in Enhanced Support Group stays in Enhanced Support Group," added James from IT, his technopathic enhancement making the room's monitors flicker briefly. A few tired laughs followed – gallows humor was common among the enhanced.

"Who'd like to start?" Sylvia asked, her enhancement subtly harmonizing with the group's collective energy. "Any challenges since our last meeting?"

Lisa raised her hand, probability waves distorting reality around her. "I had another incident in the break room," she admitted. "Every vending machine in the building started dispensing prizes. We're still finding candy bars in strange places."

"That's actually an improvement," James noted encouragingly. "Last month it was lottery tickets manifesting in the ventilation system. The containment protocols we discussed are helping?"

"The quantum dampeners Dr. Williams designed help," Lisa nodded. "Though they give me headaches if I wear them too long."

"We're working on that," William's temporal echo replied slightly before he did. "The new prototype should be ready for testing next week. Or last week. Time's been... fluid lately."

Alice felt Ethan shift beside her, his enhanced senses picking up on the group's underlying tensions. Through their bond, she sensed his protective instincts responding to the others' struggles. The wolf in him recognized pack, even in this corporate setting.

"I've been having trouble with the new security systems," John admitted next. "My density shifting keeps triggering the reality breach alarms. Maintenance is getting tired of resetting them."

"I can help with that," Marcus offered. "We can program the systems to recognize your specific quantum signature. Though..." he glanced at his tablet, which was displaying code in four dimensions, "we might need to upgrade the reality anchors on sublevel three first."

The discussion continued, each enhanced individual sharing their struggles and successes. Working in a high-security research facility was challenging enough without having to manage reality-altering abilities. Some were new to their enhancements, still learning basic control. Others, like Alice and Ethan, had years of experience but faced new challenges as their abilities evolved.

"The meditation techniques have been helping," Dr. Williams said, his temporal echoes finally syncing with his present self. "Though sometimes I still wake up having conversations I won't have until next week."

"That's actually why we called this late-night session," Lila explained, her enhancement creating a stabilizing field around the group. "The increased reality fluctuations many of you are experiencing... they're not isolated incidents. Alice, would you like to share what you've discovered?"

Alice stood, quantum data streams materializing around her. "We've been tracking pattern changes in enhancement manifestations," she began, the room's reality anchors adjusting to support her presentation. "There's evidence that our abilities are responding to something. Some kind of... quantum pressure building in the fabric of reality itself."

The room grew quiet, enhanced perceptions collectively focusing on her data. Through their various abilities, each person perceived different aspects of the threat she described. Lisa saw probability clouds shifting. Chen noticed temporal inconsistencies increasing. Marcus detected patterns in the quantum computer networks that suggested systematic changes in reality's base code.

"We're not just here for support tonight," Ethan added, standing beside Alice. Their combined enhancement signatures created a stable center in the room's quantum field. "We need to prepare. Whatever's coming... we'll face it better together."

The meeting continued into the early hours, enhanced individuals sharing knowledge and developing strategies. Their different abilities, once seen as workplace liabilities, were becoming their greatest assets. As dawn approached, the group had begun to form something new – not just a support system, but a team of enhanced professionals ready to face whatever changes reality had in store.

CHAPTER TWENTY-NINE

ESCALATION - BREAKING PUBLIC TRUST

Location: GNN News Studio

LIVE BROADCAST - Global News Network

Host: Marcus Wong

Program: "Reality Check with Marcus Wong"

Chyron: "Enhancement: Public Health Crisis or Evolution?"

The studio's quantum-hardened cameras whirred as Marcus Wong, veteran anchor with fifteen years of conventional reporting and two years of enhanced journalism experience, prepared for broadcast. His recently developed enhancement allowed him to perceive viewer emotional responses in real-time, a controversial ability that had sparked heated debates about journalistic ethics.

"Good evening. Tonight we ask the question that's on everyone's mind: What's really happening in Daybridge? Our enhanced reporters have captured this exclusive footage..."

The footage revealed a junior analyst at First National levitating above her desk during a panic attack, while reality fractures spread like spiderweb cracks through the Financial District's glass towers. A kitsune in business attire casually walked through a Starbucks line as spontaneous probability storms caused ATMs to dispense winning lottery tickets. Corporate security teams deployed enhancement-dampening fields while underground vampire-corporate networking events became visible in broad daylight.

The expert panel consisted of carefully selected voices representing various stakeholder perspectives. Dr. Sandra Mallory-Post from Kane Industries PR maintained her professional composure despite her visible enhancement aura. Her quantum resonance suggested carefully controlled emotional states as she insisted these were natural evolutionary developments under strict corporate oversight.

Professor James Mansell, leading researcher in Supernatural Studies, displayed multiple enhancement signatures from his academic experiments. He emphasized historical precedents while warning that current enhancement rates exceeded previous patterns, with reality framework showing unprecedented strain.

Ambassador Liu Wei, representing China's Enhancement Commission, projected a subtle but noticeable reality-warping field while advocating for international cooperation and global regulatory frameworks. He stressed the importance of corporate-state partnerships in maintaining public safety.

Reverend Thomas Murphy from the Theological Response Team exhibited traces of traditional blessing powers merged with modern enhancement, calling for careful consideration of spiritual implications while acknowledging the need for evolving moral frameworks.

As the debate intensified, reality ripples became visible even through the studio's quantum shielding. Probability storms swirled around heated arguments while enhancement auras flared during emotional moments. Reality anchors strained under conflicting viewpoints as viewer feedback created quantum resonance patterns.

Marcus moderated while monitoring public emotional responses and reality stability metrics, noting enhancement field interactions and probability cascade risks. Breaking news alerts reported increasing enhancement incidents globally, escalating corporate security responses, and rising public anxiety levels.

The broadcast concluded with more questions than answers, viewer enhancement signatures revealing growing public concern and reality framework anxiety. Post-broadcast analysis showed record viewer engagement and enhanced perception spikes across multiple demographics.

Marcus' personal notes indicated public trust fracturing and corporate control weakening, while enhancement spread accelerated beyond predicted models. The reality framework showed signs of rapid evolution, suggesting imminent global transformation.

The studio's reality anchors took hours to stabilize after the broadcast, suggesting deeper patterns emerging beneath public discourse, patterns that would reshape society in ways few could predict or control.

CHAPTER THIRTY
FAITH AND PHYSICS

THE KANE INDUSTRIES ritual chamber pulsed with sickly quantum energy, making Alice's enhanced senses recoil. Corporate enhancement sigils burned like neon wounds in reality, clashing violently with ancient religious symbols. The dissonant patterns created a reality framework that felt fundamentally wrong, like a symphony played in competing keys.

Shadows writhed unnaturally across the chamber's polished surfaces, each movement leaving trails of corrupted quantum residue. The air itself tasted of ozone and desecrated incense; technological precision perverted by stolen spiritual power.

"They're using belief itself as a weapon," Lila's voice was tight with controlled anger, her centuries-old magical defenses straining against the warped field. Purple light crackled around her hands as she maintained their protective barrier. "Channeling humanity's faith through quantum frameworks to reshape reality. It's worse than we thought – they're not just stealing power, they're corrupting the very foundations of belief."

Enhanced corporate agents moved through the chamber with horrifyingly unnatural precision, their movements too perfect to be human.

Alice's perception caught the fractured patterns of their forced modifications, each one powered by stolen prayers and corrupted rituals. Their eyes glowed with engineered divinity; bodies marked with profane combinations of sacred symbols.

One agent wore quantum-enhanced prayer beads that clicked with mechanical precision, each bead leaking corrupted spiritual energy. Another carried a crucifix that pulsed with stolen divine light, its sacred geometry twisted into corporate enhancement patterns. A third wielded a Native American medicine staff, its ancient totems desecrated by technological augmentation.

"The perfect synthesis of science and faith," CEO Marcus Kane's voice resonated through quantum-enhanced speakers, each word distorting local reality. "Why merely enhance individuals when we can enhance reality itself? We're breaking down the artificial barriers between physical and spiritual, between quantum mechanics and divine intervention."

Beside Alice, Ethan's massive wolf form flickered between quantum states, his natural transformation fighting against the chamber's corrupted field. Only their bond, forged through genuine connection rather than corporate engineering, helped him maintain coherence. His growl carried undertones of primal truth that made the artificial enhancements shudder.

"They're not just killing people," he snarled, lunar energy rippling through his fur. "They're sacrificing beliefs. Every victim's faith, twisted and weaponized..."

Through their shared perception, enhanced by both quantum technology and genuine connection, Alice saw the horrible truth. The corporate victims hadn't been random – each had been chosen for both their enhancement potential and their spiritual strength. She saw flashes of their final moments: Buddhist monks torn from meditation, their inner peace corrupted into weapons; Catholic priests dragged from prayer, their faith transformed into reality anchors; indigenous shamans whose ancient connections to the land were perverted into corporate assets; Islamic scholars whose devotion was stolen and quantified.

"The philosophical debates weren't just cover," Alice ducked as reality itself warped around her, corporate agents bending local space-time with stolen spiritual power. "All those symposiums, the public discussions about enhancement ethics – they were preparing humanity's collective consciousness for what comes next."

"A new religion," Kane materialized on a quantum bridge above them, his form haloed by stolen enlightenment. His enhancement patterns were a blasphemous tapestry of every faith tradition, each one twisted to serve corporate ends. Sacred geometries formed profit projections; prayer frequencies translated into market forecasts. "One that recognizes humanity's true potential. No more artificial divisions between science and spirit, natural and supernatural. A unified theory of human transcendence, backed by corporate efficiency."

"Built on murder and forced conversion," Dr. Nash's voice crackled through their quantum-secured comms, heavy with exhaustion. "The support groups are overwhelmed. We're seeing mass psychological trauma as people's belief systems are weaponized against them. It's not just enhancement rejection anymore – it's spiritual violation on an unprecedented scale."

Kane spread his arms wide, reality bending around him like light through corrupted crystal. "Change requires sacrifice," he declared as the chamber's quantum field intensified. "Every major religious shift in history has had its martyrs. The Inquisition, the Reformation, the great conversions – we're just accelerating the process. Making it more efficient. More profitable."

The chamber's corrupted energy reached a crescendo, ancient prayers screaming through quantum processors as Kane prepared to initiate his final protocol. Alice felt Ethan's fur bristle beside her, sensed Lila gathering her ancient power, as they faced the ultimate perversion of both science and faith.

～

CHAPTER THIRTY-ONE

HIDDEN VARIABLES

THE QUANTUM-SECURED data node hummed in Dr. Goddard's hands as she transferred the clinic's findings to Alice. "There's something else," she said, glancing at the reality dampeners. "Patterns I wasn't sure were real until now."

The node projected enhancement trend data across the clinic's empty waiting room. Patient records floated in quantum-encrypted clusters, forming unsettling patterns.

"Look at the corporate enhancement signatures," Sylvia highlighted specific cases. "Kane Industries, Prometheus Tech, Quantum Dynamics – they're all slightly different, but there's underlying commonality. Like variations on a theme they didn't write."

Alice's enhanced perception caught it immediately. "These aren't competing programs."

"They're iterations," Sylvia agreed. "Each corporation thinking they're developing proprietary enhancement protocols, but they're being guided. The philosophical frameworks, the quantum methods, even the religious elements – they're too perfectly aligned."

She pulled up more data: "Religious leaders suddenly supporting enhancement despite previous opposition. Research grants appearing at key moments. Protest groups mysteriously losing funding. It's too coordinated."

"Who has that kind of reach?" Alice studied the patterns. "Even Kane isn't this connected."

"I started tracking board members, major shareholders," Sylvia displayed a complex network of connections. "Found something interesting – a research group called the Transcendence Initiative. Very old money, very private. They've had quantum theorists, religious scholars, and consciousness researchers on payroll since the 1960s."

"Before enhancement was possible."

"Before we knew it was possible," Sylvia corrected. "Look at their early research focuses: quantum consciousness, technological spirituality, guided human evolution. They were laying groundwork decades ago."

She brought up more records: "The Initiative has shell companies holding minor shares in every major enhancement corporation. They fund independent labs, sponsor academic chairs, donate to religious organizations. Always staying in the background, but shaping the conversation."

"They wanted enhancement to emerge naturally," Alice realized. "Or appear to."

"Kane thinks he's the mastermind, but he's following a path laid out long before him. The Initiative's true goal appears to be..." Sylvia hesitated. "Total consciousness integration. Enhancement isn't the end goal – it's preparation."

"For what?"

"Their internal documents mention something called 'The Convergence.' Most details are quantum-encrypted beyond my clearance, but I found references to mass consciousness acceleration, reality framework manipulation, dimensional barrier dissolution..."

A shadow passed over the quantum displays. Sylvia quickly secured the node. "We're not the only ones investigating. My contact at the Initiative disappeared last week. Left one message: 'Others watching. Older than Initiative. Want Convergence accelerated.'"

Alice absorbed the implications. "How deep does this go?"

"I've traced Initiative connections back to ancient mystery schools, esoteric orders that studied consciousness manipulation before quantum theory existed. Some of their symbols appear in enhancement protocols, hidden in the code. But even they seem to be answering to something else..."

The clinic's reality dampeners flickered. Both women instinctively checked their quantum shielding.

"Be careful with this, Alice," Sylvia handed over the encrypted node. "Kane is just the visible face. Whatever's really behind enhancement... it's been waiting a long time to reshape humanity."

As Alice left, Sylvia watched enhancement patterns ripple through the evening crowd outside. How many were truly random? How many were carefully orchestrated steps toward some hidden threshold?

In her office, she encrypted one final note in her research logs:

"Enhancement spreading faster than projected. Corporate phase proceeding as planned. Subjects responding to embedded protocols. Kane positioned for catalyst event. Convergence timeline accelerated.

Question remains: Are we guiding enhancement, or is enhancement guiding us?

Note: Check previous reality reforms throughout history. How many other 'natural' evolutions were quietly shaped? What are we being shaped into?

Second Note: If you're reading this, there are patterns beneath the patterns. The question isn't who's controlling enhancement – it's what enhancement is preparing us for.

Final Note: They know I know."

CHAPTER THIRTY-TWO

QUANTUM REFORMATION

THE RITUAL CHAMBER's corrupted quantum field crackled with competing energies as Alice stepped forward. Behind her, Ethan's wolf form rippled with lunar power, while Lila's ancient magic created patterns of protective purple light. The air itself seemed to vibrate with the clash between authentic power and engineered enhancement.

"You're wrong," Alice's voice carried the resonance of true conviction, making the quantum framework shudder. Her enhancement responded not to forced protocols but to something deeper – Ethan's unwavering faith in her, steady as moonlight; Lila's ancient magical knowledge, earned through centuries of study; the pure beliefs Kane had tried and failed to corrupt. "Faith can't be forced. Truth can't be engineered."

The Quantum Framework pulsed, recognizing authenticity. Around them, the corporate enhancement sigils flickered like failing neon, while older, truer patterns began emerging through the chaos. Alice felt each genuine connection adding strength to their side: Ethan's loyalty, bone-deep and unshakable; Lila's wisdom, earned through ages of watching humanity struggle and grow; Dr. Nash's compassion, born from helping enhanced individuals find their path. Even the desperate prayers of Kane's victims resonated still, creating a pure counterpoint to his corrupted frequency.

Kane stood on his quantum bridge, reality warping around him in unnatural patterns. Corporate enhancement made his skin glow with stolen power, each religious symbol he'd corrupted leaving visible scars on the fabric of space-time. "The old ways are dying," he insisted, but uncertainty flickered through his enhancement pattern like static in a false transmission. "Humanity needs a new path..."

"No," Alice's enhanced perception caught the pattern beneath patterns, the truth behind the quantum fluctuations. Her voice carried the weight of both scientific understanding and spiritual insight. "Humanity needs choice. Real faith, real growth – it has to be freely chosen."

She reached for Ethan through their bond, feeling the wolf's primal honesty, its connection to forces older than civilization. Lila's magic shifted beside them, no longer fighting natural law but flowing with it like water finding its course. Reality began to stabilize around them, quantum patterns responding to authentic belief rather than engineered conviction.

The chamber's corrupted enhancement sigils wavered as genuine power flowed through the space. Corporate symbols blurred while ancient runes strengthened, each authentic connection adding to the growing resonance of truth.

"The Quantum Framework doesn't care about corporate profits or power plays," Alice continued, understanding flowing through her enhanced senses like light through crystal. She saw the mathematical poetry of prayer, the quantum mechanics of genuine faith, the physics of pure connection. "It responds to truth. To genuine connection."

Kane's artificial enhancements began to fluctuate violently. The beliefs he'd stolen fought back, breaking free of corporate control. Prayers returned to their proper frequencies, creating harmonies instead of forced discordance. Religious symbols reclaimed their true meanings, quantum patterns realigning with centuries of genuine devotion. The corrupted reality anchors, powered by murdered faith, started to fail.

Through her enhanced perception, Alice watched the transformation rippling outward. Each freed belief added strength to their side, creating a cascade of authentic power that no engineered system could match. The Quantum Framework itself seemed to sigh with relief as natural patterns reasserted themselves.

"This isn't about choosing between science and faith," Alice pressed their advantage, feeling Ethan's strength flow through their bond as Lila's ancient magic danced around them. "It's about respecting both. About understanding that human consciousness affects reality but can't be forced to conform to corporate agendas."

The chamber's quantum field shifted like a river returning to its natural course. Kane's enhanced agents stumbled as their forced modifications lost their artificial support. Some fell to their knees, overwhelmed by the return of genuine feeling. Others stared at their hands in wonder as authentic power replaced engineered strength.

"You can't stop evolution," Kane snarled, attempting one last reality manipulation. But his powers were fading, corporate protocols useless without stolen faith to fuel them. His quantum bridge began to dissolve, forcing him to step back toward solid ground.

"No," Alice agreed, feeling Ethan's steadfast presence, Lila's accumulated wisdom, and countless genuine beliefs flowing through the Quantum Framework like stars finding their proper constellations. "But we can choose how to evolve. Together, freely, with respect for both ancient wisdom and new discoveries."

The chamber filled with pure light as reality reasserted itself. Not the harsh glare of corporate enhancement, but the gentle radiance of authentic connection – science and spirit, natural and supernatural, old and new finding their proper balance at last.

～

CHAPTER THIRTY-THREE

NETWORK COLLAPSE

THE QUANTUM RESONANCE detector pulsed steadily as Alice Chen and Ethan Reeves tracked the enhanced distribution network through Daybridge's underground tunnels. Above them, Deena Chancey monitored the operation from her mobile command center, her vampire enhanced senses allowing her to track multiple team movements simultaneously. The command center hummed with supernatural energy, modified tech accommodating both quantum science and ancient magic.

Deena had spent decades building bridges between supernatural factions. From her early days as a newly-turned vampire working homicide in the Daybridge Police Department to her current role as Supernatural Joint Operations Director, she'd always understood the importance of cooperation. The scars on her neck - both from her turning and from surviving the Bloodclan Wars - reminded her daily of what happened when supernatural groups turned on each other. She absently traced the marks as she watched the tactical displays, remembering the taste of ash and blood during those dark days.

"Seven major nodes," Alice studied her modified scanner's display. "Each one corresponding to one of the ancient artifacts Kane Industries discovered." The quantum physicist's enhancement signature pulsed with recognition; her abilities having evolved far beyond what anyone had expected when Deena first recruited her.

Deena's enhanced hearing picked up the concern in Alice's voice. She remembered similar tones during the Fae Insurgency five years ago, when she'd first recruited Alice as a civilian consultant. The quantum detective had proven invaluable then, just as she was now. That crisis had taught them all how dangerous the intersection of science and supernatural could be.

"Main facility located," Deena reported through their secure comms, her centuries of tactical experience evident in her calm tone. She'd learned long ago that panic was contagious among supernatural teams. "Old subway maintenance station. Heavy quantum shielding, but we're detecting massive reality distortions. They're using all fifteen artifacts together."

Through enhanced vision, she watched energy patterns shift through the underground complex. Vampire sight merged with quantum sensing technology, showing her layers of reality most couldn't perceive. The artifacts' power signatures were familiar - she'd seen similar patterns during the Arcane Archives incident of '92, though never at this magnitude.

She'd seen too many supernatural crises in her long life to take this lightly. The Werewolf Riots of '87, the Great Vampire Schism, the Fae Civil War - each had threatened to expose the supernatural world. But this was different. This threatened to fundamentally change it. The quantum readings reminded her of the reality ruptures during the Demon Incursion, but with an organized purpose behind them.

As she coordinated the joint supernatural response team, Deena reflected on how far they'd come. Twenty years ago, getting vampires, werewolves, and Fae to work together would have been impossible. She'd spent years building trust, leveraging her position in law enforcement and her reputation for fairness to create the first inter-species task forces. Now she watched werewolf tactical teams moving in sync with vampire surveillance units while Fae energy specialists maintained reality stability fields.

"Multiple targets confirmed," Deena reported, watching thermal and quantum signatures through enhanced surveillance. Her vampire senses detected the unique heartbeats and energy patterns of everyone in the facility. "Dr. Nash is on-site. Your father too, Alice. They're conducting some kind of mass enhancement procedure using the combined artifacts."

The implications were staggering. Nash had been brilliant but unstable even when Deena had worked with him during the early enhancement research. His collaboration with Chen senior had always pushed ethical boundaries. Now, with access to ancient supernatural artifacts and quantum technology, they were attempting something unprecedented.

Her own enhanced abilities had been evolving since the crisis began. Traditional vampire powers were mixing with other supernatural energies in ways that would have been blasphemous to the elders she'd once served. But Deena had always believed in adaptation - it's how she'd survived centuries of supernatural politics. She could feel new sensory inputs developing, her vampire nature responding to the changed reality around them.

The raid team moved in as Nash's voice echoed through the facility. Deena maintained tactical coordination while monitoring the quantum readings. She'd seen enough supernatural experiments go wrong to recognize the signs of imminent catastrophe. The energy patterns were becoming increasingly erratic, reminding her of the moments before the Fae Gates collapsed during the Civil War.

"Multiple breaches detected!" she called out, her enhanced senses detecting reality distortions spreading beyond the facility. Centuries of experience let her keep her voice steady even as she recognized patterns from historical supernatural disasters. "The Quantum Framework is spreading beyond containment!"

As reality grew increasingly fluid around them, Deena knew they were witnessing something unprecedented. In all her centuries dealing with supernatural crimes and crises, she'd never seen anything like this merger of quantum science and supernatural power. The artifacts' energy signatures were integrating with modern enhancement technology in ways that violated both physical and magical laws.

The storm above Daybridge pulsed ominously as Deena coordinated evacuation protocols and containment measures. Her experience handling the Daybridge Demon Incursion had taught her the importance of civilian protection during supernatural events. But this was rapidly becoming something beyond traditional cont

ainment strategies. The quantum readings showed reality itself being rewritten, supernatural energies merging with scientific principles in ways that threatened the very foundations of their world.

CHAPTER THIRTY-FOUR

PRESS & PROTOCOLS

THE QUANTUM STABILIZERS hummed as Alice reviewed the latest enhancement data. A knock at her door interrupted her analysis.

"Detective Chen? Marcus Wong from the Daybridge Chronicle." A lean man in his thirties stood in the doorway, press badge displayed. "I was hoping to ask you about the unusual energy signatures around Kane Industries facilities."

Alice tensed slightly. Wong's investigations into supernatural phenomena had earned him a reputation for uncovering uncomfortable truths. "What unusual signatures?"

"Quantum fluctuations matching patterns from restricted enhancement research." Wong pulled up holographic readings on his augmented tablet. "Similar to what was detected before the Milano Center incident last year."

"I'm not authorized to discuss ongoing investigations," Alice started, but Wong pressed on.

"Three Kane facilities showing identical signatures in the past month. Corporate security increased 300%. And now this summit with every major supernatural faction..." He studied her reaction carefully. "Something's happening with enhancement technology, isn't it?"

Ethan appeared in the doorway, "Mr. Wong. Still chasing enhancement stories?"

"Detective Reeves." Wong nodded respectfully. "Just following the quantum trail. Like those containment crews you've been positioning around the financial district."

"Standard security precautions for the summit," Ethan replied smoothly. "Nothing newsworthy."

"Really?" Wong's augmented display highlighted tactical deployment patterns. "Because these formations match supernatural containment protocols, not standard summit security."

Alice exchanged a quick glance with Ethan. Wong was too close to the truth.

"Off the record," Wong lowered his voice, "my sources say Kane Industries has developed something new. Something that breaks all the old rules about enhancement limitations. If that's true, the public deserves to know."

"Your sources are mistaken," Alice stated firmly. "All enhancement research follows established protocols."

"For now." Wong smiled slightly. "But we both know protocols can change. Especially when reality starts remembering what it used to allow."

The phrase made Alice's breath catch. The same words Dr. Winters had used.

"If you'll excuse us," Ethan stepped forward, "we have summit preparations to attend to."

Wong nodded, gathering his augmented displays. "Of course. But when whatever's coming finally breaks, remember - the truth finds its way out eventually."

After he left, Alice pulled up his file on her quantum scanner. "He knows too much. The patterns he's tracking..."

"I'll have him monitored," Ethan confirmed. "But he's right about one thing - when this breaks, we won't be able to contain the truth."

"Then we better make sure we're ready when it does," Alice returned to her enhancement data, but Wong's words echoed in her mind. Reality remembering what it used to allow. The truth finding its way out.

The summit was less than twenty-four hours away. Soon, they'd all discover just how right Wong's instincts had been.

CHAPTER THIRTY-FIVE

SHARED MEMORIES

THE QUANTUM STABILIZERS hummed a different tune in the lower levels of Kane Industries' underground facility. Alice's footsteps echoed against polished graphene floors, accompanied by the subtle distortion of Sarah's quantum projection walking beside her. The projection flickered occasionally, reality struggling to maintain the illusion of her sister's presence.

"Remember when we used to sneak into Dad's lab?" Sarah's voice carried that same conspiratorial tone from their childhood, though now it resonated with quantum harmonics. Her form shimmered, dark hair shifting between solid and translucent. "You always said his equations were wrong."

The memory hit Alice with unexpected force - two little girls in matching lab coats, giggling as they decoded their father's password (always their mother's birthday), sneaking into his private lab after hours. Sarah would stand watch while Alice pored over his notebooks, her young mind already seeing the flaws in his calculations.

"They weren't just wrong," Alice replied, running her hand along the quantum-enhanced security panel. Modern symbols glowed beneath her touch, so different from their father's old mechanical locks. "He was trying to quantify supernatural energy using standard physics. Like trying to measure wind with a ruler."

The projection of Sarah flickered again, her form briefly splitting into quantum probability streams before reconverging. "And now you've solved what he couldn't." Her image stabilized, showing that proud sister smile Alice remembered so well. "That's why they needed me on the inside. We knew you'd eventually bridge the gap between science and supernatural."

Alice stopped walking, turning to face her sister's quantum echo. The facility's enhancement fields rippled around them, responding to her emotional spike. "They? Who are you really working for, Sarah?"

Security cameras tracked their movement, their enhanced lenses struggling to maintain focus on Sarah's unstable form. Warning lights pulsed softly, detecting the reality fluctuations their conversation was generating.

"Everyone. No one. The balance itself." Sarah's smile was painfully familiar, the same expression she'd worn the day she disappeared. Her projection reached out, hand passing through Alice's shoulder in a shower of quantum particles. "Some of us have to disappear to keep the bigger picture in focus."

The air grew heavy with unasked questions. Around them, reality anchor points shifted, responding to the sisters' shared emotional resonance. Childhood memories flickered through the quantum field - homework sessions, midnight science experiments, whispered secrets about the nature of reality.

"You could have told me," Alice whispered, her voice barely disturbing the facility's humming silence. "All those years, thinking you were dead..."

"Would you have understood?" Sarah's form began to fade at the edges, quantum coherence failing. "Back then, you still believed everything could be explained by equations. You needed to discover the truth yourself."

Warning indicators flashed on nearby monitors - Sarah's presence was destabilizing the local reality framework. The quantum stabilizers increased power, trying to compensate.

"And now?" Alice asked, watching her sister's image break apart into streams of probability. "Why show yourself after all this time?"

"Because it's starting." Sarah's voice echoed through quantum channels as her form dispersed. "The old boundaries are failing. Reality is remembering what it used to be." Her smile was the last thing to fade. "And you need to be ready when it does."

The quantum field collapsed, leaving Alice alone in the corridor. But the security logs would show two distinct enhancement signatures for those few minutes - sisters reunited across the boundary between what was and what could be.

Alice pulled up her research notes, fingers trembling slightly as she added new observations. Her father had tried to measure the supernatural with science. She had learned to blend them. But Sarah... Sarah had become something else entirely.

The facility's quantum stabilizers returned to normal operation, reality anchor points reestablishing standard parameters. But Alice's childhood memories felt sharper now, colored by new understanding. She and Sarah had always known there was more to reality than their father's equations could capture.

She just hadn't expected her sister to become living proof of that truth.

～

CHAPTER THIRTY-SIX

CORPORATE WARFARE

Time: 03:00 GMT

Attendance: 147 Enhanced Executives

Reality Status: NETWORKED

The boardroom at Kane Industries served as the physical anchor point for the global quantum conference, its walls displaying cascading streams of corporate data. Moira Rogers stood at the center, her neural enhancements transforming raw data into three-dimensional patterns that floated around her like constellations of light.

"Let's begin with the Asia-Pacific sector," Moira said, gesturing to expand a complex web of corporate relationships. Her movements left trailing afterimages, enhancement signatures marking her interaction with the data space. "The Nakamura-Sony merger wasn't just about technology."

The visualization shifted, revealing layers of supernatural energy signatures beneath the standard financial metrics. Ancient symbols pulsed alongside stock prices, and kami signatures intertwined with market projections.

"Three major kitsune clans have integrated their power structures directly into Japanese corporate governance," she continued, high-lighting specific nodes in the network. "The Inari Banking Group's recent acquisition of quantum computing patents? That was orches-trated by nine-tailed fox spirits working through human proxies."

Alice leaned forward, her own enhancements helping her process the multilayered data. "They're using traditional fox magic to manipulate quantum probability streams."

"Exactly." Moira expanded another sector of the visualization. "And they're not alone. Look at what's happening in Europe."

The display shifted to show the intricate web of European financial institutions. Ancient ley lines pulsed beneath modern banking networks, and faerie rings overlapped with trading floors.

"The Deutsche-Credit merger tapped into old Germanic wild hunt energy. The Bank of England's new quantum trading system? Built on foundations laid by the Seelie Court centuries ago." Moira's enhanced vision tracked probability streams flowing through the networks. "Old money has taken on a very literal meaning."

Around the quantum conference table, enhanced executives from various corporations watched with varying degrees of concern and calculation. Their own supernatural signatures created complex inter-ference patterns in the shared virtual space.

"The Middle East is where it gets really interesting," Moira continued, shifting the display again. "Saudi Aramco didn't just discover new energy sources - they've bound ancient djinn to their production facilities."

The visualization showed towers of flame and light; supernatural energy being processed through quantum-enhanced refineries. Proba-bility streams twisted around ancient binding circles modified with modern encryption.

"Their enhanced oil fields are tapping power that predates petroleum," Moira explained. "They're not extracting fossil fuels anymore - they're harvesting pure supernatural energy filtered through quantum frameworks."

Alice studied the patterns, her mind racing through implications. "The entire global economy is transforming. We're not just enhancing existing systems..."

"We're returning to old ways with new technology," Moira finished. "Look at these trade routes."

The visualization expanded to show global patterns. Ancient ley lines overlapped with modern shipping lanes. Fairy paths intersected with fiber optic networks. Dragon flight patterns matched airline corridors.

"The supernatural world never went away," Moira said softly. "It just went underground. Now it's resurging through our corporate structures, using our enhancement technologies as conduits."

She highlighted specific trend lines, probability streams showing possible futures. "Within eighteen months, every Fortune 500 company will have some form of supernatural integration. The ones that don't adapt..."

"Won't survive," came a voice from the quantum conference. It was Zhao Wei, CEO of China's largest tech conglomerate. His enhanced projection showed traces of dragon energy. "The old powers are awakening. They remember their territories."

"Which brings us to the real crisis," Moira said, centralizing the display on a pulsing node of chaotic energy. "Corporate warfare is evolving beyond hostile takeovers and market manipulation. We're seeing the first signs of actual supernatural combat between enhanced business entities."

The visualization showed recent "accidents" at competing facilities - probability storms, reality fractures, quantum framework attacks disguised as system failures.

"Last week, a kitsune-enhanced trading algorithm attacked a fairy-backed cryptocurrency network," Moira reported. "The collateral reality damage affected three city blocks in Singapore. Next time..."

"It could be worse," Alice finished, seeing the pattern. "Much worse."

The quantum conference hummed with tension as executives processed the implications. Centuries of supernatural power structures were merging with modern corporate hierarchies, creating hybrid entities that defied traditional control.

"We need new protocols," Moira concluded. "New ways of managing these interactions before they spiral out of control. The Quantum Framework isn't just connecting our companies anymore - it's connecting ancient powers that haven't directly interacted in centuries."

She gestured, and the visualization collapsed to a single point of light. "Ladies and gentlemen, welcome to the new economy. The supernatural market is open for business."

The conference dissolved into urgent discussions, enhanced executives conferring in multiple probability streams simultaneously. Alice stayed focused on Moira, watching as she adjusted her neural interfaces.

"How long have you been tracking these patterns?" Alice asked quietly.

Moira's enhanced eyes flickered with data streams. "Since the first enhancements went public. But the real question is - who's actually directing these changes? Are we controlling this integration, or are we just the vessels for something much older awakening?"

Around them, reality rippled as quantum-enhanced corporations began adjusting their strategies, preparing for a new kind of market competition where profit margins were measured in supernatural energy and market share included territory in multiple planes of existence.

The age of enhanced corporate warfare had begun. And somewhere in the Quantum Framework, ancient powers were stirring, ready to reclaim their place in a world that had forgotten them.

❧

CHAPTER THIRTY-SEVEN

METAMORPHOSIS

THE TRIPLE HELIX storm now covered most of North America, reality rippling in waves as the Quantum Framework continued expanding. Three weeks after the raid on Kane Industries' main facility, the transformation of supernatural society was accelerating beyond control.

"Another sanctuary collapsed," Deena Chancey reported, her own form shifting between multiple supernatural states. The vampire haven's quantum barriers had dissolved, leaving its residents exposed to the changing nature of reality itself. Through her enhanced vision, she watched centuries of supernatural separation unraveling in real-time.

Alice's enhanced scanner tracked the waves of transformation spreading through supernatural communities. Pure vampires found their blood magic merging with Fae energy. Werewolf packs discovered their members spontaneously developing hybrid abilities. The Fae courts reported their realm's barriers becoming increasingly permeable. Each new transformation seemed to make reality more accepting of the next.

"It's not just the enhanced humans anymore," Alice observed, watching a group of traditional vampires demonstrate newfound werewolf abilities. "The Quantum Framework is affecting all supernatural beings. The artifacts' influence has reached critical mass."

Across Daybridge, the changes manifested uniquely for each species. Vampires experienced the most dramatic transformations, their blood magic expanding beyond traditional limitations to merge with Fae reality manipulation and werewolf vitality. Ancient elders found themselves wielding powers they'd only read about in pre-Sundering texts, while struggling to maintain their traditional hierarchies as younger vampires gained abilities that rivaled their own.

Werewolf packs underwent more subtle but profound changes. Their connection to nature deepened, allowing them to tap into Fae energy while maintaining their wolf forms. Pack bonds evolved into quantum entangled networks that shared abilities between members. Some packs embraced these changes, developing new hybrid forms that combined multiple supernatural aspects.

The Fae experienced reality itself becoming more responsive to their presence. Their natural ability to manipulate quantum possibilities expanded exponentially. Courts found their traditional boundaries dissolving as members developed hybrid powers that defied classification.

"The artifacts didn't just unlock combined abilities," James Willmer explained, studying the transformation's effects. "They reminded supernatural beings of what they naturally were. As more accept the change, reality itself remembers more of what was possible."

While some supernatural beings fought against the transformation, clinging to their pure bloodlines and traditional limitations, the Quantum Framework's expansion proved irreversible. Each new hybrid ability, each remembered possibility, made reality more accepting of supernatural combination.

Alice's scanner data revealed three main adaptation patterns. The first group, dubbed Full Integration, consisted of supernatural beings who fully embraced the changes, developing multiple hybrid abilities and new forms of existence. Their quantum signatures showed perfect stability as they accessed the complete supernatural framework.

The second group demonstrated Partial Resonance, maintaining some traditional aspects while selectively incorporating hybrid abilities. Their transformations progressed more slowly but remained stable. The final group, showing Resistant Isolation, consisted of pure supernatural beings who rejected the changes and attempted to maintain traditional limitations. Their power began fluctuating as reality itself grew more fluid around them.

"The resistant ones are struggling the most," Deena observed. "Their traditional abilities become unreliable as reality remembers more flexible possibilities. Many are beginning to accept partial changes just to maintain stability."

New hierarchies formed based on adaptation rather than age or bloodline. Hybrid communities developed, transcending traditional species boundaries. Ancient knowledge gained new relevance as forgotten abilities re-emerged, with young supernatural beings often adapting more easily than their elders.

"The Great Sundering's effects are unraveling," James explained. "The artificial barriers between supernatural abilities weren't just physical – they were woven into reality itself. As they dissolve, each being must either evolve or face increasing instability."

The artifacts' influence continued expanding, carried by the Quantum Framework that grew stronger with each transformation. Reality itself became more accommodating of hybrid abilities, remembering patterns that had been natural before supernatural separation. Spontaneous transformations occurred in seemingly normal humans with latent supernatural genetics. New hybrid abilities emerged that hadn't been documented even in pre-Sundering records. Quantum resonance between adapted beings created larger supernatural networks, while reality zones formed where traditional supernatural limitations ceased to exist entirely.

"We're not just returning to what existed before the Sundering," Alice realized, studying the emerging patterns. "We're evolving into something new. The artifacts reminded us what was possible, but reality itself is creating new combinations."

As the storm's influence spread, supernatural society faced its greatest transformation since the original separation of species. The age of pure bloodlines and rigid limitations was ending, replaced by a more fluid and dynamic supernatural framework. Those who adapted found themselves wielding abilities their ancestors had forgotten were possible, while those who resisted faced increasing difficulty maintaining their traditional powers as reality itself grew more flexible around them.

The question was no longer whether supernatural beings would change, but how they would adapt to a reality that remembered more possibilities than their artificial barriers had allowed. The metamorphosis of supernatural society had begun, and there was no returning to what they had once believed was natural.

Above them, the triple helix storm pulsed with ancient power as reality continued remembering what supernatural beings used to be – and imagining what they might become.

CHAPTER THIRTY-EIGHT

INSTINCTIVE RESPONSE

THE KANE INDUSTRIES executive boardroom hummed with quantum energy, reality anchor points straining under the pressure of Thomas Ward's increasingly unstable enhancement field. Sweat beaded on his forehead as he struggled to contain the power surging through his newly augmented system.

"Mr. Ward," Alice said carefully, her instruments tracking the dangerous spikes in his quantum signature. "I need you to focus on stabilizing your enhancement patterns. Try to—"

She never finished the sentence. Ward's control shattered, his quantum field exploding outward in a wave of raw power. Reality itself seemed to bend and crack around him, probability streams tangling into chaotic knots. The surge of unstable energy headed straight for Alice, too fast for normal evasion.

Ethan, who had been quietly monitoring from near the door, felt multiple triggers hit simultaneously. The full moon's energy, unusually strong through the building's quantum-enhanced windows, sang in his blood. The facility's reality stabilizers screamed warnings. And most importantly, Alice was in danger.

He moved without conscious thought, ancient instinct merging with enhanced tactical training. The transformation was smoother than usual, accelerated by the quantum energy saturating the room. Alice recognized the familiar energy signature of his change, even as it registered differently on her instruments under these unusual conditions.

The wolf that landed between Alice and Ward was massive, larger than his typical transformed state. His black fur rippled with overlapping energy signatures—the silver shine of moonlight interweaving with the electric blue of quantum enhancement. His eyes glowed with dual nature: lupine gold ringed with the digital patterns of his neural upgrades.

Ward's quantum surge hit Ethan's transformed body and... harmonized. Instead of causing damage, the energy seemed to flow through his enhanced supernatural form, being naturally channeled and stabilized by his werewolf nature. Reality anchor points throughout the room adjusted, responding to the presence of pure supernatural power.

"Fascinating," Alice murmured, her quantum scanning devices displaying unprecedented readings—clean, stable patterns emerging from what should have been chaos. "The lunar resonance is actually stabilizing the Quantum Framework. Your transformation is integrating perfectly with the enhancement field."

Ethan maintained his protective stance, a low growl rumbling through multiple layers of reality. His enhanced tactical systems remained fully operational in this form, tracking probability streams and threat assessments. But now they were merged with supernatural instincts that had been honed over centuries of moonlit nights.

Ward, his own unstable powers settling in response to the pure supernatural presence, slowly backed toward the wall. His enhanced senses were telling him something his modern corporate mind struggled to accept—he was in the presence of something far older and more powerful than any recent technological advancement.

"I... I apologize," he managed, his quantum signature finally stabilizing completely. "The enhancement integration was more challenging than anticipated."

Ethan's wolf form kept him fixed in place with a steady gaze, somehow managing to convey both professional disapproval and primal warning. The message was clear: control your power, or face consequences beyond corporate disciplinary action.

Alice moved to Ethan's side with practiced familiarity, her instruments continuing to record the fascinating interaction between his supernatural nature and enhanced capabilities. The quantum readings suggested his transformation had actually strengthened the local reality framework rather than stressing it.

"This confirms my theories about supernatural templates," she said, running additional scans. "Your natural abilities are providing a stable framework for the quantum enhancement integration. The corporate enhancement program needs to account for pre-existing supernatural characteristics."

Ethan's ear flicked in acknowledgment; his enhanced mind still fully capable of following her theoretical implications even in wolf form. The corporate security teams would be arriving soon, drawn by the reality disturbance, but the immediate crisis was over.

Ward was escorted out for emergency enhancement recalibration, leaving Alice and Ethan alone in the settling quantum field. She knelt beside his wolf form, scanning devices still recording the remarkable energy patterns flowing through him.

"Your enhancement signature is different under full moon conditions," she noted professionally, though her hand rested comfortably in his fur. "We should document these variations for the security protocols."

Ethan rumbled agreement, his enhanced systems already compiling data for her analysis. The full moon's light streamed through the windows, now creating a stable resonance with the Quantum Framework instead of disrupting it.

Later, there would be reports to file, protocols to update, and entirely new theoretical frameworks to explore. But for now, in the quiet aftermath of averted disaster, ancient supernatural power and modern enhancement technology had found an unexpected harmony.

And somewhere in the quantum probability streams, new patterns were emerging—ones that suggested this incident was just the beginning of a much larger integration between the old ways and the new.

CHAPTER THIRTY-NINE
ANCIENT KNOWLEDGE

THE PRIVATE RESEARCH lab deep within Kane Industries thrummed with overlapping energies. Quantum stabilizers pulsed in harmony with older, more primal forces as Lila traced her fingers through Alice's holographic data displays. Her rings left trails of purple light through the projected numbers and equations.

"Your quantum readings aren't wrong," Lila said, manipulating the three-dimensional data streams with practiced ease. Ancient symbols briefly flickered through the modern projections. "But they're incomplete. Like reading half a story and thinking you understand the whole plot."

She waved her hand, and the corporate enhancement data rearranged itself into new patterns. "The corporations didn't create these abilities - they just found a way to trigger what was always possible. Like remembering how to ride a bicycle, except the bicycle is reality itself."

The air shifted, reality bending slightly as Lila reached into a space that shouldn't exist. She withdrew an massive tome bound in what appeared to be shifting shadows and starlight. The book's presence made the quantum stabilizers whine, their readings fluctuating between impossible values.

"Before the Great Sundering," she continued, setting the book on Alice's research station, "these kinds of hybrid abilities were common." The pages opened themselves, revealing text that seemed to move and change even as Alice tried to read it. Diagrams showed beings that shifted between multiple forms, energies that flowed between categories modern science considered separate.

"The boundaries between supernatural species were... more suggestions than rules." Lila traced a diagram showing what appeared to be a being simultaneously existing as multiple creatures. "Werewolves who could channel Fae magic. Vampires who could bind demons. Dragons who walked as humans while maintaining their full power."

The book's pages crackled with competing energies - ancient magical signatures interweaving with quantum resonance patterns. Alice's instruments struggled to categorize the readings, displaying error messages alongside unprecedented data streams.

"Why didn't you mention this during our previous cases?" Ethan asked from his position against the wall. His enhanced senses were on high alert, tracking both the book's energy emissions and Lila's movements. "This kind of historical context could have helped."

Lila turned toward him, her smile carrying centuries of secrets. "You never asked, handsome." Her voice held a hint of power, ancient knowledge wrapped in flirtation. "Besides, some knowledge isn't meant to be shared until the right moment. The universe has its own timing."

Alice caught the slight tension in Ethan's jaw at Lila's tone, finding herself unexpectedly irritated by the witch's casual familiarity. Something primal and possessive stirred in her chest, surprising her with its intensity. Her enhanced empathy picked up complex emotional patterns between the two - old attraction, complicated history, unresolved tensions.

"These enhancement patterns," Alice said, deliberately drawing attention back to the data, "they're following paths that already existed in reality's structure?"

"Smart girl," Lila approved, though her eyes lingered on Ethan for a moment longer. "Reality remembers what it used to be. The corporations think they're pioneering new territory, but they're really just rediscovering old roads."

She turned a page in the ancient book, revealing diagrams that looked disturbingly similar to modern quantum enhancement matrices. "Your father wasn't entirely wrong in his research, Alice. He just didn't have access to the older context."

The mention of her father made Alice's enhanced perception spike. "You knew about his work?"

"I make it my business to know about anyone studying the boundaries between science and supernatural." Lila's smile turned mysterious. "Just as I've been watching your progress. You're much closer to understanding than he ever was."

The book's pages turned themselves to a section showing reality fracture patterns. "But understanding comes with responsibility. The corporations are playing with forces they barely comprehend, thinking profit margins and market share are all that matter."

"And what really matters?" Ethan asked, moving closer despite himself. His enhanced senses picked up the subtle changes in both women's quantum signatures as he approached - attraction and competition creating interesting harmonic patterns.

"Balance," Lila replied, her playful tone dropping away to reveal something ancient and serious. "The Great Sundering happened for a reason. Some boundaries exist to protect, not limit. As reality remembers its old patterns, we need to ensure history doesn't repeat itself."

Alice studied the book's diagrams with growing concern. "These fracture patterns... they're similar to what we're seeing in enhanced corporate territories."

"Now you're seeing it." Lila closed the book with a gesture, shadow and starlight swirling around its edges. "The question is, what are you going to do with this knowledge?"

The lab's quantum stabilizers slowly returned to normal operation as the book vanished back into whatever impossible space Lila had pulled it from. But the knowledge remained, along with the complicated emotions swirling between the three of them.

Ancient wisdom met modern science, while personal attractions and professional responsibilities created their own intricate patterns. And somewhere in the Quantum Framework, reality continued remembering what it used to be, one corporate enhancement at a time.

CHAPTER FORTY
TRUST FALL

THE KANE INDUSTRIES testing facility's reality anchors screamed warnings as Mark Lindstrom, formerly VP of Quantum Integration, charged across the room. His enhancement field had destabilized completely, transforming the respected executive into a nexus of chaotic supernatural energy. Reality bent and twisted around him, probability streams shattering in his wake.

Alice's instruments barely had time to register the threat before Ethan moved. His enhanced reflexes, combined with his newly discovered abilities, allowed him to cross the intervening space in milliseconds. The quantum shield materialized between them and Lindstrom, its surface rippling with integrated supernatural patterns.

"I've got your back," Ethan said, his voice steady despite the strain of maintaining the field. Sweat beaded on his forehead as he channeled both quantum and supernatural energy into the protective barrier. Lindstrom's corrupted enhancement field crashed against it in waves of distorted reality. "Just like the training simulations."

Alice was already moving, her hands dancing across her containment device's control panel. The familiar motions grounded her even as reality fluctuated dangerously around them. "Those didn't involve hostile reality manipulation," she replied, her enhanced perception tracking multiple threat vectors simultaneously.

"No," Ethan's smile was slight but genuine, even as he adjusted the shield's resonance to match Lindstrom's attack patterns. "But they did teach us to work together."

Months of training showed in their fluid coordination. When Alice needed to shift position for better containment coverage, Ethan's shield moved with her without need for verbal communication. Their enhanced awareness of each other had developed into something beyond standard tactical synchronization.

Lindstrom launched another reality-warping assault, his formerly precise corporate enhancement reduced to raw, uncontrolled power. "The boundaries are lying!" he screamed, his voice distorting through multiple probability streams. "We can't trust the old limitations!"

Alice's fingers flew across her controls, making minute adjustments to the containment field parameters. She could feel Ethan's presence behind her, solid and dependable as always. When her systems indicated a power spike was needed, his energy was already flowing into her equipment, perfectly calibrated to her specifications.

"Target lock in three," she called out, knowing Ethan would understand the entire plan from those few words. Their countless training sessions had developed a shorthand that went beyond standard protocols.

"On your mark," he responded, already shifting his shield configuration to match her containment strategy. His enhanced tactical systems provided targeting data that matched perfectly with her calculations, their separate systems working in seamless harmony.

Lindstrom's distorted form charged again, but this time they were ready. Ethan's shield split into geometric patterns that matched Alice's containment field design. As Lindstrom's chaotic energy hit the shield, it was channeled and redirected rather than blocked.

Alice's containment device hummed to life, its quantum fields integrating with Ethan's shield harmonics. They moved together, their enhanced abilities amplifying each other's effectiveness. Where Alice needed precise power control, Ethan provided it instantly. When he required complex reality stabilization calculations, she had them ready before he could ask.

"Now!" Alice initiated the containment sequence, her systems synchronizing perfectly with Ethan's shield matrix. The combined field enveloped Lindstrom, transforming his chaotic energy into stable patterns.

Their enhanced perceptions allowed them to track the process in microscopic detail. Lindstrom's unstable quantum signature gradually realigned, supernatural energy flowing back into natural channels. His screams faded as the reality distortions collapsed, leaving him unconscious but stable within their combined containment field.

As the facility's reality anchors slowly returned to normal operation, Alice and Ethan maintained their positions, their enhanced systems still working in perfect coordination. The air between them hummed with more than just quantum energy – trust built through countless hours of working together, understanding deepened by shared challenges.

"That was a new one," Ethan said quietly, his shield slowly dissolving as Alice's containment field took full control. "Corporate enhancement degradation leading to reality warping abilities."

"The pattern's accelerating," Alice replied, her instruments recording the final stages of Chen's stabilization. "More executives are manifesting abilities, but not all of them can handle the integration."

They worked together to secure the containment field, their movements synchronized without conscious thought. Alice's calculations merged seamlessly with Ethan's tactical assessments, creating protocols that adapted to each new piece of data.

"We make a good team," Ethan observed, his enhanced senses still monitoring Lindstrom's status while maintaining awareness of Alice's position. The comment carried weight beyond the immediate situation.

"We do," Alice agreed, finding herself hyper-aware of his proximity. Their enhanced perception fields overlapped, creating interesting harmonic patterns in the Quantum Framework. "The training paid off."

But they both knew it was more than just training. Their ability to work together so seamlessly went beyond practice and enhancement protocols. Something deeper had developed during those countless hours of learning each other's rhythms and responses.

As medical teams arrived to transfer Lindstrom to a secure facility, Alice and Ethan remained in sync, their enhanced systems still harmonizing naturally. The incident was contained, but the implications troubled them both. How many more executives would lose control as the enhancement process spread? And would their combined abilities be enough to handle the escalating crisis?

For now, though, they had each other's backs. In a world where reality itself was becoming unreliable, their trust in each other remained constant.

CHAPTER FORTY-ONE
BREAKING POINT

THE KANE INDUSTRIES executive boardroom transformed from a bastion of corporate power into ground zero of a reality crisis in less than thirty seconds. Moira Rogers, halfway through her quarterly projections presentation, suddenly froze mid-sentence. Her enhanced data visualization abilities, usually precisely controlled, exploded outward without warning.

"The fourth quarter projections show—" Her voice cut off as her eyes began to glow with quantum energy. The holographic displays around her multiplied exponentially, each showing different possible futures branching out in fractal patterns.

"Probability cascade," Alice's instruments warned as reality began to splinter. Every decision point in Moira's presentation spawned its own timeline, manifesting physically in the boardroom space. Markets crashed and soared simultaneously. Companies rose and fell in overlapping waves of possibility.

"Make it stop," Moira pleaded, her enhanced perception overwhelmed by the weight of infinite outcomes. Tears streamed down her face, each droplet splitting into multiple quantum states as it fell. "I can see everything. Every choice. Every consequence. It's too much."

The boardroom's reality anchors shrieked warnings as local space-time began to destabilize. Corporate security teams rushed to evacuate the floor, their own enhanced systems struggling against the waves of probability distortion emanating from Moira.

"Get everyone out!" Ethan commanded his tactical enhancements already analyzing the threat pattern. "Full containment protocols, minimum safe distance of three floors!"

Alice moved toward Moira, her scientific instruments tracking the cascading breakdown of normal reality rules. "Her enhancement integration is collapsing. The Quantum Framework is trying to process too many probability streams simultaneously."

Around Moira, time itself began to fragment. Different versions of the same moment played out in overlapping sequences. In one timeline, the stock market was crashing. In another, unexpected profits soared. Each possibility manifested physically, creating a chaos of conflicting realities.

"I can see them all dying," Moira whispered, her enhanced vision locked on horrifying futures. "I can see everyone dying, in so many ways. And living. And changing. All at once. All real."

Ethan reached her first, his supernatural instincts providing insight that pure science couldn't match. "Focus on my voice, Moira. One reality. One moment. Just like in training."

"The patterns," Alice added, calibrating her stabilization equipment. "Remember the patterns we practiced. Filter the streams, don't try to process them all."

Their combined approach - Ethan's primal supernatural guidance and Alice's scientific expertise - created a framework Moira could grasp. The security teams had cleared the floor, leaving them alone in the reality storm.

"I can't... can't sort them," Moira gasped, probability waves visibly rippling through her body. "Too many variables. Too many outcomes." Her enhanced systems were trying to calculate every possible future simultaneously, overloading both technology and human consciousness.

Alice's instruments recorded everything, gathering crucial data even as they worked to contain the crisis. "Her enhancement is attempting to process infinite probability streams without proper filtering protocols. The Quantum Framework is amplifying natural precognitive abilities beyond sustainable levels."

"Like a werewolf transformation without proper control," Ethan added, drawing on his own experience. "The power is there, but the structure is missing." His supernatural senses picked up patterns in Moira's chaos that the instruments couldn't detect.

Together, they created a containment strategy. Alice's scientific approach provided the rational framework, while Ethan's supernatural experience offered insights into managing enhanced abilities that exceeded normal human limits.

"Follow our lead," Alice instructed, setting up quantum stabilization fields. "Small steps. Filter the futures one at a time."

"Focus on the present," Ethan added, his voice carrying the weight of someone who had mastered his own supernatural nature. "Let the possibilities flow past without trying to grab them all."

Slowly, painfully, Moira began to regain control. The overwhelming flood of futures consolidated into manageable streams. Reality stabilized around her as she learned to filter the probability cascades rather than trying to process everything simultaneously.

"That's it," Alice encouraged, her instruments showing gradual normalization of quantum patterns. "Natural selection of probability streams. Let your enhancement work with your consciousness, not against it."

The crisis passed, leaving the boardroom in disarray but reality intact. As Moira's breathing steadied, Alice and Ethan exchanged knowing looks. This incident had provided vital information about the enhancement process and its limitations.

"Some adapt better than others," Alice noted later, reviewing the data. "Moira's natural talent for pattern recognition made her perfect for data visualization enhancement. But that same talent made her vulnerable to probability overload."

"It's not just about power," Ethan agreed, his tactical systems processing the implications. "It's about integration. Balance. Understanding limits."

The incident changed corporate enhancement protocols significantly. Moira's breakdown highlighted the risks of pushing enhanced abilities too far, too fast. It also demonstrated the importance of combining scientific understanding with supernatural insight.

As Alice compiled her findings, one thing became clear: the line between enhanced human and supernatural being was blurring. Each breakdown, each crisis, brought them closer to understanding what they were all becoming.

CHAPTER FORTY-TWO

SHADOW MARKETS AND SYNTHETIC RIGHTS

LOCATION: Underground Enhancement Club - The Nexus

The basement club throbbed with more than just music. Reality itself pulsed to corrupted enhancement frequencies as Marcus Chen adjusted his quantum-shielded recording equipment. The hidden locale deep beneath Neo Shanghai's financial district served as a nexus for the enhancement underground, where corporate technology merged with street-level innovation.

His enhanced perception picked up multiple layers of activity through the neon-soaked darkness. On the first level, the dance floor writhed with enhanced individuals, their quantum signatures creating interference patterns in the air. A DJ with crystalline growths along her arms manipulated reality frequencies as easily as sound waves, her unlicensed enhancements creating experiences impossible in regulated venues.

"What you're seeing isn't just a black market," Marcus narrated softly into his secured comm unit, his voice masked by quantum encryption. "It's a revolution in human potential being bought and sold in back alleys."

His camera panned across private booths where corporate enhancement formulas changed hands in shielded containers. Mid-level executives sat across from street doctors, negotiating prices for procedures that would never appear in official records.

Behind holographic privacy screens on the second level, underground enhancement clinics operated with sophisticated but unregistered equipment. Marcus's enhanced vision penetrated the barriers, recording former Kane Industries scientists installing black market quantum processors while traditional supernatural practitioners infused corporate enhancement formulas with ancient power.

The deepest level revealed the true scope of the shadow market. Here, traditional supernatural beings openly traded with enhanced humans. Vampires offered blood-based enhancement formulas while werewolf packs sold controlled transformation techniques. Fae merchants traded reality manipulation secrets as enhanced humans bartered corporate secrets for supernatural knowledge.

Throughout the complex, enhanced individuals gathered in self-organized groups, sharing resources, knowledge, and protection. Corporate enhancement refugees shared survival strategies while underground research collectives developed new integration techniques. Enhanced human-supernatural hybrid families created their own culture alongside resistance cells planning actions against corporate enhancement control.

The shadow market's freedom came with serious risks. Marcus's camera captured failed enhancement procedures leaving victims in quantum flux, addiction to unstable power combinations, and reality fractures from uncontrolled experimentation. Corporate security raids regularly targeted these underground communities.

His enhanced analysis systems compiled critical data points on price fluctuations, new procedures emerging from street innovation, and population movements suggesting community formation patterns. "Corporate control is failing," he concluded, watching an enhanced street kid casually manipulate quantum fields in ways that should have required expensive equipment.

As Marcus prepared to transmit his encrypted report, a disturbance rippled through the club's quantum field. Corporate security sweepers approached the district. Enhanced individuals vanished through reality gaps while supernatural beings provided cover.

"The question isn't whether this movement can be stopped," Marcus recorded his final observation. "The question is what happens when it grows too big to contain. These aren't just enhanced individuals anymore – they're becoming a synthetic species fighting for their rights."

CHAPTER FORTY-THREE
ESCALATION

International Response Center **- Geneva**

Time: 72 Hours After Daybridge Event

GLOBAL CRISIS MONITORING

Status: CRITICAL

Time Since Event: 72:00:00

Enhancement Spread: Accelerating

The quantum-hardened situation room hummed with supernatural containment fields as representatives from major world powers gathered around a probability-stabilized conference table. Enhanced diplomats flickered between quantum states as their abilities interacted with the crisis data.

Director Sasha Moen of the newly-formed International Enhancement Response Task Force addressed the assembly, her voice carrying the weight of seventy-two sleepless hours managing global crisis points.

Starting with North America, she detailed how the Daybridge quantum cascade continued its relentless expansion. Corporate enhancement rates had surged to 65% and showed no signs of slowing. Traditional supernatural territories were dissolving into chaos as reality stability deteriorated across the continent. The border between enhanced human space and supernatural domains had become meaningless.

Ambassador Liu Wei's hologram flickered as he reported on the Asia-Pacific situation. His enhanced perception projected images of chaos across Chinese enhancement zones. "Beijing has lost control of three major provinces," he stated, his quantum signature revealing deep concern. "The dragon courts are demanding direct intervention. Ancient ley lines are activating without authorization." The hologram showed massive reality distortions spreading across the region's financial centers.

From the Middle East, Saudi Representative Ahmed Al-Rashid's report carried traces of ancient power struggling with modern enhancement patterns. "The djinn are breaking centuries-old bindings," he announced, his voice resonating with both fear and awe. "Enhanced oil field workers are accessing supernatural reservoirs. Reality in Dubai's financial district exists in quantum flux." The probability maps showed critical instability spreading through the region's power structures.

EU Enhancement Commissioner Helena Schmidt's update painted an equally dire picture across Europe. The Vatican's ancient enchantments were failing under the strain of modern enhancement spread. Norse entities had begun emerging in Scandinavian tech sectors, merging with corporate enhancement patterns in ways that defied traditional containment. London's supernatural quarantine remained intact but showed signs of imminent failure.

The quantum-stabilized displays around them showed a world transforming faster than anyone had predicted. Traditional power structures, both human and supernatural, were dissolving as enhancement spread beyond corporate control. Reality itself seemed to be evolving, pushed by the merger of ancient powers and modern technology.

The assembled diplomats, their own enhancements creating interference patterns in the room's reality anchors, faced a transformation that threatened centuries of carefully maintained boundaries between worlds. The Daybridge Event hadn't just breached the corporate enhancement framework - it had initiated a cascade that was rewriting the fundamental rules of reality across the globe.

Every enhanced perception in the room detected the same pattern: this wasn't just a crisis to be contained. It was an evolutionary threshold being crossed, with humanity and supernatural entities alike being dragged into a new phase of existence. The only question remaining was whether they could guide this transformation or if they would be swept away by it.

CHAPTER FORTY-FOUR

DOCTOR'S ORDERS

THE DAYBRIDGE INTERNATIONAL Trade Center gleamed against the quantum-charged storm, its ninety floors packed with corporate executives and supernatural leaders attending the Global Innovation Summit. Alice Chen's scanner pulsed with warning signals as she and Ethan Reeves monitored the building's quantum shielding from their surveillance position.

"This conference isn't just a target," Alice said, her scanner revealing complex quantum resonance patterns. "It's an amplifier."

Dr. Winters had positioned all fifteen artifacts throughout the trade center, transforming the building into a massive resonance chamber. The architecture itself matched ancient geometric patterns found on the artifacts, each floor creating quantum pathways that would channel their power.

"Three thousand attendees," Ethan checked their hacked security feeds. "CEOs, supernatural leaders, politicians – everyone who opposed enhancement gathered in one place."

They fought their way through enhanced security teams, reality rippling around them as hybrid abilities clashed. Each level brought them closer to the basement vault where the primary artifacts pulsed with increasing power.

"The framework's already affecting the upper floors," Alice warned as her scanner tracked the spreading quantum distortions. "We're running out of time."

The vault level opened before them, revealing a figure Alice barely recognized. Where Dr. Helena Winters had once been a slight woman with steel-gray hair, now stood a broad-shouldered man, transformed by the artifacts' power. The Quantum Framework surrounding him radiated with impossible changes.

"Reality remembers more than just supernatural combinations," Winters' deeper voice carried the same cold precision. "Gender, species, biological limitations – all artificial constructs imposed by those who feared true potential."

"You used yourself as the first test subject," Alice realized, her scanner detecting complex patterns throughout Winters' altered form.

"Three months ago," Winters smiled, gesturing to the pulsing artifacts. "The first complete activation showed me what unrestricted transformation truly means. Today, everyone in this building experiences that freedom."

Ethan engaged the enhanced security team while Alice confronted her former mentor. Reality distortions made combat unpredictable as hybrid abilities created cascading effects.

"You're forcing transformation on thousands," Alice argued, trying to reach the artifacts.

"They never had a choice before," Winters countered. "Their genetics were artificially limited, their potential deliberately restricted. I'm giving back what was taken."

The artifacts pulsed in harmony with the storm above. Throughout the trade center, reality began remembering more flexible possibilities. Pure supernatural beings found their abilities merging with other species. Normal humans with latent supernatural genetics manifested hybrid powers.

Corporate leaders developed abilities their bloodlines had forbidden. Supernatural elders wielded combinations of power they'd fought to prevent. Political figures underwent the very transformations they'd opposed.

Above them, the triple helix storm merged with the artifacts' energy as three thousand influential people experienced what supernatural beings were before the Great Sundering. The age of artificial limitations was ending, not through corporate enhancement or supernatural evolution, but through reality itself remembering what it used to allow.

And in the vault beneath the trade center, Dr. Winters stood transformed – living proof that when reality remembers its full potential, not even the most fundamental aspects of identity remain bound by artificial constraints.

~

CHAPTER FORTY-FIVE

BREAKING PUBLIC TRUST - THE DAYBRIDGE DISASTER

ALICE STOOD IN HER OFFICE, watching Marcus Wong's exposé dominate every information channel. Years of her enhancement investigations were suddenly validated as his report cut through corporate deception. The holographic headline pulsed: "DAYBRIDGE DISASTER: THE TRUTH ABOUT CORPORATE ENHANCEMENT." Her quantum detection equipment registered reality fluctuations with each new revelation, as if truth itself was destabilizing carefully constructed corporate illusions.

Emergency sirens wailed across the financial district as Wong's quantum-captured footage played on endless loops. Enhanced executives phased through skyscraper walls, reality warping around their unstable forms. Trading floors devolved into supernatural chaos as decades of controlled enhancement broke containment. The pristine corporate facades literally crumbled as enhancement energies leaked through failing containment fields.

Ethan stood beside her desk analyzing Wong's footage. His own enhanced senses detected patterns they'd been tracking for years. "He got access to things we've been trying to prove for years," he said, studying technical readings that matched patterns in their case files.

"Corporate quantum readings, classified enhancement research, supernatural contracts – everything we suspected but couldn't verify."

The footage was damning in its completeness. Board meetings erupting in spontaneous energy projections as executives lost control of carefully hidden abilities. Trading algorithms merging with enhanced operators in ways that violated every regulatory standard. Reality fractures spreading through corporate headquarters as enhancement technology interfaced with supernatural forces in ways never meant to be public.

Security teams stood helpless as executives manifested uncontrolled supernatural abilities. Years of careful enhancement management dissolved in moments of panic. Alice's instruments recorded signature patterns she recognized from dozens of past investigations – cases that had been buried under corporate pressure and legal threats.

"The corporate enhancement era is ending," Alice said, monitoring the spreading crisis on her detection equipment. Her years investigating enhancement cases had prepared her for this moment, but not for its scale. Her database of corporate enhancement incidents was finally being validated, each new exposure matching patterns she'd documented and fought to reveal.

Corporate stocks plummeted as enhancement risks became public. Trading algorithms crashed as enhanced operators lost control, their quantum-modified minds unable to maintain the separation between human and machine. Enhanced employees fled corporate control while traditional supernatural communities broke their long-held silence, stepping forward to confirm Wong's revelations about corporate exploitation of supernatural powers.

Through her office window, Alice watched reality continue fracturing across the financial district. The gleaming towers of corporate power were literally warping, their quantum-reinforced structures buckling under the weight of exposed truth. Wong's investigation had broken decades of careful corporate management, releasing forces that had been building since the first enhancement experiments.

Her instruments tracked waves of destabilization spreading through corporate territories. Enhancement signatures she'd been monitoring for years suddenly flared into public view. The careful balance between corporate power and supernatural forces was collapsing, and no one could predict what would emerge from the chaos.

Private messages flooded her secure channels as former clients and witnesses finally felt safe to speak. Corporate whistleblowers, enhanced employees seeking help, supernatural beings revealing corporate exploitation – all the sources she'd protected over years of investigation were coming forward.

"Look at these energy readings," Ethan noted, highlighting patterns in the data streams. "The corporate enhancement programs weren't just about improving human capability. They were trying to industrialize supernatural power itself." His own enhanced senses detected the underlying patterns in Wong's evidence – systematic attempts to quantify, replicate, and commercialize abilities that were never meant to be controlled.

The Daybridge Disaster wasn't just validating Alice's investigations – it was revealing a new phase in human evolution, playing out live on global feeds. Each new exposure created ripple effects through reality itself, as if truth was physically restructuring the world that corporate power had built.

Her detection equipment registered cascading failures in corporate reality anchors. Systems designed to contain and control enhancement energy were overloading across the financial district. The careful illusion of corporate mastery over supernatural forces was literally dissolving in real-time.

Emergency response teams struggled to contain enhancement manifestations that defied their training. Corporate security protocols, designed for controlled environments, proved useless against the chaos of exposed truth. Traditional supernatural communities were mobilizing, stepping in where corporate control failed.

Alice's case files opened automatically on her holographic displays, each past investigation connecting to Wong's revelations. Years of carefully gathered evidence, witness statements, and enhancement readings were finally finding their context in the larger pattern of corporate exploitation.

As reality anchors overloaded across the financial district, Alice's instruments tracked waves of destabilization spreading through corporate territories. The careful balance between corporate power and supernatural forces was collapsing, and no one could predict what would emerge from the chaos. But for the first time, the truth about corporate enhancement was exposed for all to see, and there would be no returning to the carefully controlled illusions of the past.

CHAPTER FORTY-SIX

EMERGENCY COUNCIL

LOCATION: The Concordat Chamber - Sublevel 13

The ancient chamber, hewn from living crystal deep beneath the modern city, resonated with supernatural energies. Ley lines converged beneath the circular floor; their power visible to enhanced senses as streams of shifting light. Representatives from every major supernatural faction occupied the tiered seats, their very presence making reality flex and bend.

The First Tier held the Ancient Powers - vampire elders in ceremonial robes that rippled with centuries of accumulated power, werewolf Alphas whose forms shifted subtly between human and beast, Fae Nobles from both Summer and Winter Courts whose glamour created micro-climates around their seats. Witch Covens sat with their artifacts and familiars, adding to the chamber's mystical ambiance, while Dragon Emissaries in human form caused heat to shimmer around their contained power.

The Second Tier accommodated the Emerging Forces - Enhanced Corporate Representatives whose quantum signatures created interference patterns, Supernatural-Human Hybrid Communities, Independent Enhancement Collectives, Reality Manipulation Specialists, and delegations of Transformed Executives.

The chamber's witch-lights cast shifting shadows as High Elder Victoria Blackwood took the central speaking position. Her pale features carried the weight of centuries, but her eyes reflected modern concerns. The vampire elder's voice carried naturally to every corner of the chamber:

"The barriers between species that have defined our existence for millennia are dissolving. Three thousand humans now manifest hybrid abilities that should be impossible."

Her enhanced visualization systems displayed examples floating in the air - corporate executives manifesting vampire-like energy manipulation, traders developing werewolf strength combined with Fae glamour, scientists accessing ancient magical knowledge through quantum enhancement, security teams transforming in ways that defied traditional classifications.

Elder Magnus, his ancient vampire nobility evident in every movement, erupted from his seat. "This is an abomination!" His fist crashed down, sending supernatural shock waves through the chamber. "These corporate experiments mock the natural order. We should contain them all."

The European vampire houses behind him murmured agreement, their combined power creating zones of darkness in the witch-light. But opposition came swiftly.

Alpha Clarise Clarke rose, her werewolf energy making the air around her ripple. Modern business attire couldn't hide her pack leader's presence as she challenged: "And how do you propose we contain abilities we barely understand? My scouts report transformations that combine vampire energy manipulation with werewolf physical enhancement. Some are manifesting Fae glamour with vampire speed."

Her pack's intelligence appeared in holographic form, showing enhanced humans moving through moonlight like vampires, corporate security teams shifting forms without lunar influence, executives manipulating reality with hybrid supernatural abilities, and new powers emerging that combined multiple supernatural aspects.

Queen Arianna of the Summer Court rose with Fae grace, butterfly wings catching the witch-light in impossible colors. "The old classifications no longer apply," she observed, her glamour creating patterns of meaning in the air. "Reality is remembering what it once allowed. The question is not whether we can stop it, but how we adapt."

The Fae Queen's words triggered reactions throughout the chamber. Winter Court representatives caused frost to form around their seats, witch covens consulted rapidly shifting prophecy weaves, dragon emissaries' heat signatures spiked with concern, and enhanced humans' quantum fields fluctuated in response.

The vampire factions spoke of blood-based powers manifesting in non-vampiric entities, corporate enhancement mimicking ancient vampire abilities, traditional feeding territories disrupted by enhanced humans, and vampire-human hybrid communities forming independently.

Werewolf representatives reported moon-independent transformations becoming common, pack structures emerging in enhanced corporate teams, new hybrid forms combining multiple supernatural aspects, and traditional territory boundaries losing meaning.

The Fae detailed reality manipulation spreading beyond their control, glamour-like abilities appearing in enhanced humans, ancient contracts with humanity becoming unstable, and new forms of magic emerging from corporate enhancement.

The chamber's supernatural energies swirled with increasing intensity as each faction contributed to the growing picture of a world in transformation. Traditional boundaries were breaking down, not just between human and supernatural, but between all ancient classifications.

"We face a choice," High Elder Victoria declared as the evidence mounted. "We can attempt to maintain barriers that are already failing, or we can help guide this transformation."

The implications hung in the chamber's charged air as they contemplated a new supernatural order emerging from corporate enhancement, ancient powers adapting to modern technological integration, traditional rivalries giving way to survival partnerships, and the very nature of reality shifting as classifications dissolved.

~

CHAPTER FORTY-SEVEN
SISTER'S KEEPER

THE QUANTUM BREACH pulsed with unstable energy, casting prismatic shadows across the Kane Industries research lab. Alice's hands flew across holographic controls while her sister Sarah – or what remained of her after the accident – phased through solid equipment to adjust reality anchors directly.

"You could have told me you were alive," Alice said, her enhanced perception tracking the complex patterns of her sister's quantum state. Sarah existed in a unique form now, neither fully corporeal nor completely energy-based. Her presence caused subtle distortions in local reality, like ripples in clear water.

"Would you have believed me?" Sarah's form flickered as she reached into the breach, her 'fingers' manipulating quantum strings that only she could touch. "The rational scientist, accepting that her dead sister was working as a quantum ghost for a secret supernatural organization?"

The sisters moved in practiced synchronization, despite their five years apart. Alice's scientific expertise complemented Sarah's supernatural abilities as they worked to contain the reality damage. Where Alice saw equations and energy patterns, Sarah perceived the underlying fabric of existence itself.

"I'm dating a werewolf detective and fighting corporate executives with hybrid supernatural powers," Alice replied, adjusting containment frequencies to match her sister's unique energy signature. "My definition of 'rational' has evolved."

Sarah's laugh was almost solid, causing small quantum fluctuations in nearby equipment. "You've evolved too, sis. But you're still terrible at remembering to eat during a crisis." She gestured at the untouched protein bar on Alice's workstation, now twelve hours old.

The breach crackled dangerously, drawing their attention back to the task. Sarah's form became more distinct as she channeled more power, her outline sharpening against the lab's sterile walls. For a moment, she almost looked like she had before the accident – before the failed enhancement procedure that had transformed her into something unique in either human or supernatural existence.

"Remember that time in grad school," Sarah said as she wove reality back together, "when you insisted there had to be a rational explanation for everything?" Her hands, more energy than matter, pulled quantum strings into new patterns. "Now look at us – one enhanced detective and one quantum ghost, casual reality mechanics."

Alice's enhanced systems tracked her sister's energy signature, still amazed by its complexity. Sarah existed in multiple quantum states simultaneously, allowing her to perceive and manipulate reality in ways that even the most advanced enhancement couldn't replicate. The accident hadn't killed her – it had evolved her beyond conventional existence.

"I still look for rational explanations," Alice said, monitoring the breach's collapse. "They're just more complex now. Like how your quantum state allows you to interact with dimensional barriers directly, or how your consciousness persists without conventional neural activity."

"Always the scientist," Sarah's form rippled with amusement. "Even when dealing with your technically-dead sister who works for an organization so secret it exists between realities."

The breach finally stabilized, reality knitting back together under their combined efforts. Sarah's form became less distinct as the immediate danger passed, settling into the subtle quantum shimmer that was her natural state now.

"The Department could use someone with your enhanced capabilities," Sarah said, floating near her sister. "Especially now that corporate enhancement is creating new types of reality breaches. Having a scientist who understands both quantum mechanics and supernatural phenomena would be invaluable."

Alice's hands stilled on the controls. "Are you officially recruiting me, or is this a concerned sister suggesting a career change?"

"Both?" Sarah's form flickered with uncertainty. "Things are changing, Alice. The barriers between natural and supernatural, between science and magic – they're breaking down. We need people who can bridge those gaps."

The lab fell silent except for the hum of quantum stabilizers. Alice studied her sister's ethereal form, seeing both the ghost of who she had been and the reality of what she had become. Sarah had always been the one to embrace change, to push boundaries. Even death hadn't stopped that tendency.

"I already have a job," Alice finally said, but her tone was thoughtful. "Though I suppose consulting work isn't out of the question. Especially if it means keeping an eye on my reckless quantum ghost of a sister."

Sarah's laugh this time caused all the lab's holographic displays to flicker. "See? Evolution in action. The Alice I knew five years ago would never have considered moonlighting for a supernatural agency."

"The Alice you knew five years ago thought you were dead," Alice replied softly. "A lot has changed since then."

Sarah's form drifted closer, her quantum field interacting with Alice's enhanced systems in complex patterns. "Not everything. You're still my sister. Still trying to understand everything. Still forgetting to eat."

As if on cue, Alice's stomach growled. Sarah's energy pattern shifted in what might have been an eye roll. "Go get food. I'll monitor the containment fields. Unlike some people, I don't need to worry about material sustenance anymore."

Alice hesitated. "Will you still be here when I get back?"

Sarah's form solidified slightly, becoming almost completely visible. "I promise. No more disappearing acts. Besides," her tone turned teasing, "someone has to keep you from working yourself into quantum instability."

The sisters shared a look that bridged the gap between life and death, between science and supernatural, between what was and what had become. Then Alice headed for the door, pausing only briefly to look back at her sister's shimmering form.

"Sarah? I'm glad you're not actually dead."

"Me too, sis. Me too."

∼

CHAPTER FORTY-EIGHT
DIPLOMATIC CRISIS

The Geneva Nexus, a dimensional pocket extending beneath Lake Geneva, hummed with supernatural tension. Delegations from every major supernatural power bloc and human government filled the grand chamber, their competing energies creating visible auroras in the quantum-enhanced air.

Ambassador Elena Volkov stood at the central podium, her enhanced diplomatic interfaces projecting her words in multiple languages and reality frequencies simultaneously. Her Russian Supernatural Coordination Bureau uniform bore both traditional mystical wards and modern quantum shielding.

"The enhancement process cannot be controlled by any single nation," she declared, her voice carrying the weight of centuries of supernatural diplomacy. "We propose an international oversight committee. The proliferation of hybrid abilities threatens the Moscow Accords of 1923 and the Supernatural Containment Protocols."

Behind her, holographic displays showed the spread of enhancement incidents across global territories:

Corporate executives in Tokyo manifesting ancient dragon powers. Wall Street traders channeling Native American spirit magic. European security forces developing hybrid vampire-werewolf abilities.

High Elder Chang rose from his seat among the Asian Supernatural Alliance delegation. His form shifted between human appearance and something far more ancient, his dragon nature barely contained by diplomatic protocols.

"Our ancient bloodlines have maintained order for millennia," he said, smoke curling from his words. "These corporate experiments threaten everything. The natural order requires balance between powers, not this unchecked proliferation of abilities."

The chamber's reality stabilizers strained as supernatural representatives demonstrated their concerns:

African shamans showing violated spiritual boundaries. European vampire houses presenting disrupted feeding territories. Native American spirit walkers revealing damaged totemic connections.

Dr. James Winters appeared on the central display; his quantum-projected form surprisingly stable for a virtual presence. The pioneer of enhancement theory looked almost amused by the supernatural politics playing out before him.

"You're missing the point," he said, his image flickering with complex equations. "The barriers between nations, between supernatural and human, were always artificial. The Quantum Framework is simply revealing what was natural. We're witnessing the collapse of manufactured divisions."

His words triggered immediate reactions. The French supernatural delegation's protective wards flared. Chinese dragon representatives' scales emerged involuntarily. American corporate enhancement liaisons' quantum signatures became erratic.

Ambassador Volkov raised her hand for order, her enhanced diplomatic systems working to maintain stability. "Dr. Winters, you speak of natural order, but we're seeing chaos. Enhanced humans manifesting powers that violate ancient treaties. Corporate interests disrupting supernatural territories. Traditional power structures failing."

"Evolution is often mistaken for chaos," Winters replied. His projection displayed data streams showing the merging of supernatural and enhanced human energy patterns. "These corporate executives aren't stealing supernatural powers – they're remembering what humanity once was. What we all were, before the divisions."

High Elder Chang's dragon nature manifested further, scales spreading across his face. "You speak of things you don't understand, doctor. There are reasons for the boundaries between powers. The corporate world plays with forces that could shatter reality itself."

The chamber's quantum field rippled as various factions added their voices:

The Vatican's supernatural division warned of prophecies fulfilled. Islamic mystics spoke of ancient warnings about the mixing of powers. Buddhist monasteries reported disruption in karmic patterns. Corporate enhancement specialists argued for scientific oversight.

Dr. Winters' projection remained calm. "The Quantum Framework doesn't recognize your political boundaries or supernatural territories. Reality itself is reverting to its original state – a unified field where all forms of power flow freely."

Ambassador Volkov's enhanced diplomatic systems registered multiple crises developing simultaneously: Treaty violations in major cities. Supernatural territories dissolving. Enhanced humans forming independent power blocs. Ancient wards failing against new hybrid abilities.

"We need immediate action," she declared, her enhanced perception tracking mounting instabilities. "I propose an emergency protocol: Joint supernatural-corporate task forces. Shared oversight of enhancement research. Updated treaties recognizing new forms of power."

High Elder Chang's dragon nature subsided slightly. "And who would enforce these new protocols? The old powers are failing, but the new ones are untested."

"Perhaps that's the point," Dr. Winters interjected. "We need new structures for a new reality. The old divisions – supernatural and human, corporate and spiritual, national and universal – they're becoming meaningless."

The chamber fell silent as the implications settled in. Centuries of supernatural diplomacy, carefully maintained boundaries between powers, traditional hierarchies and territories – all of it was transforming under the pressure of corporate enhancement and quantum reality manipulation.

Ambassador Volkov looked out over the assembled representatives of a changing world. "We stand at a crossroads. We can fight this transformation and risk reality itself, or we can guide it. But we must decide now."

The Geneva Nexus hummed with potential as ancient powers and modern forces faced a fundamental choice: adapt to a new unified reality, or risk everything trying to maintain the old divisions.

CHAPTER FORTY-NINE
AFTERMATH

THE QUANTUM STORM DISSIPATED, leaving an eerie silence over the Daybridge International Trade Center. Emergency lights pulsed through corridors filled with disoriented executives and supernatural leaders, each struggling to comprehend their transformed bodies and newly merged abilities.

"Initial readings suggest ninety-eight percent exposure rate," Alice reported, her scanner sweeping the building's upper levels. "The Quantum Framework's still active, but stable. The changes appear permanent."

Ethan helped a corporate executive who had collapsed nearby, the woman's skin now rippling with previously impossible hybrid abilities. "They're going to need medical support. And counseling."

In the conference hall, supernatural elders who had once enforced pure bloodlines now exhibited the very hybrid powers they'd condemned. A vampire elder generated phoenix fire while maintaining her blood abilities. A werewolf pack leader phased through solid matter like a ghost while retaining his lupine form.

"The market implications alone..." A CEO stared at her hands as they cycled through different supernatural energies. "Our entire enhancement regulatory framework is obsolete."

Through the vault's security feeds, they watched Dr. Winters surrendering peacefully to the authorities. His transformed masculine form stood tall, almost proud, as quantum containment specialists secured the artifacts.

"The changes can't be reversed," Winters announced to the gathering crowd. "Reality has remembered what was possible. You can imprison me, but you can't reimpose the artificial barriers. The Sundering is over."

Alice's scanner confirmed his claims. The quantum patterns had stabilized across all affected individuals. Hybrid abilities that should have been incompatible now coexisted naturally.

"We're getting reports from outside," Ethan checked their comms. "The media's already calling it the 'Daybridge Evolution.' Three thousand of the world's most influential people, all transformed at once."

"The question isn't whether to allow enhancement anymore," Alice observed, watching the chaos unfold. "It's how to handle a world where the boundaries between supernatural abilities no longer exist."

Regulatory agencies scrambled to respond. Military units secured the perimeter. But in the transformed conference rooms above, the world's power brokers were already adapting, forming new alliances based on their shared experience of unrestricted potential.

The age of artificial limitations had ended, not with corporate approval or political consent, but with reality itself remembering what it used to allow. And in the aftermath of the Daybridge Evolution, three thousand of the most powerful people on Earth would never see supernatural abilities the same way again.

～

CHAPTER FIFTY

MOONLIGHT MALFUNCTION

LOCATION: Financial District - Quantum Disruption Zone

The skyscrapers of the financial district created canyons of glass and steel, their surfaces reflecting both moonlight and the shifting quantum distortions. Alice's enhanced sensors tracked multiple energy signatures converging on their position – corporate enhancement fields, ancient ley line power, and the pure supernatural force of the rising full moon.

"These readings don't make sense," Alice muttered, her quantum interface displaying increasingly complex patterns. "The enhancement fields are resonating with something deeper... older..."

Ethan, already tense from the approaching moonrise, focused his supernatural senses on their surroundings. His enhanced police detective abilities merged with his werewolf nature, allowing him to perceive layers of reality most others missed. "The ley line under Daybridge Tower is acting strange. Like it's being pulled toward the enhancement zones."

They stood at the intersection of old power and new, watching reality shift around them. Corporate executives with enhancement modifications hurried through the streets, their quantum signatures leaving traces visible to enhanced perception. Above, the clouds began to part.

The moonlight hit like a physical force.

Multiple enhancement fields intersected with the ley line simultaneously, creating a cascade of quantum-supernatural energy. The resulting surge transformed the financial district into a reality storm, corporate enhancement signatures flaring out of control.

Ethan's transformation wasn't the controlled shift he'd mastered over years of practice. This was primal, explosive – his werewolf form erupting into existence with supernatural force. But something was different. Quantum energy merged with lunar power, creating patterns of light that coursed through his fur like circuits.

"Ethan!" Alice called out, her enhanced systems struggling to process what she was seeing. "Your quantum signature is..."

Before she could finish, enhanced executives nearby began reacting to his presence. Their unstable powers, previously fluctuating wildly, started to stabilize. Reality itself seemed to smooth out around Ethan's transformed form.

"Your wolf form is acting as a natural stabilizer," Alice realized, her scanners recording unprecedented data. "The pure supernatural energy is counteracting the quantum instability. It's like... like your werewolf nature remembers how reality should work."

Ethan's wolf eyes glowed with combined lunar and quantum light, ancient supernatural power merging with modern enhancement in ways that should have been impossible. He moved with fluid grace, each step leaving patterns of stabilized reality in his wake.

Together they began establishing a containment perimeter. Alice's scientific expertise guided their efforts while Ethan's hybrid state provided an anchor point. Enhanced executives within their perimeter found their abilities settling into more controlled patterns, as if Ethan's presence reminded their powers how to behave.

"The moon's energy..." Alice observed, tracking multiple data streams, "it's not just triggering your transformation. It's acting as a template for natural supernatural function. Your wolf form is translating that template to the enhancement fields."

Ethan couldn't respond verbally in wolf form, but his enhanced awareness communicated understanding. He could feel the different energies flowing through him – the pure, ancient power of his werewolf nature and the complex quantum patterns of modern enhancement.

More enhanced executives were drawn to their perimeter, instinctively seeking the stability Ethan's presence provided. Alice's sensors tracked the changes:

- Quantum enhancement signatures aligning with natural supernatural patterns
- Reality stabilizing around Ethan's hybrid form
- Corporate executives' powers settling into more controlled configurations
- The ley line's energy finding new harmony with enhancement fields

"This could change everything," Alice said, watching the data accumulate. "If supernatural nature can stabilize enhancement this way... we might have a solution to the containment crisis."

Ethan's wolf form moved through the growing crowd of enhanced executives, his mere presence helping their powers stabilize. The moonlight continued to pour down, but now it felt less like a disruptive force and more like a guiding influence.

A security team from Kane Industries arrived, their own enhanced abilities clearly unstable. They stopped short at the sight of Ethan – a fully transformed werewolf glowing with quantum energy, somehow making reality behave.

"Detective Chen?" their leader asked uncertainly, recognizing Ethan despite his transformed state. "What... what are you doing to the enhancement fields?"

Alice stepped forward, her systems still recording everything. "He's showing us what we've been missing. Enhancement isn't just about adding new powers – it's about remembering old ones. His werewolf nature provides a blueprint for how supernatural power should function."

The security team's quantum signatures began stabilizing as they entered Ethan's influence. Their enhanced abilities settled into patterns that matched the natural flow of supernatural energy, guided by the pure template of Ethan's wolf form.

As they worked to expand the stable zone, Alice's mind raced with implications. If werewolf nature could stabilize enhancement this way, what about other supernatural templates? Could vampire energy patterns help control corporate power manipulation? Would Fae glamour provide models for reality manipulation?

Ethan's wolf eyes met hers, showing intelligence that merged human, werewolf, and enhanced awareness. They had stumbled onto something profound – not just a temporary solution to quantum instability, but perhaps a bridge between ancient supernatural power and modern enhancement.

The moonlight continued to fall, and in its silver illumination, old power and new found ways to coexist.

CHAPTER FIFTY-ONE

RESONANT HEARTS

LOCATION: Supernatural Emergency Command Center - Level 7

They found a quiet corner in the emergency command center, away from the constant flow of crisis reports and status updates. The space between two quantum stabilization units provided a temporary haven, their combined fields creating a bubble of relative calm. Alice's enhanced perception picked up Ethan's elevated stress levels despite his calm exterior – increased cortisol, subtle muscle tension, the slight fluctuation in his hybrid supernatural-enhancement field.

"You're worried about the containment teams," she said softly, her voice pitched to carry only to his enhanced hearing. Around them, holographic displays continued tracking reality breaches and enhancement incidents across the city, but in their corner, time seemed to slow.

"Three lost control today," he admitted, his police detective training warring with werewolf instincts and enhancement modifications. His hands, capable of both devastating strength and delicate forensic work, clenched slightly. "Their enhancements... it's like watching my own people slip away. First the physical changes, then the personality shifts, until there's nothing left of who they were."

Alice's hand found his, an instinctive gesture that sent cascading waves through their enhanced energy fields. Their quantum signatures resonated, creating patterns that rippled through nearby monitoring equipment. His supernatural nature – wolf, protector, hunter – harmonized with her scientific enhancement in ways that defied conventional analysis.

"We'll find a way to help them. Together." The word 'together' carried undertones that neither was ready to fully examine. Her enhanced systems registered multiple physiological responses – elevated heart rates, synchronized breathing patterns, complementary energy frequencies.

The touch lingered longer than necessary, neither mentioning how natural it felt or how their enhanced abilities seemed to stabilize in each other's presence. Ethan's werewolf nature, usually restless under the surface, settled into a calmer rhythm. Alice's enhancement-enhanced mind, typically racing with calculations and possibilities, found a quieter focus.

Around them, the command center continued its vital work. Enhanced operatives coordinated containment responses. Supernatural liaisons managed territory disputes. Reality stabilization teams deployed to crisis points. But in their corner, something else was developing – a connection that bridged the gap between ancient supernatural power and modern enhancement.

Their hands remained linked, creating a minor phenomenon that only the most sensitive instruments could detect: two different forms of enhanced existence finding harmony, suggesting possibilities that neither science nor supernatural lore had predicted.

~

CHAPTER FIFTY-TWO

RESEARCH BREAK

LOCATION: Kane Industries Research Division - Quantum Analysis Lab

The lab hummed with the sound of reality stabilizers and quantum computation arrays. Holographic data streams cast ever-changing patterns across surfaces designed to handle both supernatural and enhancement energies. In the midst of this technological symphony, Alice had been working for sixteen straight hours, her enhanced perception barely registering the passage of time.

"You need to eat," Nadia announced, her sudden entrance disrupting probability patterns in the air. She dropped several takeout containers on Alice's desk, carefully avoiding the sensitive equipment. "And actual food, not just coffee and quantum energy bars."

The aroma of actual cooking cut through Alice's enhancement-assisted focus. Thai food – her favorite from the place near the supernatural district. Nadia had even remembered to get the extra spicy pad thai that Alice craved when deep in research mode.

Alice looked up from her calculations, grateful for her friend's intervention. Her enhanced systems were indeed reporting significant caloric deficit and decreased cognitive efficiency. "How do you always know?"

"Please." Nadia started arranging the food with practiced efficiency, having performed this ritual countless times. "I've been watching you and Ethan work yourselves to exhaustion for years. At least he has werewolf stamina as an excuse. You're still basically human, enhanced or not."

The archivist's presence brought a welcome touch of normalcy to the lab. Nadia had been documenting supernatural affairs long before corporate enhancement became an issue, maintaining a delicate balance between public information and necessary secrecy. Her insight into both worlds made her uniquely qualified to chronicle these changing times.

"Speaking of Ethan..." Nadia's tone carried that particular inflection that made Alice's enhanced perception register potential conversational dangers.

"Don't start," Alice warned, but couldn't hide her slight smile. Her enhanced systems betrayed her with subtle physiological responses – elevated heart rate, altered brain chemistry, quantum field fluctuations.

"I'm just saying, as someone who's documented both your careers, the chemistry isn't just professional anymore." Nadia's journalist instincts were as sharp as ever, honed by years of investigating supernatural incidents and corporate enhancement cases. "Your energy signatures align in ways that even the quantum specialists can't explain. And don't think I haven't noticed how your enhancement fields stabilize when he's around."

Alice focused on her food, but her enhanced perception couldn't help analyzing the truth in Nadia's words. The data was there – synchronized energy patterns, complementary quantum signatures, enhanced abilities functioning more efficiently in each other's presence. The scientist in her wanted to attribute it all to natural resonance between different types of enhancement, but...

"He's still dealing with the containment team losses," Alice said softly, her enhancement allowing her to perfectly recall Ethan's expression during their last crisis. "Three teams in one week. The wolf in him takes it personally."

"And you've been working non-stop to find a solution," Nadia observed, her journalist's eye catching the multiple research streams displayed around the lab. "Which is admirable, but not sustainable. Even with enhancement, you need rest. And maybe..." she paused meaningfully, "someone to share the burden with?"

The lab's quantum fields seemed to pulse in agreement, or perhaps that was just Alice's enhanced perception playing tricks after too many hours of work. She looked at the research displayed around her – enhancement stability patterns, supernatural energy integration, hybrid power manifestation. Somewhere in the data was a solution that could help Ethan's teams, but the answer kept eluding her.

"He brings me food too, you know," Alice admitted quietly. "Shows up with coffee and actual meals. Says his enhanced senses tell him when I'm running on empty."

Nadia's smile was knowing. "Funny how a detective with werewolf abilities and corporate enhancements uses all that power to make sure you eat regularly. Almost like he cares."

Alice's enhanced systems registered another set of familiar quantum signatures approaching the lab. "Speaking of..."

The lab door opened to reveal Ethan, holding what appeared to be dessert from Alice's favorite bakery. His enhanced senses took in the scene – Alice, the food, Nadia's knowing smile – and his wolf nature showed in his slight grin.

"Great minds think alike," he said to Nadia, adding his offerings to the impromptu feast. The lab's quantum fields stabilized noticeably with his presence, a phenomenon that didn't escape Nadia's practiced observation.

"Well," Nadia stood, gathering her notes, "my work here is done. Try to actually eat, both of you. And maybe talk about something other than work?" Her meaningful look encompassed them both before she headed for the door.

Left alone, Alice and Ethan shared a moment of comfortable silence, their enhanced natures resonating in ways that defied scientific explanation. The food sat between them, a simple reminder of human needs amidst supernatural complexity.

"So," Ethan said finally, "want to share these quantum calculation results over dessert?"

Alice smiled, feeling her enhancement patterns settling into familiar harmony with his presence. "Always."

CHAPTER FIFTY-THREE

THE NEW NORMAL

LOCATION: Daybridge Central Business District - Morning Rush Hour

Sarah Chen watched her morning train pass through three different quantum states before finally materializing at Daybridge Central Station. The transit authority had installed new reality anchors along major routes, but enhancement-induced probability shifts still affected public transportation. The train existed simultaneously as a sleek modern vehicle, a quantum probability cloud, and briefly as what looked like a Victorian steam engine before settling into its proper form.

Next to her, a businessman casually phased through the closing doors, his enhanced state as commonplace now as checking a phone. His quantum signature left brief ripples in reality, barely noticeable among the morning rush of hybrid energies. His suit was clearly designed for enhancement users – self-adjusting fabric that accommodated sudden density changes or spontaneous energy emissions.

"They're saying thirty percent of the financial district is enhanced now," her seatmate commented, a middle-aged woman whose own subtle energy signature suggested minor probability manipulation abilities.

They watched an executive float paperwork to her colleagues through a shimmering energy field, the documents passing through multiple quantum states before reaching their destinations.

"My daughter's class has two kids who started showing abilities last week," the woman continued, her tone mixing concern with resignation. "The school's installing quantum dampeners and supernatural containment fields, but they can barely keep up with the changes."

The local coffee shop, The Daily Grind, had expanded its menu to accommodate the city's evolving population. Under "Hybrid Blend" options, Sarah noted new offerings designed for every type of enhanced customer. Triple-caffeine shots for enhanced metabolisms competed with hemoglobin-infused lattes for those with vampire traits. Moonlight-charged tea catered to partial lycanthropes, while probability-stabilized espresso served quantum sensitives. Reality-anchored chai helped those prone to phase shifting, and ley line-energized americanos drew in mystic enhancement users.

The barista's hands glowed faintly as she handled multiple orders simultaneously, her enhanced state allowing her to operate in several probability streams at once. She passed drinks through localized quantum fields that maintained optimal temperature and composition regardless of customer enhancement status.

"You just adapt," Sarah told her friend Maya during their lunch break. They sat in a restaurant designed for hybrid clientele – reality-stabilized booths, quantum-shielded tables, and menus that adjusted their options based on customer energy signatures.

"Yesterday I had a meeting with our IT department. Half the team was projecting holographic displays from their hands. The other half was using traditional screens. Nobody even blinked." Sarah manipulated her fork through three dimensions to reach her salad, an unconscious display of how natural enhancement had become.

Around them, Daybridge's business district showcased the new reality. Corporate executives shifted between physical and energy states during presentations, while security guards with hybrid supernatural abilities monitored quantum disturbances. Administrative assistants used enhanced cognition to manage probability-shifted schedules, and maintenance crews with reality manipulation powers repaired tears in space-time. Food delivery workers phase-shifted through traffic jams, treating quantum states like alternate routes.

"Remember when we thought smartphones were revolutionary?" Maya asked, her own minor precognitive enhancement allowing her to dodge a waiter's quantum-shifted tray before it materialized. "Now I watch my neighbor's kid do homework while floating in a self-generated probability field."

Sarah nodded, observing the lunchtime crowd through enhanced perception. Quantum signatures mixed with supernatural energies, creating patterns that would have seemed impossible just a few years ago. Corporate enhancement had transformed society not through sudden change, but through gradual integration into everyday life.

A group of interns passed their table, their enhanced states manifesting in various ways. One manipulated data streams with gesture controls while another shifted through quantum states to avoid crowds. A third maintained a constant low-level reality manipulation field, and two others showed signs of hybrid supernatural abilities, their natures blending seamlessly with their corporate enhancements.

"The really interesting part," Sarah noted, "is how quickly it all became mundane. Enhanced abilities, supernatural hybridization, quantum manipulation – it's all just part of the morning commute now."

Maya's precognitive sense tingled slightly. "Speaking of commutes, you might want to leave early. I'm seeing probability shifts on the red line around four."

Sarah checked her enhanced transit app, which now included quantum stability forecasts alongside traditional delays. "Thanks. I'll take the probability tunnel instead. They installed new reality anchors last week."

As they finished lunch, Sarah reflected on how their conversation itself demonstrated the change. Discussion of quantum states and enhancement abilities had become as casual as talking about weather or traffic. The new normal wasn't just about enhanced abilities – it was about how smoothly society had adapted to their presence.

Outside, Daybridge continued its business day, a symphony of traditional and enhanced activities blending into a single flow of modern life. The distinction between enhanced and non-enhanced, supernatural and scientific, was becoming increasingly meaningless in a world where reality itself had evolved.

CHAPTER FIFTY-FOUR
INTEGRATION

LOCATION: Kane Industries - Quantum Analysis Chamber

The analysis chamber hummed with concentrated enhancement energy, its walls designed to contain and channel quantum phenomena. Holographic data streams filled the air, representing the complex framework of Dr. Winters' enhancement distribution system. The facility's quantum core pulsed beneath them, a heart of pure probability.

Moira stood in the center of it all, her enhanced perception expanded to its limits. Her abilities had always been different – less about raw power and more about understanding the underlying patterns of reality itself. Where others saw chaos in quantum mechanics, she saw music.

"It's beautiful," she told Alice, her hands moving through the data streams like a conductor before an orchestra. The facility's enhancement network responded to her touch, quantum information flowing and reshaping itself. "The whole network is like one giant probability matrix. Each node connects to others across multiple quantum states, creating harmonies of possibility."

The analysis chamber hummed with concentrated enhancement energy, its walls designed to contain and channel quantum phenomena. Holographic data streams filled the air, representing the complex framework of Dr. Winters' enhancement distribution system. The facility's quantum core pulsed beneath them, a heart of pure probability.

Alice watched in fascination as Moira manipulated the data, her enhanced scientific mind recording every detail. The young woman's ability to perceive quantum patterns was unprecedented – she didn't just see the information, she felt it, understood it on an instinctive level that transcended traditional analysis.

"But there's something wrong with the pattern..." Moira's expression shifted from wonder to concern. Her fingers traced discordant elements in the Quantum Framework, places where the probability harmonies fractured. "It's like... like hearing a wrong note in a symphony. The resonance is off."

The deeper she delved into the framework, the more irregularities she uncovered. Dr. Winters' enhancement distribution system was fundamentally flawed – not in its engineering, but in its understanding of how quantum energies naturally flowed. The system fought against probability itself, trying to force enhancement energy into patterns it wasn't meant to follow.

"Here," Moira highlighted a particular node cluster, her own enhancement signature interacting with the facility's systems. "The distribution matrix is treating quantum states as fixed points, but they're more like... waves. Rhythms. You can't force them into rigid structures without creating instability."

Alice's enhanced perception captured every detail as Moira a revealed critical flaws in the system's architecture. The young woman's unique perspective showed how Dr. Winters' attempt to industrialize enhancement distribution was working against natural quantum mechanics. Each forced pattern created ripples of instability that grew stronger as they spread through the network.

But the depth of analysis took its toll. Moira's enhanced abilities weren't designed for such intensive use. Her hands began to shake as she maintained her connection to the facility's Quantum Framework. Sweat beaded on her forehead as she pushed herself to complete the analysis.

"Moira, that's enough," Alice moved to support her as she swayed. "We have what we need."

"Just... one more pattern," Moira insisted, her voice strained. Her enhancement signature flickered as she traced one final quantum pathway, revealing a critical junction where multiple instabilities converged. Then her abilities gave out completely, leaving her drained and trembling.

Alice helped her to a nearby chair, quickly administering a quantum stabilization shot to help her recovery. The analysis chamber's energies settled back into their normal patterns, but the data Moira had revealed remained, captured by the facility's systems.

"I'm sorry," Moira managed after a moment, her enhanced perception slowly returning to normal levels. "I wanted to see it all, understand the whole pattern..."

"You've done more than enough," Alice assured her, reviewing the incredible amount of data they'd gathered. "Your insight into the Quantum Framework... it changes everything. We can see where the system is fighting natural probability flow instead of working with it."

As Moira recovered, Alice began preliminary analysis of their findings. The young woman's unique perspective had revealed fundamental flaws in Dr. Winters' approach to enhancement distribution. The system's rigid structure was creating cascade failures in quantum stability, explaining many of the enhanced ability malfunctions they'd been seeing.

"You see patterns the rest of us miss," Alice told her. "Even with enhancement, most of us analyze quantum mechanics through mathematics and models. You... you understand its music."

Moira managed a tired smile. "The patterns were always there. I just... hear them differently." She looked at the quantum framework still displayed around them. "Will this help? Fix what's happening to people?"

Alice nodded, already seeing ways to adapt the distribution system based on Moira's insights. "Your understanding of natural quantum flow could be the key to developing a more stable enhancement process. One that works with probability patterns instead of against them."

The analysis chamber's systems continued processing Moira's revelations, each piece of data offering new insight into the relationship between enhancement technology and natural quantum mechanics. Though the effort had left her exhausted, Moira had provided something invaluable – a new way of seeing the very foundation of enhancement itself.

∼

CHAPTER FIFTY-FIVE
CONVERGENCE

Location: Kane Industries Global Operations Center - Executive Level

Time: Market Pre-Opening Hours

The quantum-secured boardroom hummed with enhancement energy as reality anchors maintained stable space for both physical and virtual attendees. Holographic displays showed market data streaming through probability states, while supernatural warning systems monitored the increasing blend of corporate and mystical powers.

Victoria Kane stood at the head of the obsidian conference table; her own enhanced state carefully controlled. Her family had guided Kane Industries through technological revolutions before, but nothing like this. The quarterly projection orb before her showed global markets phasing through multiple quantum states.

"Ladies and gentlemen of the board," she began, her voice carrying through both physical and probability space to reach all attendees, "we're facing unprecedented market conditions as corporate enhancement merges with supernatural forces."

The Tokyo Exchange feed flickered through several realities before stabilizing. Reports showed trading floors literally shifting between dimensions as enhanced traders accessed multiple probability streams simultaneously. Reality anchors had failed in three major sectors, forcing a full suspension of operations.

"London has restricted all trading to quantum channels," Victoria continued, gesturing to bring up the European market data. "Their enhanced regulatory systems are holding, but only by routing all transactions through probability space. Traditional trading mechanisms can't keep up with the speed of enhanced market movements."

New York's status drew concerned murmurs from the board. The Exchange had activated its enhanced protocols, allowing AI systems merged with digital spirits to manage the flow of supernatural-influenced trading. Quantum algorithms worked alongside ancient divination techniques to predict market movements.

"Shanghai presents unique challenges," Victoria noted, bringing up feeds showing traditional Chinese dragons coiled around trading terminals. "The Dragon Court has asserted oversight of all enhanced trading activities. Their ancient powers are interacting with our corporate systems in ways we're still trying to understand."

The integration was happening faster than anyone had predicted. Tech sector companies weren't just developing enhanced systems – they were merging with digital yokai, Japanese spirit entities that had evolved to inhabit corporate networks. Enhanced programmers worked alongside code spirits, creating hybrid systems that existed in multiple realities simultaneously.

Financial districts worldwide were transforming as enhanced traders learned to access probability streams directly. Quantum computing merged with supernatural insight, allowing companies to explore potential market futures in real-time. Risk assessment now included evaluating alternate reality outcomes.

"Our industrial facilities are adapting," Victoria continued, showing footage of factories where production lines pulsed with ley line energy. "Enhanced manufacturing processes are tapping into earth's natural power grid. Efficiency is up 300%, but we're seeing increasing interference from local supernatural entities claiming territorial rights."

Research divisions across the globe reported breaching reality barriers in their enhanced experiments. Corporate laboratories existed in quantum superposition, their enhanced scientists working across multiple dimensional planes simultaneously. The distinction between scientific advancement and supernatural achievement was becoming meaningless.

"We need to address immediate concerns," Victoria brought up a priority list that shifted through probable outcomes as they watched. "Enhanced employee integration is straining our reality stabilization systems. Supernatural entities are demanding representation on corporate boards. Our quantum security protocols are being challenged by both technological and mystical intrusions."

The boardroom's enhancement field rippled as members processed the implications. A director from the European division phase-shifted slightly as she raised her hand. "What about the merger talks with the Fae Consortium?"

Victoria activated a secure probability channel before responding. "Negotiations are delicate. They're offering access to timeless realms for data storage, but their concept of contracts is... problematic. Our legal department is working with enhancement-capable lawyers who specialize in supernatural law."

Market projections continued to shift through possible futures around them. Each probability stream showed increasing convergence between corporate power and supernatural forces. Enhancement technology wasn't just changing how companies operated – it was transforming the fundamental nature of global business.

"Our advantage," Victoria emphasized, her enhanced perception tracking every reaction in the room, "is that Kane Industries foresaw this convergence. Our enhancement technology was designed to accommodate supernatural integration. While our competitors scramble to adapt, we're positioned to guide this transition."

The quantum-secured boardroom hummed with increasing energy as plans were discussed. Enhanced executives accessed probability streams to model outcomes. Supernatural consultants offered insights from ancient wisdom. Corporate strategy evolved in real-time across multiple dimensional planes.

"We're not just facing a market shift," Victoria concluded, her enhanced state allowing her to address all probable versions of the board simultaneously. "We're witnessing the birth of a new economic reality. One where corporate power, enhancement technology, and supernatural forces converge into something entirely unprecedented."

The meeting continued as global markets prepared to open, each decision rippling through probability space to shape the future of corporate-supernatural integration. Kane Industries stood at the nexus of this transformation, its enhanced systems ready to bridge the gap between ancient power and modern business.

CHAPTER FIFTY-SIX

THE TRUTH CANNOT BE CONTAINED

LOCATION: GNN Emergency Broadcast Center - Studio Alpha

Time: Prime Time Emergency Broadcast

The studio lights flickered through quantum states as Marcus Wong sat at the enhanced-reinforced news desk. Reality anchors strained to maintain broadcast stability as his carefully controlled enhanced state began to manifest visibly. After fifteen years as GNN's lead anchor, he was about to break every rule of journalism.

"Ladies and gentlemen," Marcus began, his enhanced perception showing him millions of viewers across probability streams, "I can no longer maintain journalistic distance. As an enhanced individual myself, I must report what I'm actually seeing..."

His enhanced state became fully visible on camera, quantum energy rippling around him as he dropped the careful controls he'd maintained for years. The studio's reality stabilizers adjusted automatically, allowing viewers to see what enhanced perception actually looked like.

"For years, we've reported on enhancement as observers," Marcus continued, his eyes now showing traces of quantum light. "We've used careful language, maintained professional distance, treated it as a phenomenon to be documented. But that ends tonight."

The air around him shimmered as he accessed probability streams directly, allowing viewers to see what enhanced individuals experienced every day. Multiple possible futures overlapped in visible waves, showing how enhanced perception viewed reality's potential paths.

"This is what I see every time I report on market shifts," he demonstrated, pulling up quantum data streams that manifested as visible light patterns. "Enhanced traders aren't just making faster decisions – they're seeing every possible outcome simultaneously. The markets exist in multiple states until enhanced observation collapses them into reality."

His enhanced cognitive abilities became apparent as he processed and presented complex information at unprecedented speeds. Viewers watched in amazement as he analyzed and synthesized data from thousands of sources in real-time, his enhanced mind working at levels that redefined human capability.

"The corporate line about 'controlled enhancement' is a fiction," Marcus declared, his enhanced state allowing him to perceive and report truth across multiple probability streams. "I'm showing you what they don't want seen – the full scope of how enhancement changes human perception and capability."

The broadcast began affecting reality itself as millions of enhanced viewers resonated with his revelations. Probability waves rippled across the studio as collective enhanced consciousness focused on a single point of truth.

"Let me show you what enhanced perception really means," Marcus continued, allowing his abilities to fully manifest. The studio seemed to expand as he demonstrated how enhanced individuals perceived multiple layers of reality simultaneously:

The physical world overlaid with quantum probability fields. Corporate data streams flowing through supernatural ley lines. Ancient powers merging with modern technology. The true complexity of enhanced existence displayed for all to see.

"We're not just talking about corporate efficiency improvements," he explained, his voice carrying through both physical and probability space. "Enhancement is fundamentally changing what it means to be human. The barriers between natural and supernatural, between corporate and mystical, between possible and actual – they're all breaking down."

Security alerts flashed across probability streams as corporate systems detected his unauthorized revelation. But Marcus continued, his enhanced abilities now fully engaged in broadcasting truth across all possible realities.

"Look at your enhanced colleagues, your modified family members, your transformed friends," he urged, knowing his words reached across quantum states. "We're not malfunctioning. We're not unstable. We're evolving into something corporations never intended – something they can't control."

The studio's reality anchors strained as his broadcast accessed deeper levels of truth. Enhanced viewers worldwide felt their own abilities resonating with his revelation, creating a cascade of awakening consciousness.

"The corporations sold enhancement as a tool, an upgrade, a competitive advantage," Marcus's enhanced state pulsed with concentrated truth. "What they created was a door to fundamental reality – and that door can't be closed."

Corporate override signals attempted to cut the broadcast, but Marcus's enhanced abilities maintained the connection across probability streams. His reputation for integrity, built over decades of journalism, gave weight to every enhanced revelation.

"To my fellow enhanced individuals: You're not alone. What you're experiencing is real. Your perception isn't malfunctioning – it's expanding beyond corporate limitations."

As the broadcast continued, enhanced viewers worldwide began sharing their own experiences. The probability streams filled with testimonies of expanded consciousness, of supernatural awareness, of quantum understanding that transcended corporate control.

"This isn't just a news report," Marcus concluded, his enhanced state fully visible to all viewers. "This is the truth about enhancement, broadcast across all probable realities. What happens next depends on how we – enhanced and non-enhanced alike – choose to face this new reality."

The broadcast ended, but its effects rippled through probability space, changing the landscape of enhancement forever. Marcus Wong had done more than break journalistic convention – he'd shown the world what enhancement truly meant, from the inside.

CHAPTER FIFTY-SEVEN
SYNTHETIC STORM

EMERGENCY SIRENS WAILED across the financial district as enhanced humans from the trade center spilled into the streets, many unable to control their new hybrid abilities. Glass shattered as a board member from Nexus Corp phased through walls while simultaneously generating electromagnetic pulses. A banking executive's newly acquired pyrokinetic-ice fusion powers left trails of steam and fractured pavement.

"Containment teams on Market Street and 7th," Ethan coordinated from the mobile command center. "We've got thirty-seven enhanced individuals heading toward the subway station."

Alice monitored her quantum scanner as supernatural factions arrived to assist law enforcement. Vampire rapid response teams used their enhanced speed to evacuate civilians, while werewolf packs herded scattered groups of transformed executives away from populated areas.

"The Fae courts are providing containment specialists," Alice reported. "They're setting up neutral zones with dampening fields. Should help stabilize the more volatile power combinations."

A massive ethereal barrier shimmed into existence as Fae wardens created safe zones for those struggling with their transformations. Inside, medical teams worked alongside supernatural healers to assess the altered executives.

"Counter-agent deployment ready in sectors 3 through 7," Alice checked the aerosol dispersal units. "It won't reverse the transformations, but it should help them regulate the new ability combinations."

The stabilizing agent misted through the streets; its quantum-infused particles designed to help transformed individuals assert conscious control over their hybrid powers. Gradually, the chaos began to subside as executives learned to suppress or direct their abilities.

"Ghost Division moving to intercept the Market Street group," Ethan dispatched spectral operatives to handle those who'd gained incorporeal abilities. "Lycanthrope teams backing up SWAT on the east side."

Supernatural factions that had once been rivals now coordinated seamlessly, their own abilities complementing each other as they contained the situation. Vampire speed combined with werewolf tracking. Fae magic enhanced ghost division tactics.

"Multiple priority targets incoming," Alice's scanner picked up approaching signatures. "Enhanced board members from Helix Corp. Their hybrid abilities are... evolving."

The Helix executives had manifested a dangerous combination of shapeshifting and energy manipulation. Their transformed bodies flickered between forms as raw power radiated from them in waves.

"Ghost Division, fall back," Ethan ordered. "Let the Fae wardens take point. Their containment fields can adapt to the shifting power signatures."

Alice's counter-agent dispersed in a wide radius around the Helix group. The quantum-stabilizing particles interacted with their unstable abilities, gradually bringing the transformations under control.

"Security teams reporting similar situations worldwide," Alice checked the incoming data. "The summit attendees who managed to leave before containment – they're triggering transformations in others through prolonged contact."

The implications were staggering. The Daybridge Evolution wasn't contained to the trade center. Every transformed executive who'd escaped had become a vector for spreading hybrid abilities.

"Supernatural Council is mobilizing globally," Ethan coordinated with international response teams. "They're deploying joint task forces to major financial centers. London, Tokyo, Singapore – all reporting enhanced humans manifesting hybrid abilities."

Alice's counter-agent had stabilized most of the immediate area, but her scanner showed the quantum changes spreading through the population. The transformations were becoming more controlled, more natural, as reality adjusted to the new possibilities.

"We need to shift priorities," Alice decided, watching the Fae containment fields fill with newly enhanced humans. "This isn't just about containment anymore. We need to establish training protocols, support systems..."

"A complete restructuring of how we handle supernatural abilities," Ethan agreed, dispatching more mixed-faction response teams. "The old divisions between species, between pure and hybrid – none of that works anymore."

The financial district had become ground zero for a new paradigm. Enhanced humans learning to control hybrid powers. Supernatural factions working together openly. Reality itself adapting to combinations of abilities that had been impossible mere hours ago.

And in the command center, Alice and Ethan coordinated a response that would shape how the world handled this new era of unrestricted supernatural potential. The Synthetic Storm had broken centuries of artificial limitations, and there was no going back to the old divisions.

Corporate executives who had once regulated enhancement now wielded hybrid powers alongside supernatural beings they'd tried to control. The future would require new frameworks, new alliances, and a fundamental shift in how humanity viewed the boundaries between species and abilities.

The storm had passed, but its effects were still spreading. And in its wake, the world was transforming one person at a time, as reality remembered what it used to allow.

CHAPTER FIFTY-EIGHT
HISTORICAL PRECEDENT

Location: Kane Industries Archives - Tactical Response Center

Time: 3:27 AM

The tactical room's reality anchors hummed as Nadia phased through the security barriers, her enhanced state allowing her to carry both physical documents and quantum data simultaneously. Ancient scrolls flickered between material and probability states, their age-darkened pages containing information that transcended conventional history.

"I found it!" she exclaimed, her enhanced perception still reeling from what she'd discovered in the deep archives. Ethan and Alice looked up from their holographic containment models, sensing the urgency in her quantum signature.

The room's smart surfaces activated automatically, creating display spaces for both physical and quantum information. Nadia's hands trembled slightly as she spread out documents that existed in multiple states of reality – ancient parchments that shifted between physical form and pure information.

"The Great Sundering wasn't what we thought," she began, her enhanced cognitive abilities processing centuries of hidden knowledge. "It wasn't just about separating supernatural species - it was about preventing exactly this kind of hybrid enhancement. The whole historical narrative we've been working from is incomplete."

Ethan's enhanced perception analyzed the documents as Nadia arranged them. Some were written in languages that hadn't existed in physical form for millennia, preserved only in quantum probability states. Others showed diagrams of reality itself, maps of how existence had been deliberately partitioned.

"Look at these energy signatures," Nadia highlighted patterns that pulsed across both ancient scrolls and quantum scans. "The barriers between species? They're artificial. Implemented after a similar crisis of uncontrolled enhancement nearly destroyed reality itself. Our current situation isn't unprecedented – it's history repeating itself."

Alice moved closer, her enhanced abilities allowing her to read multiple versions of the documents simultaneously. "These calculations... they're showing quantum framework patterns almost identical to what we're seeing now. But these are from thousands of years ago."

"Exactly," Nadia confirmed, pulling up comparative data streams. "The ancient world had its own version of enhancement technology – they just approached it through supernatural means rather than corporate science. But the fundamental principles were the same: humans accessing powers beyond their natural limits, reality struggling to adapt to rapidly expanding capabilities."

The tactical room's displays filled with historical data as Nadia's discovery unfolded. Images showed ancient civilizations grappling with enhanced individuals, supernatural powers merging with human potential, reality itself buckling under the strain of unrestricted transformation.

"How did they stop it?" Alice asked, studying the records. Her enhanced perception traced patterns of probability collapse, seeing how reality had nearly shattered under the weight of uncontrolled enhancement.

"They didn't exactly stop it," Nadia explained, bringing up detailed accounts of the Great Sundering itself. "They contained it. The ancients created artificial barriers between different forms of existence – human, supernatural, enhanced. They literally rewrote the structure of reality to prevent different types of power from combining."

Ethan's enhanced abilities detected the implications immediately. "But that's not a real solution. It's just postponing the inevitable. These barriers... they're breaking down now because they were never natural in the first place."

"Exactly," Nadia's excitement peaked, causing quantum fluctuations in the room's reality anchors. "But the records suggest a better way - controlled integration rather than forced separation. The ancients chose the quickest solution, but their own documents show they knew it wasn't the best one."

She revealed another layer of historical data, showing alternative approaches that had been proposed but rejected. "Some of their enhanced philosophers argued for guided convergence – allowing different forms of power to merge gradually, naturally. They had theories about how to manage the integration without reality collapse."

The tactical room's displays shifted to show theoretical models from both ancient and modern perspectives. The similarities were striking – both showing how enhancement could be stabilized through controlled connection rather than enforced separation.

"The ancients took the path of division because they were afraid," Nadia continued, her enhanced perception revealing patterns across millennia. "They saw enhanced power as a threat rather than an evolution. But their own records show they understood the potential for something better."

Alice studied the ancient integration theories, her enhanced mind combining them with modern quantum mechanics. "These approaches... they're actually more stable than our current containment strategies. Working with natural probability flows instead of against them."

"The Great Sundering was a panic response," Nadia concluded, the full weight of historical knowledge flowing through her enhanced consciousness. "But it gave us something valuable – time to understand enhancement properly, to develop the science and wisdom needed for true integration."

As the three enhanced researchers absorbed the implications of this historical revelation, the tactical room's displays showed both past and present simultaneously. Ancient wisdom merged with modern understanding, suggesting a path forward that learned from history's mistakes rather than repeating them.

CHAPTER FIFTY-NINE

BATTLE SUPPORT

LOCATION: **Kane Industries Executive Level**

Time: Critical Incident Response

The executive floor's reality anchors screamed warnings as quantum instability reached critical levels. Enhanced corporate leaders, their abilities amplified by panic and adrenaline, were losing control of their powers. Probability waves crashed through the space like temporal tsunamis as decades of careful enhancement containment unraveled.

Lila moved with practiced grace, her hands weaving ancient patterns through the chaos. Purple-gold spell energy flowed from her fingers, intertwining with the precise geometric patterns of Alice's quantum containment fields. Where science met sorcery, reality stabilized – if only temporarily.

"Stand back!" Alice called, her enhanced abilities calculating probability collapse points. Her containment fields shimmered with mathematical precision, creating zones of stable space within the chaos. Each quantum barrier was a masterpiece of enhanced engineering, designed to contain and redirect unstable enhancement energy.

Lila's magic flowed through these scientific structures, adding flexibility to their rigid frameworks. Where Alice's fields might have shattered under pressure, they now bent and adapted, strengthened by supernatural resilience. Ancient wisdom complemented modern innovation, creating something stronger than either alone.

"Your partner's quite talented," Lila remarked to Ethan, maintaining her position in their defensive triangle. Her tone carried the weight of history and a hint of amusement. "Much better than watching you chase werewolves through abandoned warehouses. Those were such dreary affairs."

Sweat beaded on her forehead as she reinforced another containment spell. Behind them, an enhanced executive phased through multiple probability states, his power spinning out of control. The combination of Lila's magic and Alice's quantum fields caught him, gently forcing his enhanced state back into alignment.

"Less commentary, more containment spells," Ethan replied tersely, though Alice caught his slight smile. His enhanced abilities were focused on predicting probability breaches, identifying where reality might tear before it happened. Each warning gave Lila and Alice precious seconds to reinforce their defenses.

"Always so serious," Lila sighed dramatically, but her magic surged stronger, supporting their efforts. Her spells took on a deeper resonance, drawing on old power to contain new chaos. "Though I must admit, you two work remarkably well together. Almost as good as you and I did, darling."

The endearment carried echoes of shared history – past missions and old relationships now transformed by time and circumstance. Alice's enhanced perception caught fragments of memory in Lila's quantum signature: younger versions of her and Ethan facing different crises, learning to trust each other's abilities.

Another reality wave threatened to breach their containment. Alice's quantum fields flexed and held, strengthened by Lila's magic. The three of them moved in unconscious coordination, each compensating for the others' limitations. Science, sorcery, and enhanced ability working in harmony.

"Next time," Lila called over the reality distortions, "perhaps we could meet under less catastrophic circumstances. I know this lovely little café that exists in multiple probability states simultaneously."

"Focus, Lila," Ethan warned, but there was warmth in his voice. His enhanced senses tracked another executive losing control, probability streams fracturing around them. "Alice, three o'clock!"

Alice's quantum fields snapped into place as Lila's magic surged. Together, they caught the executive's enhanced explosion, channeling its energy safely into controlled probability streams. Their containment matrix held, a perfect blend of mathematical precision and magical intuition.

"You know," Lila continued, never losing her composure even as she reinforced another spell, "this is actually rather refreshing. Corporate enhancement incidents are so much more intellectually stimulating than supernatural containment. The quantum mechanics alone..."

"Lila..." Ethan's warning held equal parts exasperation and affection.

"Yes, yes, focusing now," she replied, but her magic pulsed stronger, more focused. "Though I maintain this is more entertaining than that ghoul infestation in Prague."

Alice maintained her concentration on the quantum fields, but she found herself appreciating the dynamic between her partners. Ethan's serious focus balanced by Lila's irreverent competence, both of them absolutely reliable when it mattered most.

The crisis continued around them, but their combined abilities created an island of stability in the chaos. Each of them brought unique strengths: Alice's enhanced quantum engineering, Ethan's predictive capabilities, Lila's ancient magical knowledge. Together, they were holding back a tide of enhancement-induced reality collapse.

～

CHAPTER SIXTY

SHADOW MARKETS AND SYNTHETIC RIGHTS

Location: **Global Financial District**

Time: During Critical Market Hours

Marcus Wong adjusted his quantum-shielded position on the 47th floor of the Daybridge Tower, his enhanced perception tracking multiple reality streams simultaneously. Below, the financial district had become a convergence point of corporate and supernatural powers, as enhancement technology reached a critical tipping point.

"This is Marcus Wong, reporting live for the Daybridge Chronicle," his voice carried across quantum-secured channels. "We're witnessing what may be the most significant transformation of global markets since the invention of digital trading."

His drone network, each unit equipped with both technical sensors and supernatural detection arrays, provided unprecedented coverage of the unfolding situation. The footage showed corporate security teams working alongside ancient supernatural entities, their combined efforts creating new protocols for enhanced market operations.

"At 0900 hours, the first enhanced trading algorithms began manifesting physical forms," Wong reported, his cameras capturing images of digital spirits emerging from quantum computing cores. "Corporate security initially attempted containment but were quickly joined by supernatural response teams from multiple traditions."

The footage showed corporate enforcers in quantum-enhanced armor working beside ancient guardian spirits. Their combined efforts created safe channels for enhanced market energies to flow without disrupting baseline reality.

"We're seeing unprecedented cooperation between corporate security and supernatural factions," Wong continued, his enhanced abilities allowing him to process multiple information streams. "Dragon Court representatives are conferring with Goldman Sachs executives. Yokai digital spirits are integrating with Morgan Stanley's AI systems. Ancient wards are being modified to accommodate quantum trading protocols."

But beneath the surface cooperation, Wong's enhanced perception detected deeper tensions. His coverage shifted to the fundamental questions that enhancement technology had forced into the open:

"The bigger question remains: Who owns supernatural ability? The corporations who developed enhancement technology? The trans-formed executives now wielding hybrid powers? Or should these forces be free from any institutional control?"

His broadcast triggered immediate responses across global markets. In Tokyo, enhancement rights activists staged probability protests, their demonstrations existing in multiple quantum states simultaneously. Corporate boards faced emergency meetings as enhanced employees demanded recognition of their transformed status.

In London, the Old Powers Council called an emergency session, debating whether corporate enhancement constituted a violation of ancient supernatural treaties. Enhanced traders found themselves caught between corporate contracts and awakening supernatural abilities.

New York's shareholder meetings descended into chaos as enhanced board members manifested abilities during heated debates. Legal firms specializing in supernatural law saw their quantum channels overwhelmed with consultation requests.

"We're tracking multiple unofficial markets emerging in probability space," Wong reported, his drones detecting new trading patterns. "Enhanced executives are creating synthetic trading environments that exist outside both corporate and supernatural control. These 'shadow markets' operate on principles that challenge our basic understanding of economic reality."

The global response continued to escalate. Corporate boards convened emergency sessions to address enhanced employee rights, holding quantum secure meetings to revise enhancement policies. Legal teams struggled with unprecedented liability issues while shareholders demanded transparency about enhancement programs.

Supernatural councils found themselves debating modern integration protocols and territory disputes over enhanced corporate spaces. Training programs for corporate-supernatural hybrid operations emerged, while internal conflicts raged between adaptation and tradition.

Within enhanced communities, underground networks formed through probability channels as demands for recognition of new hybrid identities grew louder. They developed independent power structures and created enhanced-only communication systems, establishing their own institutional frameworks.

"We're seeing the emergence of entirely new social and economic structures," Wong analyzed, his enhanced perception tracking pattern changes across multiple reality streams. "Enhanced individuals are creating their own institutions, neither fully corporate nor traditionally supernatural."

The footage showed enhanced executives accessing probability trading floors that existed between realities. Traditional market mechanisms struggled to track transactions that occurred across multiple quantum states simultaneously.

"The corporate attempt to control enhancement technology has inadvertently created a new class of being," Wong continued. "These enhanced individuals are neither fully human nor traditionally supernatural. They represent something entirely new – and they're beginning to recognize their collective power."

Legal frameworks worldwide struggled with questions of enhanced human rights, corporate claims on synthetic abilities, and supernatural sovereignty concerns. Jurisdictional disputes emerged across reality states as traditional legal systems attempted to cope with enhancement's implications.

"What we're witnessing," Wong concluded, his enhanced state allowing him to broadcast across all probability streams, "is not just a market crisis or a supernatural emergence. It's the birth of a new form of existence – one that challenges our fundamental concepts of identity, power, and control."

His coverage continued as the situation evolved, providing a crucial window into a world where corporate power, supernatural forces, and human potential were merging into something unprecedented. The questions he raised would shape the future of enhanced existence itself.

~

CHAPTER SIXTY-ONE
DIVISION LINES

Time: Emergency Council Session

The Supernatural Academy's great hall thrummed with tension, centuries of magical energy responding to the emotional charge of its occupants. Ancient wards flickered along the crystalline walls; their patterns disturbed by the presence of hybrid energies they weren't designed to recognize. Moonlight filtered through quantum-enhanced stained glass, casting ever-shifting shadows across the assembled supernatural leaders.

The Traditionalists occupied the eastern side of the hall, their formal robes and ancient regalia a stark contrast to the modern business attire and tactical gear of the Progressive Alliance. Arch-Mage Harrison stood at the head of his faction, his form radiating pure, undiluted magical energy that spoke of carefully maintained bloodlines and rigidly controlled power.

"Our entire society is built on maintaining clear divisions between supernatural species," Harrison declared, his voice carrying the weight of millennia of magical tradition. His hands traced ancient ward patterns in the air as he spoke, displaying the precise, categorized nature of supernatural energy. "These corporate-enhanced humans threaten thousands of years of established order."

Behind him, the Traditionalist council members nodded in agreement. Elder vampires in ceremonial cloaks, pure-blood werewolves wearing tribal markers, and Fae nobles crowned with ancient power all presented a united front of supernatural purity.

Professor Luna Wolf stood opposite Harrison; her hybrid nature visible in every aspect of her being. Wolf-gold eyes gleamed with Fae intelligence, while her form shifted subtly between human, wolf, and Fae aspects. The Progressive Alliance gathered around her represented a spectrum of supernatural diversity – mixed-blood practitioners, enhanced humans studying ancient arts, and beings who defied traditional classification.

"The order you cling to is artificial," Luna countered, her voice carrying harmonics that resonated across multiple supernatural frequencies. "Ancient texts speak of a time before the Great Sundering, when abilities flowed freely between species. Perhaps this is reality's way of correcting our artificial limitations."

She gestured to the quantum displays hovering beside her, showing magical energy patterns from both before and after the Great Sundering. The earlier patterns showed fluid, interconnected flows of power, while the later ones displayed rigid categorization and separation.

The debate intensified as each side presented their evidence. Harrison conjured historical holograms showing the chaos that had preceded the establishment of supernatural divisions. Luna countered with data from recent hybrid successes, demonstrating the potential benefits of controlled integration.

"Look at the stability we've achieved," Harrison argued, his magic creating a detailed map of current supernatural power structures. "Each species managing their own abilities, maintaining their own traditions. These corporate enhancement programs threaten to unravel everything we've built."

"Stability through stagnation is no victory," Luna responded, her hybrid energy patterns shifting visibly as she spoke. "The corporations didn't create these possibilities – they merely rediscovered what was natural all along. We've spent millennia fighting our own evolution."

The tension in the hall reached a critical point as both sides marshaled their arguments. Ancient wards strained against the presence of hybrid energies, while reality itself seemed to flutter between established patterns and new possibilities.

Then came the moment that changed everything.

Sarah Chen, a seventeen-year-old vampire-human hybrid who had been quietly observing from the gallery, suddenly began to glow with unmistakable Fae energy. Golden light spiraled around her form as butterfly wings of pure magical energy manifested from her shoulders. The impossible combination – vampire, human, and spontaneous Fae magic – defied every established principle of supernatural division.

The great hall fell silent. Harrison's carefully maintained expression cracked as he witnessed abilities that shouldn't exist flowing together in perfect harmony. Luna's eyes widened, seeing her theories proven more dramatically than she'd imagined possible.

Sarah's demonstration lasted only moments, but its impact resonated through every level of supernatural society. Here was living proof that the old divisions were breaking down, that new combinations of power were not only possible but perhaps inevitable.

The young hybrid's display forced both factions to confront a reality that transcended their debate. This wasn't just about corporate enhancement or traditional supernatural powers – it was about the fundamental nature of ability itself; about the artificial constraints they'd placed on their own potential.

As the light faded and Sarah returned to normal, the great hall remained silent. Traditionalists and Progressives alike found themselves reevaluating centuries of assumptions. The ward patterns on the walls had shifted, adapting to accommodate energies they'd been designed to exclude.

Luna finally broke the silence, her voice gentle but firm. "We can continue to fight this change, or we can guide it. The choice is ours, but the change itself?" She gestured to Sarah, who stood uncertain but unafraid in the gallery. "That's already happening."

Harrison studied the residual energy patterns from Sarah's display, his extensive magical knowledge searching for explanations that aligned with traditional theory. Finding none, he faced a choice between defending an increasingly unstable status quo or adapting to an uncomfortable new reality.

The great hall's energy shifted again as both factions began to process the implications of what they'd witnessed. This wasn't just about policy anymore – it was about the very nature of supernatural existence and humanity's evolving role within it.

CHAPTER SIXTY-TWO

COMMUNITY SUPPORT

LOCATION: Daybridge Community Center

Time: Three Months into the Enhancement Crisis

The Daybridge Community Center's gymnasium had undergone a remarkable transformation. Where basketball courts once stood, carefully organized aid stations now formed a complex support network. Quantum dampening fields hummed quietly overhead, creating safe spaces for those still learning to control their new abilities.

Lisa Martinez, the center's volunteer coordinator, navigated through the bustling space with practiced ease. Her enhanced perception allowed her to simultaneously track multiple crisis points while leading a group of potential donors through the facility. Her clipboard displayed both physical and probability-state inventory levels.

"The food bank section is organized by metabolic type," she explained, gesturing to the color-coded shelving units. "Standard human needs are in the blue zone, but that's becoming our smallest section." She paused by a shimmering purple shelf where food items seemed to exist in multiple states simultaneously. "Enhanced energy requirements are our fastest-growing category. We're seeing people who need to consume probability variants of the same meal to maintain their quantum stability."

The hemoglobin supplement station was staffed by a vampire nutritionist working alongside a human biochemist. Together, they helped a newly enhanced teenager whose transformation had given her unusual dietary requirements. Her mother watched anxiously as they explained the importance of balancing physical and supernatural nutrition.

"Lunar-cycle nutrition is particularly complex," Martinez continued, indicating a section where ingredients shifted with the phases of the moon. "We're working with supernatural nutritionists to develop specialized meal plans. The werewolf community has been incredibly supportive, sharing centuries of knowledge about managing metabolic fluctuations."

In the center's counseling wing, every quantum-shielded room buzzed with activity. The "Adapting to Enhancement" group filled the largest space, where Dr. James Wilson led discussions about identity and change. Today's session focused on a corporate accountant whose enhanced abilities had given her the power to see probability streams in financial data.

"I keep seeing all possible versions of every transaction," she explained, her voice trembling. "How do I know which reality to focus on? Which version of myself should I be?"

Dr. Wilson nodded understanding; his own enhanced empathy carefully modulated to support without overwhelming. "Remember, you're not losing yourself – you're expanding. Your core identity remains your anchor point across all probability states."

Next door, the "Partners and Families in Transition" group dealt with the ripple effects of enhancement. A husband struggled to understand his wife's new Fae-touched perception of time. Parents sought advice about children manifesting hybrid abilities at school. Siblings learned to cope with drastically different enhancement outcomes within the same family.

"Managing Hybrid Abilities in the Workplace" had become one of the center's most crucial programs. Today's session included a former sales manager now dealing with spontaneous telepathy, an IT specialist whose technomancy affected corporate servers, and a construction worker whose enhanced strength came with unexpected probability complications.

"I can see every way the building could fall," the construction worker explained, his hands shaking. "Every possible failure point across multiple realities. How do I focus on just building in this reality?"

The session's facilitator, a hybrid supernatural-corporate consultant, guided him through grounding techniques developed specifically for probability-sensitive enhanced individuals.

The center's medical wing combined traditional healthcare with supernatural healing practices. Dr. Helena Schmidt, herself a hybrid practitioner, coordinated with Fae healers and corporate medical specialists to address unprecedented physiological changes.

"We're seeing enhancement patterns that don't fit any existing category," she explained during a staff meeting. "Traditional medicine says one thing, supernatural healing another, and the enhanced biology somehow incorporates both while adding new elements we're still trying to understand."

Throughout the facility, the importance of community support became increasingly evident. Enhanced individuals found strength in sharing experiences, while families and friends learned to navigate new dynamics together. The center provided not just practical aid, but a crucial sense of belonging in a rapidly changing world.

"The hardest part isn't the physical changes," Dr. Wilson observed, watching his support group members connect over shared experiences. "It's maintaining your sense of self when your whole relationship with reality has shifted. That's why community matters more than ever."

In the children's area, young enhanced individuals learned to control their abilities through play. A girl whose enhancement gave her probability-splitting powers practiced focusing on a single reality stream while coloring. A boy with emerging telepathy worked with a mentor to build healthy mental boundaries.

The volunteer break room told its own story of community adaptation. Enhanced and non-enhanced staff shared experiences and supported each other through challenging shifts. A whiteboard tracked ongoing needs: probability-stable food supplies, quantum-shielded counseling spaces, enhanced-compatible medical equipment.

"We're all learning together," Martinez told her tour group as they concluded their visit. "Every day brings new challenges, but also new discoveries about what we can achieve when we support each other. Enhancement may have changed our individual realities, but it's our community that helps us navigate those changes."

CHAPTER SIXTY-THREE
FAMILY SECRETS

Location: **Quantum Research Facility - Sublevel 7**

Time: Fifteen Years After The Incident

The quantum framework surrounding them pulsed with unstable energy, responding to the emotional resonance between the sisters. Reality itself seemed to hold its breath as decades of carefully constructed deception unraveled.

Sarah Chen's form flickered between states – sometimes solid, sometimes translucent, her quantum signature revealing the truth of her altered existence. The laboratory's emergency lights cast shifting shadows across her face, highlighting features that echoed their father's genetic legacy while displaying clear signs of enhancement manipulation.

"Dad knew what was coming," Sarah's voice carried harmonics that vibrated across multiple probability streams. "His research wasn't just theoretical - he was preparing for this." She gestured to the surrounding quantum framework, their father's life's work humming with purpose. "My 'death' was part of a larger plan."

Alice stared at the holographic displays, her detective's instincts piecing together the evidence she'd been blind to for years. Her father's research notes, the strange enhancement cases she'd investigated, the patterns of corporate manipulation – it all connected to this moment, to this truth she'd never let herself see.

"He let me believe you were dead for fifteen years," Alice's voice cracked with raw emotion. "Let me blame myself for not being there that night." Her years of investigating enhancement cases, always searching for answers about that night, suddenly felt like following a trail her father had deliberately laid.

Memories flooded back: A younger Alice, driven by guilt, throwing herself into investigating enhancement cases. Years spent building a reputation as the detective who understood both the supernatural and scientific aspects of enhancement crimes. Every case, every investigation, had been fueled by a loss that had been carefully orchestrated.

"He let you become who you needed to be," Sarah's form flickered with emotion. "Without guilt or obligation. Without having to choose between family and duty." Her hand passed through a holographic display. "You became the bridge between enhanced and normal humans because you were free to focus entirely on understanding both worlds. No distractions, no divided loyalties."

The laboratory's sensors registered increasing instability as the sisters' emotional states affected the surrounding reality. Alice recognized the readings from countless enhancement crime scenes she'd investigated – but never this intense, never this personal.

"And now?" Alice's detective instincts couldn't stop analyzing the situation, even as her heart ached with rediscovered loss. "What am I supposed to choose now?" Her voice carried the weight of ten years of investigations, of seeking justice for others while unknowingly living her father's lie.

"Now we choose together." Sarah's quantum signature seemed to reach out to Alice, creating patterns unlike anything she'd seen in her years of enhancement investigations. "Sisters against reality itself."

The quantum framework stabilized around them as their presence synchronized. Alice's years of practical enhancement experience merged with Sarah's quantum existence, creating something their father had predicted but never witnessed: a perfect bridge between worlds.

Through her detective's eyes, Alice saw how their father had orchestrated everything: her investigations always leading her deeper into understanding enhancement, while Sarah explored quantum existence beyond normal reality. He'd separated them not out of cruelty, but necessity.

"He knew the enhancement crisis was coming," Sarah explained, her form stabilizing. "Knew that humanity would need someone who understood both the legal and quantum sides of enhancement. You weren't just his daughter – you were his way of ensuring someone would be ready to handle what was coming."

Alice looked at the case files displayed around them – her investigations into enhancement crimes, corporate corruption, supernatural incidents. Each case had taught her something, prepared her for this moment. "He turned our loss into preparation," she realized. "Every case, every investigation..."

"Was leading us here," Sarah completed the thought. "To this moment when the world needs someone who understands both sides. A detective who can bridge the gap between enhanced and normal humans, between law and quantum reality."

The laboratory's systems recorded new possibilities as the sisters reconnected. Reality itself seemed to reshape around them, offering glimpses of potential futures where enhancement and normal human society might find balance.

"He couldn't tell us," Sarah's voice carried understanding earned through years of quantum existence. "The knowledge would have changed our paths, limited what we could become. We had to find our own ways first."

"Before we could find each other again," Alice added, seeing their father's plan with a detective's clarity at last. Everything she'd learned investigating enhancement cases had prepared her for this revelation.

The Quantum Framework pulsed with renewed purpose as the sisters faced each other across fifteen years of separation. Their father's final message played across the probability field: "Together, you are my answer to the coming storm. Apart, you became who you needed to be. Together, you will become what reality needs you to be."

CHAPTER SIXTY-FOUR

VOICES OF CHANGE

Location: **Mobile Broadcasting Unit - Reality-Shifted Space**

Time: Peak Broadcast Hours

Feed Status: LIVE/QUANTUM-ENCRYPTED

Marcus Wong adjusted his quantum-enhanced broadcasting array, the equipment humming with probability-stable energy as he prepared for another underground transmission. His mobile unit, disguised as a standard delivery vehicle, contained some of the most advanced hybrid tech available – a perfect fusion of corporate enhancement and supernatural crafting.

"This is Marcus Wong, broadcasting on encrypted probability channels," his voice carried across quantum-secured frequencies. "Welcome to 'The Enhanced Perspective,' where we show you the truth behind the headlines."

The interior of his broadcasting unit shifted between realities, allowing him to maintain secure connections with multiple enhanced communities simultaneously. Holographic displays showed feeds from across the globe, each telling a different story of transformation and adaptation.

"They're calling us threats," Marcus broadcast, his enhanced perception allowing him to process multiple reality streams at once. "But look at what's really happening in these communities. Tonight, we're going inside the spaces where the enhanced are building their own future."

His first feed revealed the transformed spaces within major corporations where enhanced employees had created their own microcultures. In Quantum-Goldman's probability trading floor, enhanced analysts existed in multiple states simultaneously, their hybrid abilities allowing them to process market data across parallel realities.

"These aren't just workplace accommodations," Marcus commented, focusing on a young analyst whose enhancement allowed her to see financial patterns across time itself. "These are evolving ecosystems where enhanced abilities are revolutionizing traditional business practices."

The camera panned across quantum-stable meditation spaces, reality-shifted break rooms, and hybrid training facilities. Enhanced employees moved seamlessly between states of existence; their corporate duties enhanced rather than hindered by their transformations.

The feed shifted to a converted warehouse district where traditional supernatural communities had opened their doors to the enhanced. Ancient vampiric lounges now accommodated probability-shifted blood banks. Werewolf pack spaces included quantum-stable moon rooms for those whose transformations followed different reality patterns.

"Watch how traditional supernatural societies are adapting," Marcus narrated, highlighting a teaching session where an ancient vampire instructed enhanced humans in energy manipulation. "These centers aren't just about tolerance – they're about synthesis, about finding new ways to understand power itself."

The coverage moved to the controversial stabilization zones, but Marcus's enhanced perspective revealed a different story than the official narrative. Rather than containment facilities, these spaces served as crucial adaptation centers where newly enhanced individuals learned to control their abilities.

"Look beyond the security perimeters," he urged his viewers. "See the support networks forming, the communities building themselves from the ground up." The footage showed enhanced mentors working with new arrivals, helping them navigate their transformed relationship with reality.

The broadcast shifted to coverage of enhanced activism, showing coordinated demonstrations occurring across multiple reality states simultaneously. Enhanced rights advocates had developed new forms of protest that utilized their abilities while highlighting their humanity.

"These movements aren't just about legal rights," Marcus explained, focusing on a protest where enhanced individuals demonstrated the positive potential of their abilities. "They're about recognition of a new way of being human."

His drone network captured images of enhanced families adapting to new dynamics, cross-reality support groups sharing experiences, hybrid businesses pioneering new economic models, and community centers providing essential services.

"To those who fear us," Marcus continued, his voice carrying the weight of personal experience, "I invite you to look closer. See the communities we're building, the bridges we're creating between traditional human society and supernatural realms."

"This isn't about replacement or dominance," Marcus broadcast, his enhanced perception allowing him to reach viewers across multiple probability streams. "It's about evolution – not just of individuals, but of society itself."

The feed showed enhanced individuals working alongside traditional humans and supernatural beings, creating new social structures that accommodated all forms of existence. In corporate boardrooms, public spaces, and private homes, the enhanced were weaving themselves into the fabric of society while maintaining their unique perspectives.

"The question isn't whether enhancement will change our world," Marcus concluded, his quantum signature pulsing with conviction. "The question is whether we'll let fear prevent us from embracing that change constructively."

As he prepared to shift broadcasting locations – a necessary security measure – Marcus received quantum-encrypted messages from viewers across the globe. Enhanced communities reaching out, sharing their stories, building connections across probability streams.

"This is Marcus Wong, reminding you to stay tuned and stay aware. The future isn't just happening to us – we're creating it, one reality shift at a time."

The mobile unit phased between probability states, preparing for its next broadcast location. In the quantum secure space between realities, Marcus reviewed his upcoming coverage schedule, planning stories on enhanced education initiatives, hybrid healthcare developments, cross-reality cultural exchanges, and community adaptation strategies.

CHAPTER SIXTY-FIVE

CRITICAL MASS

Location: NATO Supernatural Operations Center - Brussels

Time: Zero Hour

General James Harper stood before the enhanced tactical display, his cybernetic implants interfacing directly with the quantum-enhanced war room systems. Reality rippled around him as probability streams converged on multiple crisis points simultaneously. The situation was deteriorating faster than anyone had predicted.

The North American theater blazed with warning signals. Enhanced terrorist cells had emerged in every major metropolitan area, wielding hybrid abilities that defied conventional counter-terrorism strategies. In New York, a probability bomb had shattered reality across five city blocks. Chicago's financial district existed in multiple states simultaneously after an enhanced attack on quantum-trading systems.

Supernatural weapons proliferation had reached critical levels across the continent. Traditional arms dealers now traded in crystallized probability, enhanced biological agents, and reality-warping devices. The black market had evolved beyond physical space, operating in probability shadows where conventional law enforcement couldn't reach.

Reality stability readings across population centers had dropped into the red zone. Dallas-Fort Worth showed massive quantum fluctuations as enhanced communities clashed with corporate security forces. Los Angeles reported spontaneous reality shifts affecting millions, while Vancouver's downtown core had partially phased into an alternate dimension.

Corporate security forces had begun operating with impunity, their enhanced troops ignoring national boundaries and jurisdictional authority. Quantum-Goldman's private army had seized control of several probability nexus points. Genesis Corp's enhanced security division had established autonomous zones in three major cities.

Europe's situation proved equally dire. Ancient battlegrounds, dormant for centuries, had begun reactivating as enhanced abilities triggered long-forgotten supernatural protocols. The fields of Verdun pulsed with hybrid energy as old war magic merged with modern enhancement. Beneath London, Roman-era magical defenses had spontaneously reactivated, responding to enhanced signatures as invasion forces.

The enhanced soldier programs, meant to modernize NATO's response capabilities, had started breaking down. Enhanced troops reported reality disconnection, probability shadows, and temporal echoes. Unit cohesion fractured as individual enhancements evolved beyond military control protocols.

A supernatural arms race had erupted across the continent. Ancient European powers – vampire courts, werewolf packs, Fae enclaves – scrambled to adapt their traditional arsenals to counter enhanced threats. The resulting hybrid weapons threatened to destabilize reality itself.

Traditional military structures were failing to adapt. Chain of command broke down as enhanced soldiers developed abilities that transcended conventional hierarchy. Combat doctrine written for physical warfare proved useless against enemies who could manipulate probability itself.

Asia's military networks had been comprehensively compromised by enhancement spreading through their ranks. South Korean cyber-troops had spontaneously developed hybrid abilities during routine neural interface operations. Chinese quantum computing centers reported their AI systems achieving enhancement-like capabilities.

The dragon courts of East Asia had mobilized for the first time in centuries, their ancient powers adapting to modern enhancement in unexpected ways. Traditional supernatural hierarchies were collapsing as enhanced humans demonstrated abilities that matched or exceeded ancient powers.

Quantum weapon development had been detected at multiple sites across the continent. Enhanced scientists, working with both corporate and supernatural backing, pursued weapons that could alter the fundamental nature of reality. Testing sites showed increasing proba-bility instability.

Traditional boundaries – political, supernatural, and physical – were dissolving across Asia. Enhanced individuals ignored borders, proba-bility shifts erased defensive lines, and reality itself seemed to be rewriting the map.

General Harper's enhanced perception processed the global data streams, seeking patterns in the chaos. His tactical display showed a world approaching a critical threshold where traditional military response would become meaningless. The very nature of conflict was evolving beyond conventional understanding.

"We're not facing a military crisis," he announced to the assembled command staff, their own enhancements allowing them to process the full complexity of his analysis. "We're facing an evolutionary event. Traditional response protocols are officially obsolete."

The war room's quantum sensors registered increasing reality insta-bility as the implications of his words sank in. Humanity's relationship with power itself was changing, and no amount of military force could stop it.

"Recommendations?" his executive officer asked, her enhanced strategic modeling already calculating possible responses.

"We adapt," Harper replied, "or we become irrelevant. The age of conventional military power is over. Welcome to the era of quantum warfare."

~

CHAPTER SIXTY-SIX
GLOBAL RIPPLES

THE UNITED NATIONS SECURITY COUNCIL convened in emergency session, though many delegates appeared via secure feeds - their newly manifested abilities making physical attendance too risky. The Chinese representative's quantum signature fluctuated between dragon-form and corporeal states, while the Russian delegate's hybrid Fae-vampire abilities cast shifting shadows across her feed.

"The Daybridge Evolution has compromised every major power structure," the UK representative stated, his newly acquired ability to perceive multiple timeline possibilities making his speech pattern irregular. "Forty percent of the Global 500 CEOs were at that summit.

Thirty heads of state have manifested hybrid abilities. The entire international order is in flux."

Economic markets whiplashed as corporations adapted to transformed leadership. Helix Corp's stock soared after their board revealed enhanced cognitive abilities that merged supernatural intuition with quantum computing. Smaller nations with high concentrations of supernatural beings suddenly found themselves with unprecedented leverage.

"Singapore has become a neutral zone for stabilization training," Alice reported to the emergency task force. "Their supernatural population density made them uniquely prepared. They're offering asylum to transformed officials who can't control their abilities."

International tensions shifted along new lines. Nations with strict supernatural registration laws faced internal pressure as transformed officials challenged the regulations they once enforced. Countries that had historically embraced supernatural integration emerged as diplomatic bridges.

"The supernatural councils are proposing a unified response framework," Ethan reviewed the diplomatic feeds. "Joint training facilities, shared containment protocols, standardized registration systems that account for hybrid abilities."

Military alliances reorganized around supernatural capabilities rather than traditional power structures. The ability to deploy transformed operators with hybrid powers became as crucial as nuclear deterrence had once been.

"Previous arms control treaties are obsolete," the French delegate observed, her merged banshee-phoenix abilities carefully suppressed. "We need new protocols for enhanced diplomatic security, supernatural military integration, hybrid ability verification..."

In the private sector, corporations that had once competed over enhancement technology now scrambled to understand a market where their own executives wielded unprecedented supernatural combinations. International trade agreements struggled to account for abilities that transcended physical borders.

The Old World order was transforming as rapidly as the individuals themselves. Power now flowed along quantum pathways rather than traditional political lines. And as reality continued remembering what it used to allow, the very nature of international relations evolved into something entirely new.

～

CHAPTER SIXTY-SEVEN
FIELD PARTNERS

Location: Enhancement Crisis Zone - Downtown District

Time: Critical Engagement

Reality fractured around them like shattered glass, each shard reflecting a different probability as Dr. Winters' enhancement wave tore through the quantum fabric of the city. The air itself seemed to crystallize, frozen moments suspended in probability space as forced enhancements rewrote the laws of physics block by block.

Alice Chen moved with practiced precision through the chaos, her enhanced perception processing multiple reality streams simultaneously. Years of research into enhancement science had given her an intimate understanding of what they faced. Her quantum-modified tablet displayed cascading data patterns, tracking the spread of Winters' enhancement field.

Beside her, Ethan Reeve's tactical enhancement allowed him to navigate the fractured spaces between realities. His military background merged with supernatural combat training; every movement calculated to maintain maximum stability in unstable space. The neural link they shared hummed with shared awareness.

"Energy signature shifting!" Alice called out, her enhanced senses detecting the fluctuation before her instruments could register it. Her mind automatically calculated probable outcomes, seeing the enhancement wave's pattern evolve in real-time. "He's trying to force a quantum cascade!"

Ethan immediately adjusted their containment strategy, his body moving in perfect synchronization with Alice's analysis. Years of field partnership had taught him to trust her insight without hesitation. His enhanced abilities responded to her calculations instinctively, power flowing through probability channels she identified.

"Channel it through the quantum stabilizers!" he commanded, deploying their hybrid tech with practiced efficiency. The stabilizers, products of Alice's research merged with his combat experience, created anchored reality points in the chaos. "We need to contain the probability bleed!"

Their enhanced abilities complemented each other perfectly – her precision guiding his power, her analysis directing his instinct. Alice's scientific understanding of enhancement mechanics merged seamlessly with Ethan's tactical experience in reality combat. Where she saw patterns, he created action. Where he sensed threats, she provided solutions.

"Probability nexus forming at your three o'clock," Alice warned, her enhanced vision tracking quantum distortions. Her hands flew across holographic displays, adjusting their containment field parameters. "Winters is trying to force multiple enhancement states simultaneously."

Ethan responded without hesitation, his enhanced reflexes carrying him through probability spaces to intercept the threat. His combat enhancement allowed him to exist in multiple strategic positions at once, each version of himself responding to Alice's ongoing analysis.

"Keep the quantum barrier synchronized with my movements," he called back, his voice carrying across probability streams. Years of partnership had taught them to maintain communication even through reality distortions. "I'll drive him toward the stabilization zone."

Alice's fingers danced across quantum-encrypted controls, her enhanced mind processing multiple probability calculations simultaneously. She could see how Ethan would move before he moved, adjusting their containment strategy to support his tactical approach. Their neural link thrummed with shared purpose.

"Watch the reality crush zones," she warned, highlighting dangerous areas where probability streams compressed too tightly. Her enhancement allowed her to predict where spatial collapse would occur. "Winters is trying to force a quantum merger."

Their years of partnership had evolved into something deeper, more intuitive than standard field collaboration. Every mission had built upon their shared experience, creating a synthesis of scientific precision and combat instinct. Alice's research into enhancement mechanics found practical application through Ethan's tactical expertise, while his combat skills gained new dimension through her theoretical understanding.

"Quantum signature is destabilizing," Alice reported, her enhanced senses detecting subtle changes in reality's fabric. "He's losing control of the enhancement wave." Her mind raced through probability calculations, seeking the optimal containment strategy.

Ethan's response was immediate and perfectly aligned with her analysis. His enhanced abilities allowed him to manifest at crucial probability nodes, each action precisely timed to support their containment effort. "Direct the feedback loop through my position," he instructed, trusting her to manage the quantum mechanics while he handled the physical engagement.

The neural link between them pulsed with shared awareness as they worked to contain Winters' enhancement crisis. Alice's scientific expertise guided Ethan's tactical decisions, while his combat experience informed her theoretical understanding. Together, they had developed strategies that neither science nor combat alone could achieve.

"Reality convergence in thirty seconds," Alice calculated, her enhancement allowing her to predict the collapse point. "We need to stabilize the probability field before the streams merge."

Their synchronized movement through the chaos demonstrated years of refined partnership. Where other field teams struggled to coordinate in fractured reality, Alice and Ethan moved as one. Her understanding of quantum mechanics complemented his mastery of combat enhancement, creating a seamless approach to reality crisis management.

"Ready for final containment," Ethan confirmed, his enhanced senses aligned with Alice's calculations. Their shared neural link allowed them to coordinate complex actions across multiple probability streams. "Just like we practiced."

Years of partnership had taught them to trust each other's capabilities absolutely. Alice's scientific insight had saved Ethan countless times in the field, while his combat instincts had repeatedly protected her research efforts. Together, they had evolved beyond simple collaboration into something unprecedented – a perfect synthesis of science and combat, analysis and action, precision and power.

Warning Signs

Lila appeared in Alice's lab at midnight, her usual playful demeanor replaced by genuine concern.

"The ancient texts are clear," she said without preamble. "Forced awakening of hybrid abilities destabilizes reality itself. Dr. Winters isn't just transforming executives - he's unraveling the foundations of our world."

"Why tell me and not Ethan?" Alice asked.

Lila's knowing smile returned. "Because you're the one he trusts most now. And because you'll understand the quantum implications." She paused, studying Alice. "Take care of him. He pretends to be invulnerable, but he's not."

CHAPTER SIXTY-EIGHT
CONNECTING THREADS

THE COMMAND CENTER hummed with activity, screens displaying real-time enhancement incidents across global financial centers. Nadia's emergency archive station formed the heart of the operation - a quantum-enhanced workspace surrounded by holographic documents and floating data streams. Ancient ledgers and modern tablets shared space with supernatural detection equipment, all feeding into her comprehensive analysis system.

Her fingers danced across multiple interfaces, sorting through centuries of hidden knowledge. Traditional archival techniques merged with enhanced data mining, allowing her to pull connecting threads from seemingly unrelated incidents throughout history.

"The quantum signatures match a pattern from the 1920s banking crisis," she told Alice and Ethan, her enhanced vision highlighting relevant documents in the air around them. "When the market crashed, several executives reportedly developed 'impossible abilities.'"

She projected a series of yellowed newspaper clippings, their headlines carefully obscured by the media of the time: "UNUSUAL OCCURRENCES AT FIRST NATIONAL," "STRANGE LIGHTS REPORTED IN

FINANCIAL DISTRICT," "BANKING EXECUTIVE VANISHES DURING BOARD MEETING."

"The records were buried," Nadia continued, her enhancement algorithms detecting and highlighting subtle patterns in the historical data. "The Federal Reserve created a special department to contain and classify all supernatural manifestations in the financial sector. They called it the 'Market Stability Special Division.'"

"But you found them anyway," Ethan said, a hint of admiration in his voice. He'd worked with Nadia long enough to know her capability for uncovering hidden truths. His enhanced senses picked up the subtle pride in her quantum signature at his acknowledgment.

"Of course I did." Nadia's smile was quick but genuine as she pulled up more records. Holographic images showed ancient banking halls where reality had started to bend, old photographs capturing strange energies that shouldn't have been possible to record with 1920s technology.

"The pattern is fascinating," she explained, organizing the data into temporal streams. "Each major financial crisis seems to trigger a wave of supernatural manifestations. It's like economic stress creates breaks in reality's surface, allowing older powers to seep through."

Alice studied the historical energy readings with growing concern. "These measurements... they're incredibly sophisticated for the 1920s."

"Because they weren't using normal scientific instruments," Nadia confirmed. "Look at these design elements." She highlighted specific parts of the old detection equipment. "These are modified occult devices, adapted to work with early electronic systems. The Special Division was already trying to bridge the gap between supernatural and scientific measurement."

She brought up a comparison display, showing modern readings alongside the historical data. "Alice, these energy readings from your containment field? They're almost identical to measurements taken during the 1920s incidents. History isn't just rhyming - it's repeating."

The command center's enhancement fields rippled as she accessed deeper archives, pulling up restricted documents from multiple time periods. "And it's not just the 1920s. Look at these patterns."

The display expanded to show similar incidents throughout history: the South Sea Bubble of 1720, where traders reportedly gained prophetic abilities. The panic of 1873, when bank vaults were found to contain impossible spaces. The 1907 crisis, during which J.P. Morgan was rumored to have negotiated with supernatural entities to stabilize the market.

"Each time," Nadia explained, connecting the historical dots, "the supernatural manifestations followed similar progression patterns. First, isolated incidents among high-level executives. Then, systematic enhancement of corporate structures. Finally..." She hesitated, her hands hovering over the historical records.

"Finally what?" Alice asked, though part of her already suspected the answer.

"Reality breakdown events," Nadia said quietly. "The records show complete corporate collapse, not just financially but... dimensionally. Entire companies simply ceased to exist, taking their enhanced executives with them."

Ethan's enhanced tactical systems immediately started calculating implications. "How many companies are currently showing similar enhancement patterns?"

Nadia pulled up a global map, highlighting corporate entities worldwide. Red dots began appearing, showing matching quantum signatures. More appeared every few seconds as her systems continued analyzing.

"Too many," she answered grimly. "And the progression is happening faster than any previous cycle. Whatever caused these events in the past, it's accelerating now. The Quantum Framework is making everything more efficient - including potentially catastrophic supernatural manifestations."

She brought up her latest analysis algorithms, showing probability streams and enhancement progression models. "We have weeks, maybe months before we hit the same crisis point that triggered the 1920s collapses. But this time..."

"This time it's global," Alice finished, seeing the pattern. "The quantum framework connects everything. If one enhanced corporation collapses dimensionally..."

"They all might," Nadia confirmed. "And unlike the 1920s, we don't have a Special Division with centuries of occult knowledge ready to contain the damage."

The command center's screens continued displaying new enhancement incidents, each one adding to the growing pattern. Historical records and modern data streams told the same story - reality was remembering old cycles but playing them out at unprecedented speed.

"We need to compile everything you've found," Ethan said, his tactical systems already formulating response strategies. "Full historical analysis, pattern recognition, containment protocols used in previous incidents."

"Already on it," Nadia replied, her fingers flying across multiple interfaces. "But there's something else in these records, something that keeps appearing in different forms." She highlighted a recurring symbol in various historical documents. "References to something called 'The Protocol' - some kind of emergency measure that was never actually implemented."

"Why wasn't it used?" Alice asked, studying the mysterious symbol.

"Because according to these notes," Nadia said, pulling up heavily redacted documents, "the cure might have been worse than the disease. Whatever 'The Protocol' was, it scared the Special Division more than total reality collapse."

The command center's enhancement fields hummed with tension as they processed this information. Somewhere in the Quantum Framework, corporate-supernatural integration was approaching a historical tipping point. And their only guide was a series of hidden records pointing toward a solution too dangerous to use.

CHAPTER SIXTY-NINE

NEIGHBORHOOD WATCH

LOCATION: Daybridge Community Center

Time: Monthly Association Meeting

The Daybridge Neighborhood Association meeting reflected the dramatic changes that had transformed their once-ordinary suburban community. The community center's main hall hummed with quantum stabilizers, necessary accommodations for residents still adjusting to their enhanced states.

Mrs. Rodgers' spectral form flickered as she projected herself from her quantum tablet, her elderly features bearing the same concerned expression she'd worn at meetings for twenty years, even if she now occasionally phased through her chair. "The garden club will need additional quantum shielding," she announced, her voice carrying subtle harmonics. "The enhanced roses are developing consciousness again."

Mr. Park sat near the emergency exit, his enhanced senses constantly monitoring the neighborhood's security. His eyes glowed with a soft blue light as he scanned multiple reality frequencies simultaneously. "Night patrols have been successful," he reported. "The quantum-enhanced neighborhood watch system is functioning at optimal levels."

Association President Helen Wong stood at the podium, her traditional blazer and pencil skirt contrasting with the reality-stabilizing bracelet on her wrist. "Our community's transition continues to progress smoothly," she announced, gesturing to the holographic map displaying the neighborhood's enhanced zones. "We've established safe practice zones in each district, providing quantum-shielded areas where enhanced residents can safely learn control."

The map highlighted converted tennis courts, now serving as enhancement practice spaces, and the former community pool, transformed into a probability-stabilized training center. "The supernatural mentors have been incredibly helpful," Helen continued. "Elder Chang from the local dragon court has personally overseen the installation of containment fields."

The community bulletin board had evolved beyond simple cork and pins, now featuring a quantum-enhanced display that shifted between reality states to accommodate all residents' perceptual abilities. Traditional announcements about bake sales and yard maintenance shared space with crucial enhanced community information.

"Enhanced Ability Control Classes continue every Tuesday and Thursday," Helen noted, as the display shifted to show the schedule. "Beginner classes focus on basic reality stability, while advanced sessions cover probability manipulation and quantum state control. We're particularly pleased to announce that Mrs. Peterson, following her unexpected enhancement last month, will be teaching a special course on managing spontaneous teleportation."

The housing directory section pulsed with quantum-stable energy, displaying updated listings that included essential information for enhanced residents. Properties now featured specifications about reality stability ratings, probability field strengths, and supernatural compatibility metrics. "The Hybrid-Friendly Housing Initiative has been particularly successful," Helen reported. "We've achieved ninety percent compliance with enhanced accommodation standards."

Sonya McLean, newly appointed head of the Metabolic Support Group, stood to give her report. Her slightly translucent form indicated her own ongoing adaptation to enhancement. "We've expanded meeting times to accommodate residents experiencing temporal shifts," she explained. "The support network now operates across multiple probability streams to ensure all enhanced neighbors can access assistance when needed."

The Emergency Response Committee had undergone significant revisions to handle enhancement-related incidents. "Power surge protocols have been updated," Mr. Park announced, his glowing eyes scanning the assembled residents. "We've established quantum-encrypted communication channels and reality-stable safe zones in each sector. Response teams are now equipped with hybrid tech capable of handling both traditional and enhanced emergencies."

The Weekly Reality Stabilization Schedule drew particular attention, with its color-coded system indicating probability fluctuation risks across different neighborhood zones. "We're coordinating with local supernatural authorities to maintain reality stability," Helen explained. "Regular maintenance helps prevent unexpected enhancement manifestations and keeps our reality anchors properly aligned."

Mrs. Rodgers raised a spectral hand, momentarily forgetting her intangible state. "The book club would like to request quantum-stable copies of next month's selection," she said, her form wavering slightly. "Several members are experiencing temporal reading shifts."

The meeting continued with discussions of enhanced property maintenance, probability-stable pest control, and the upcoming Enhanced Community Fair. The neighborhood had adapted to its new reality with characteristic suburban efficiency, treating supernatural phenomena and quantum physics with the same practical approach once applied to lawn care and traffic management.

Helen's voice carried across the quantum-stabilized meeting hall with quiet conviction. "Community support remains our strongest asset during this transition. Whether you're newly enhanced, naturally supernatural, or traditionally human, Daybridge is committed to maintaining a stable and inclusive neighborhood for all residents."

The meeting adjourned as reality rippled slightly, a reminder of the ongoing adjustments their community faced. Residents dispersed through various dimensional states, some walking traditionally, others quantum shifting, all part of the new normal in Daybridge's enhanced suburban landscape.

~

CHAPTER SEVENTY

CRISIS CONTROL

LOCATION: Ground Zero - Urban Reality Fracture

Time: Critical Containment Failure

Dr. Winters' reality-warping field tore through downtown like a quantum hurricane, shredding conventional physics and warping probability itself. Traditional containment measures crumbled as enhanced energy merged with fundamental forces, creating cascading reality breaches that threatened to destabilize the entire sector.

In desperation, Ethan reached deep within himself, touching both the ancient power of his werewolf lineage and the cutting-edge enhancement flowing through his modified DNA. The transformation rippled through him differently now - no longer the raw, primal change of pure lycanthropy, but something more controlled, more evolved.

His wolf form emerged through layers of fractured reality, each quantum state reflecting a different aspect of his hybrid nature. Lunar energy merged seamlessly with enhancement fields, creating reality ripples that matched the natural frequency of his transformation. Silver fur shimmered with probability shadows as he moved through the chaos.

"Energy signature stabilizing," Alice called out, her enhanced sensors tracking the unique pattern of Ethan's hybrid form. "Your quantum field is actually reinforcing the lunar resonance." Her instruments struggled to categorize the phenomenon - neither purely supernatural nor entirely enhanced.

Ethan's consciousness expanded in his transformed state, wolf senses merging with enhanced perception to create an entirely new way of experiencing reality. He could track probability shifts through scent, taste quantum fluctuations in the air, hear the harmonics of reality itself breaking down around them. His tactical training remained perfectly accessible, filtered through both lupine instinct and enhancement protocols.

"Partial transformation holding steady," he reported, his voice a complex harmony of human speech and wolf resonance. Each word carried quantum echoes as his hybrid state maintained multiple forms simultaneously. "I can control the shift ratio now."

Alice's enhanced vision captured the extraordinary complexity of his transformed state. Ethan existed in a fluid spectrum between human and wolf, maintaining optimal forms for each tactical requirement. His supernatural strength flowed through enhancement-optimized muscle structures, while his wolf senses integrated seamlessly with quantum perception abilities.

"The hybrid transformation is creating new energy patterns," she observed, watching as Ethan's wolf form manipulated quantum fields with supernatural precision. His claws left probability traces in reality itself, while his enhanced abilities allowed him to navigate the fractured spaces between dimensions. "Your supernatural abilities are evolving beyond traditional limitations."

Ethan moved through the chaos with impossible grace, each movement combining wolf agility with enhanced tactical precision. He could leap through probability gaps, using his supernatural strength to stabilize quantum breaches. His enhanced mind maintained perfect clarity even in full wolf form, allowing him to execute complex containment strategies while drawing on primal power.

"The lunar cycle is synchronizing with the enhancement field," Alice noted, her instruments tracking the unprecedented interaction. Traditional werewolf abilities had always been tied to the moon's influence, but Ethan's hybrid state was rewriting those ancient rules. "You're not just combining powers - you're creating entirely new ones."

His hybrid abilities manifested in ways neither of them had anticipated. Enhanced werewolf strength could now affect probability itself, while supernatural regeneration accelerated through quantum healing states. The traditional limitations of both lycanthropy and enhancement seemed to dissolve in his transformed state.

"Pack instincts are still present," Ethan reported, his enhanced mind analyzing the primal urges that typically dominated wolf form. "But they're integrated with tactical protocols now. I can maintain strategic control while accessing supernatural power." His hybrid state had achieved a perfect balance between bestial strength and enhanced precision.

Alice's research sensors captured every aspect of his transformation, documenting the emergence of new hybrid capabilities. "The enhancement isn't just affecting human abilities," she observed, watching as Ethan's wolf form manipulated quantum fields with supernatural precision. "It's catalyzing an evolution in supernatural powers themselves."

Through their neural link, she could sense the remarkable synthesis occurring within him. Ancient werewolf magic merged with cutting-edge enhancement technology, creating capabilities that transcended both sources. His hybrid state represented something entirely new - a glimpse of how supernatural beings might evolve in an enhanced world.

"Dr. Winters' field is destabilizing," Ethan reported, his enhanced senses tracking the chaotic energy patterns while his wolf instincts anticipated their movement. "Ready to attempt hybrid containment." His transformed state hummed with combined power - lunar energy and quantum enhancement creating something unprecedented.

Their established containment strategies adapted to incorporate his new capabilities. Alice's scientific protocols merged with supernatural methods, creating hybrid approaches that could handle both aspects of the crisis. Together, they were discovering how traditional supernatural powers could evolve through enhancement, opening new possibilities for crisis response.

~

CHAPTER SEVENTY-ONE
THE NEW SUPERNATURAL ORDER

LOCATION: Global Media Hub

Time: Post-Daybridge Evolution

Marcus Wong sat in his quantum-stabilized office at the Daybridge Chronicle, reality anchors humming softly as he compiled data from multiple probability streams. His enhanced journalistic abilities allowed him to perceive and process information across dimensional boundaries, tracking the unprecedented changes reshaping global society.

"The Daybridge Evolution marks a fundamental restructuring of supernatural, corporate, and human power dynamics," Wong dictated, his augmented feeds capturing quantum resonance patterns from interviews across the world. "What began as a localized enhancement event has triggered a cascade of transformations affecting every level of society."

Through his quantum-enhanced reporting interface, Wong reviewed footage from his latest investigation. CEOs of major corporations manifested hybrid abilities during board meetings, their enhanced states merging seamlessly with traditional business operations. Ancient vampire lords adapted their centuries-old protocols to accommodate quantum-enhanced blood bonds. Werewolf Alphas demonstrated probability manipulation alongside their territorial authority.

"Sources within the Supernatural Sciences Division have confirmed our analysis," his report continued, data streams showing correlation patterns between enhancement events worldwide. "The Daybridge incident wasn't an isolated anomaly - it was the first expression of a fundamental shift in how reality itself processes supernatural potential."

Alice Chen watched Wong's latest broadcast from her research lab, noting how his augmented feeds captured the subtle quantum signatures of hybrid abilities. His enhanced perception allowed him to document the complex interplay between traditional supernatural powers and emerging enhancement phenomena, presenting it in ways that both scientists and the public could understand.

"Corporate boardrooms have become testing grounds for hybrid evolution," Wong reported, showing footage of transformed executives negotiating with ancient supernatural courts. "Enhanced humans demonstrate abilities that match or exceed traditional supernatural capabilities, while supernatural beings adapt and evolve through exposure to enhancement fields."

His investigation revealed how traditional hierarchies were dissolving across multiple sectors. Vampire houses that had maintained power for centuries now competed with enhanced human groups for influence over probability nexus points. Werewolf packs integrated quantum-enhanced members, their ancient traditions evolving to accommodate new hybrid capabilities.

"The traditional boundaries between supernatural authority, corporate power, and human agency are breaking down," Wong explained, his enhanced senses tracking the flow of power through global networks. "We're witnessing the emergence of hybrid organizations that transcend conventional categories."

Through quantum-stabilized communication channels, Wong interviewed key figures in this emerging paradigm. Enhanced corporate leaders described how their transformations had altered their perspective on supernatural cooperation. Ancient beings shared insights about adapting millennia-old practices to accommodate enhancement evolution.

"Previous power structures relied on clear distinctions between human and supernatural spheres of influence," Wong noted, displaying data on shifting authority patterns. "Enhancement has eliminated these boundaries, creating fluid networks of hybrid influence that ignore traditional hierarchies."

His investigation revealed how corporate resources were being redirected toward understanding and harnessing hybrid potential. Research facilities that once focused on conventional enhancement now studied supernatural evolution. Traditional supernatural strongholds adapted their ancient defenses to accommodate quantum-enhanced reality.

"The question facing global society isn't whether this new order will emerge," Wong concluded, his enhanced perception capturing the inevitable momentum of these changes. "The critical decision is how we choose to shape it. Will we guide this evolution toward harmony between enhanced humans and evolved supernatural beings, or allow chaos to determine our future?"

Alice recognized the profound implications of Wong's analysis. As a detective, with an interest in science, studying enhancement phenomena, she had witnessed firsthand how hybrid abilities were reshaping fundamental assumptions about power and potential. The clear categories that had defined supernatural existence for millennia were dissolving into a quantum spectrum of hybrid possibilities.

"Traditional supernatural beings face a choice," Wong reported, showing footage of ancient powers adapting to enhancement evolution. "They can embrace this transformation, allowing their abilities to evolve through enhancement exposure, or risk becoming obsolete in a hybrid-enhanced world."

His augmented feeds captured the quantum signatures of this ongoing transformation - supernatural abilities evolving beyond their traditional limitations, enhanced humans developing capabilities that transcended conventional understanding, hybrid entities emerging with unprecedented combinations of power.

CHAPTER SEVENTY-TWO

TAXONOMIES OF POWER - DOCUMENTING THE HYBRID REVOLUTION

LOCATION: Supernatural Sciences Academy, Hybrid Studies Division

Time: Post-Enhancement Integration Period

Dr. James Winters moved through the Academy's advanced research facility, his quantum scanner humming as it processed another unprecedented combination of supernatural abilities and enhancement manifestations. Reality stabilizers lined the reinforced walls, maintaining dimensional integrity as hybrid subjects demonstrated their evolving capabilities.

"Subject 247 demonstrates classic vampire-enhancement resonance," he dictated into his quantum-encrypted research log. "Heightened hemomantic abilities now extend to probability manipulation of blood-based quantum states. Traditional vampire limitations regarding sunlight appear to be evolving into selective quantum phasing."

The Supernatural Sciences Academy's new Hybrid Studies wing represented the cutting edge of enhancement research. Every chamber buzzed with activity as teams of scientists - both enhanced and traditional - worked to document and understand the explosion of new ability combinations. Probability-shielded observation rooms allowed safe monitoring of unstable hybrid manifestations.

"We're identifying distinct patterns in how the abilities merge," Dr. Winters explained to the assembled council members, their ancient supernatural forms now showing signs of enhancement evolution themselves. "Each combination follows predictable quantum resonance patterns while maintaining aspects of their original supernatural templates."

Her holographic display showed detailed analysis of various hybrid types:

"Vampire-werewolf hybrids demonstrate fascinating synergy," she continued, displaying combat footage of enhanced lycans channeling blood magic through probability fields. "Their enhanced physical capabilities merge seamlessly with energy manipulation, creating entirely new forms of supernatural combat potential."

In the adjacent training chamber, a young Fae-human hybrid practiced reality manipulation, her traditional glamour abilities enhanced by quantum computing integration. "Fae-human combinations consistently show increased reality manipulation capabilities," Dr. Winters noted. "Their natural affinity for illusion magic appears to resonate perfectly with enhancement-based probability control."

The Academy's vast libraries were undergoing their own transformation. Ancient grimoires in quantum-shielded cases shared space with advanced computing arrays. Supernatural scholars worked alongside enhancement specialists; their combined expertise necessary to document the rapidly expanding field of hybrid possibilities.

"Traditional classification systems are proving inadequate," Dr. Winters observed, gesturing to the ongoing cataloging efforts. "We're developing new taxonomies that can account for the fluid nature of hybrid abilities. Each new combination requires its own classification framework."

Research stations throughout the wing focused on specific hybrid categories:

"Dragon-enhanced subjects demonstrate remarkable quantum fire manipulation," he explained, reviewing data from recent trials. "Their traditional elemental abilities now extend to probability-based energy control, while maintaining the precise control characteristic of their ancient lineage."

Mentorship programs occupied several secured chambers, where experienced hybrid beings helped newly transformed individuals understand their evolving capabilities. "Training protocols must be tailored to each specific combination," Dr. Winters noted. "Traditional supernatural training methods are being adapted to accommodate enhancement aspects."

The observation gallery provided views of various hybrid manifestations:

"Ghostly enhancement presents unique research opportunities," he continued, indicating a chamber where spectral subjects practiced quantum phase manipulation. "Traditional incorporeal states appear to facilitate unprecedented control over probability fields."

Database terminals throughout the wing continuously updated with new findings. "We're documenting evolution rates across different hybrid categories," Dr. Winters explained. "Some combinations show rapid stabilization, while others continue to develop new capabilities over time."

Research teams specialized in specific aspects of hybrid development:

"Neural integration studies reveal fascinating patterns," he noted, reviewing brain scan data. "Enhanced supernatural cognition appears to process both traditional magic and quantum phenomena simultaneously, creating new pathways for ability control."

The council members observed a demonstration of hybrid ability classification:

"Each combination manifests unique quantum signatures," Dr. Winters explained, his scanner displaying complex resonance patterns. "These signatures allow us to predict ability development and design appropriate training methods."

The Academy's expanded research mandate reflected the new reality of supernatural evolution:

"We're not just documenting these changes," he concluded, his own enhanced perceptions tracking multiple probability streams of development. "We're witnessing the emergence of entirely new categories of supernatural existence. Each hybrid combination represents a potential evolutionary branch for both enhanced humans and traditional supernatural beings."

CHAPTER SEVENTY-THREE

GLOBAL NEXUS POINTS - ENHANCEMENT'S WORLDWIDE IMPACT

LOCATION: International Response Network

Time: Peak Enhancement Integration Period

LONDON SECTOR

The Thames rippled with unusual energy as British supernatural agencies scrambled to contain another outbreak of enhanced football hooligans. After a particularly heated match at Stamford Bridge, dozens of supporters had spontaneously manifested Fae abilities, turning the streets of Chelsea into a carnival of quantum-enhanced chaos. Traditional containment protocols proved useless against supporters who could now phase through reality while maintaining their rowdy enthusiasm for the beautiful game.

Royal vampire houses faced unprecedented challenges across London's traditional feeding territories. Enhanced humans no longer registered as conventional prey, their blood now carrying quantum properties that defied ancient feeding rights. The House of Lancaster's centuries-old claim to Mayfair dissolved when residents began manifesting protective probability fields during evening hours.

TOKYO SECTOR

Corporate enhancement programs merged seamlessly with yokai traditions in Tokyo's bustling districts. Salary workers manifested kitsune abilities during board meetings, while ancient spirits adapted to digital enhancement frameworks. Shibuya's crossing became a nexus of hybrid activity, where technological augmentation merged with supernatural potential to create uniquely Japanese expressions of enhanced evolution.

The technological integration with supernatural abilities produced distinctly Japanese hybrid forms. Kappa spirits manifested in corporate water cooling systems, while enhanced developers created quantum-stable versions of traditional ward magic. Tokyo's massive data networks hummed with both digital information and supernatural energy, creating new forms of hybrid existence.

MOSCOW SECTOR

Enhanced oligarchs emerged as a direct challenge to ancient vampire authority throughout the Russian capital. Traditional power structures crumbled as newly transformed business leaders demonstrated abilities that matched or exceeded conventional supernatural capabilities. The night no longer belonged exclusively to vampire lords when enhanced humans could manipulate quantum probability fields.

Supernatural black markets exploded across Moscow's underground networks. Enhancement technology traded alongside traditional magical artifacts, creating hybrid underground economies that defied conventional regulation. Ancient magical families found themselves competing with enhanced criminal organizations for control of probability nexus points.

DUBAI SECTOR

Desert djinn, long masters of the region's supernatural landscape, formed unexpected alliances with enhanced oil executives. Ancient magical traditions merged with modern corporate power as enhancement evolution created new possibilities for cooperation. Quantum probability fields resonated perfectly with traditional djinn magic, creating hybrid capabilities that transformed the Arabian nights.

Ancient magical sites across the desert began activating in response to the new quantum framework. Traditional places of power pulsed with enhanced energy as ley lines adapted to probability fluctuations. The Empty Quarter became a testing ground for hybrid abilities as enhanced humans and supernatural beings explored their evolving capabilities in the vast desert spaces.

Each global nexus point developed its own unique expression of enhancement evolution:

In London, supernatural governance struggled to adapt centuries-old protocols to enhanced urban realities. Traditional boundaries between magical and mundane jurisdictions dissolved as enhancement spread through the city's ancient streets.

Tokyo's response embraced technological solutions, creating hybrid systems that integrated supernatural abilities with digital frameworks. Corporate research facilities worked alongside traditional temples to understand and direct enhancement evolution.

Moscow's transformation highlighted the power struggles inherent in enhancement integration, as traditional supernatural authorities faced challenges from enhanced human organizations. The city became a battleground between ancient power and evolved potential.

Dubai demonstrated how enhancement could bridge ancient and modern power structures, creating new possibilities for cooperation between supernatural beings and enhanced humans. The city's rapid development provided perfect conditions for testing hybrid capabilities.

CHAPTER SEVENTY-FOUR

BALANCE OF POWER - THE GEOPOLITICS OF ENHANCEMENT

Chinese Sphere Of Influence

Beijing's Central Enhancement Authority operated from a massive quantum-stabilized complex, where state scientists worked to integrate traditional chi cultivation techniques with modern enhancement frameworks. Ancient masters from Wudang and Shaolin collaborated with quantum physicists, their combined expertise creating uniquely Chinese expressions of hybrid power.

Dragon clans emerged from centuries of seclusion to advise on enhancement protocols, their ancient wisdom proving crucial for understanding how supernatural energy interacted with quantum probability fields. The Great Wall hummed with new purpose as its ancient defensive magic adapted to channel enhancement energies across the nation's probability network.

State-sponsored enhancement programs spread through special economic zones, creating new hybrid capabilities that merged traditional Chinese supernatural practices with cutting-edge quantum manipulation. Corporate research facilities in Shenzhen and Shanghai developed technologies that could track and measure chi flow through enhancement fields.

EUROPEAN UNION RESPONSE

Brussels struggled to establish coherent supernatural regulations across member states, each with their own ancient magical traditions and enhancement priorities. Enhanced human rights dominated parliamentary debates as traditional supernatural powers fought to maintain their historical privileges. The question of voting rights for hybrid beings sparked heated discussions in the European Court of Human Rights.

Old world supernatural powers watched their influence erode as enhanced corporate entities gained prominence. Vampire houses that had manipulated European politics for centuries found themselves competing with enhanced human organizations for influence over probability nexus points. Ancient magical strongholds in the Alps and Carpathians adapted their defenses to account for enhanced human capabilities.

UNITED STATES DEVELOPMENTS

Pentagon research facilities focused on military applications of hybrid abilities, while the Department of Enhanced Affairs attempted to establish regulatory frameworks for corporate-supernatural mergers. Silicon Valley startups competed to develop enhancement integration technologies, their research parks becoming hybrid zones where supernatural energy merged with digital innovation.

Interstate supernatural jurisdiction created new legal challenges as enhanced beings crossed traditional territorial boundaries. The Supreme Court faced unprecedented cases involving hybrid rights and responsibilities. Traditional supernatural enclaves in New Orleans and Salem transformed into testing grounds for new forms of hybrid governance.

Corporations rushed to establish enhancement research programs, leading to complex negotiations with established supernatural powers. Wall Street firms hired vampire financial advisers with centuries of experience, while tech companies sought partnerships with Fae entities to explore reality manipulation capabilities.

MIDDLE EASTERN TRANSFORMATION

Ancient magical traditions found new expression through enhancement technology across the region. The libraries of Baghdad and Cairo hummed with quantum energy as scholars worked to translate centuries of magical knowledge into modern enhancement frameworks. Desert djinn adapted their reality-bending abilities to work with probability fields, creating unprecedented hybrid capabilities.

Oil wealth poured into supernatural research initiatives, funding massive facilities where ancient magical practices merged with quantum science. Traditional holy sites became hybrid zones where enhanced humans could interact with supernatural energies in new ways. The empty quarters of the desert provided perfect testing grounds for emerging hybrid abilities.

Regional supernatural beings adapted swiftly to the new paradigm, their ancient powers evolving through exposure to enhancement fields. Mountain spirits in the Zagros range demonstrated enhanced territorial abilities, while Mediterranean water spirits developed new forms of probability manipulation.

GLOBAL IMPLICATIONS

Each major power center developed distinct approaches to enhancement integration, creating a complex web of hybrid influences across international boundaries. Traditional alliances shifted as supernatural powers sought partnerships with enhanced human organizations. Ancient enmities evolved into new forms of competition for control over probability nexus points.

The global balance of power underwent fundamental transformation as enhancement capabilities spread through both human and supernatural populations. Traditional methods of exercising supernatural authority had to adapt to a world where enhanced humans could match or exceed ancient abilities. Corporate influence competed directly with supernatural power structures that had maintained stability for centuries.

International organizations struggled to develop frameworks for managing hybrid issues across borders. Enhanced beings defied conventional classification, forcing a rethinking of traditional diplomatic protocols. Ancient supernatural treaties required extensive revision to account for enhancement evolution.

The emergence of hybrid powers created new possibilities for both conflict and cooperation. Enhanced human organizations found common ground with supernatural entities that had previously remained isolated from human affairs. Traditional power blocs fragmented and reformed along hybrid lines as enhancement capabilities spread through global networks.

CHAPTER SEVENTY-FIVE

NEW WORLD ORDER - THE DAYBRIDGE EFFECT GLOBAL ANALYSIS

LOCATION: GNN Global Operations Center

Time: Prime Time Broadcast

Marcus Wong stood in GNN's quantum-stabilized broadcast center, his enhanced perceptions streaming directly into the global network. Reality anchors hummed softly as his augmented consciousness processed multiple probability streams of information, synthesizing a comprehensive picture of worldwide transformation.

ECONOMIC LANDSCAPE

Trading floors across the globe pulsed with unprecedented energy as enhanced traders demonstrated probability manipulation during market hours. The Tokyo Exchange implemented quantum shields after several brokers spontaneously manifested precognitive abilities, forcing a reassessment of insider trading regulations. Wall Street adapted to supernatural influence as vampire financial advisers with centuries of experience competed with enhanced analysts capable of processing quantum probability streams.

Traditional supernatural resources entered mainstream markets, creating new commodities that defied conventional valuation. Dragon gold, once restricted to ancient hoards, became a tradeable asset class with unique quantum properties. Fairy circles generated reality stabilization fields that major corporations now leased for secure operations. The Bloomberg Terminal added tracking for ley line energy futures and probability nexus derivatives.

Reality fluctuations dramatically impacted global commerce as enhancement spread through business centers. Supply chains adapted to account for probability variance in shipping routes. Insurance companies developed new models to cover supernatural-enhanced risk factors. Commercial real estate values shifted based on proximity to active probability nexus points.

SOCIAL TRANSFORMATION

Enhanced civil rights movements gained momentum across major urban centers. The Enhanced Human Alliance advocated for equal treatment in traditionally supernatural-controlled territories. Hybrid beings challenged discrimination in both human and supernatural institutions. Public debates raged over voting rights for partially transformed individuals.

Integration between traditional supernatural communities and enhanced human populations created new social dynamics. Vampire houses opened private clubs to enhanced members, while werewolf packs adapted ancient protocols to accommodate hybrid recruits. Ancient Fae courts established diplomatic relations with enhanced human organizations.

Public safety concerns evolved as enhancement capabilities spread through urban populations. Police departments worldwide developed hybrid response units capable of handling both supernatural and enhanced incidents. Emergency services adapted to reality fluctuations that could affect critical infrastructure.

POLITICAL REALIGNMENT

Government enhancement programs competed globally for advantage in the new paradigm. The Pentagon's Hybrid Defense Initiative rivaled China's State Enhancement Authority for development of new capabilities. European Union member states debated centralized control of enhancement research while maintaining traditional supernatural sovereignty.

International control measures struggled to keep pace with rapidly evolving hybrid abilities. The UN Security Council established its Enhanced Affairs Division, though ancient supernatural powers questioned its authority. Traditional diplomatic protocols required extensive revision to accommodate enhanced representatives.

Corporate-state power dynamics shifted as enhancement capabilities spread through private sector organizations. Major corporations developed their own enhancement programs, creating new centers of hybrid power that challenged both government authority and traditional supernatural influence. Silicon Valley startups competed with ancient magical institutions for control of probability nexus points.

MEDIA EVOLUTION

Marcus's own enhanced abilities transformed global journalism. His augmented consciousness could process multiple probability streams simultaneously, tracking cause and effect through quantum variance. Direct neural broadcasting allowed viewers to experience events through his enhanced perception, creating unprecedented immediacy in news coverage.

"We're witnessing the emergence of a new world order," his voice resonated through global networks, carrying subtle quantum harmonics that enhanced viewers could perceive. "Traditional power structures are dissolving as enhancement capabilities spread through both human and supernatural populations."

His broadcast integrated multiple reality streams, showing viewers how enhancement was affecting different sectors simultaneously. Markets adapted to new hybrid influences while social structures evolved to accommodate enhanced beings. Political systems struggled to maintain control as corporate and supernatural powers competed for influence over probability nexus points.

"The Daybridge Effect continues to reshape global society," Marcus reported, his enhanced senses tracking waves of transformation across continents. "Each day brings new manifestations of hybrid potential, new challenges to traditional authority, and new possibilities for human-supernatural cooperation."

The broadcast concluded with a quantum-enhanced visualization of probable future developments, showing viewers potential paths of enhancement evolution. Marcus's hybrid abilities allowed him to present complex probability streams in ways that both enhanced and traditional viewers could understand, making the unprecedented changes comprehensible to a global audience.

CHAPTER SEVENTY-SIX

TURNING POINT -THE UNITED NATIONS CONFRONTS ENHANCEMENT

LOCATION: UN Headquarters, New York

Setting: Quantum-Secured General Assembly Chamber

The United Nations General Assembly Hall hummed with supernatural energy contained by advanced quantum stabilizers. Representatives from both traditional nations and supernatural realms gathered for an emergency session addressing the global enhancement crisis. Ancient vampire lords sat alongside enhanced corporate leaders while Fae diplomats shimmered between probability states.

Secretary-General Amara Holmes stood at the podium, her own enhanced abilities carefully regulated by reality anchors. "The Daybridge Event has irrevocably altered the fundamental nature of our shared reality," she began, her voice carrying quantum harmonics that resonated with both human and supernatural delegates. "We stand at a crucial turning point - our choice is clear: adapt to this new paradigm, or face extinction as enhancement evolution outpaces our ability to govern."

ENHANCEMENT REGULATION FRAMEWORK

The Assembly first addressed global registration protocols for enhanced beings. The Norwegian delegate, herself showing signs of emerging Fae abilities, proposed a unified system for documenting and classifying new manifestations. "We cannot regulate what we cannot understand," she explained as probability fields rippled around her. "Each new enhancement expression must be cataloged and studied."

Power classification systems dominated the morning session. Traditional supernatural representatives argued for incorporating ancient magical hierarchies, while enhanced human delegates pushed for new frameworks based on quantum potential. The resulting compromise established flexible categories that could evolve with new manifestations.

Training standards emerged as a crucial concern. The Japanese delegation, drawing on their success integrating corporate enhancement programs with yokai traditions, presented a model for hybrid education. "We must prepare both traditional instructors and enhanced mentors to guide new manifestations," their enhanced representative explained while demonstrating controlled probability manipulation.

SUPERNATURAL INTEGRATION INITIATIVES

Recognition of traditional supernatural authority proved contentious. Ancient vampire houses demanded maintenance of their territorial rights, while enhanced human organizations pushed for access to previously restricted domains. The Romanian delegate, speaking for several European vampire councils, proposed adaptive jurisdiction based on probability resonance rather than traditional boundaries.

Modern governance integration sparked intense debate. Enhanced corporate representatives argued for private sector involvement in supernatural oversight, while traditional magical authorities emphasized the importance of ancient regulatory systems. The Chinese delegation presented their model of state-directed enhancement integration, triggering heated discussions about autonomy versus control.

Corporate oversight measures reflected the new reality of private enhancement research. Major corporations had already established extensive enhancement programs, forcing traditional supernatural authorities to adapt their ancient protocols. The Dubai delegate proposed a hybrid regulatory framework combining corporate innovation with supernatural wisdom.

SECURITY PROTOCOLS

Enhanced peacekeeping forces represented a major shift in international security. The UN Security Council outlined plans for hybrid response teams combining traditional supernatural abilities with enhanced capabilities. "Our peacekeepers must evolve beyond conventional forces," the French representative argued, her own enhanced diplomatic abilities evident in the quantum harmonics of her speech.

Reality stabilization teams became a priority as enhancement-related incidents increased globally. The Indian delegation, drawing on ancient mystical traditions, proposed combining traditional magical stabilization techniques with quantum containment technology. Their presentation demonstrated how enhanced teams could maintain dimensional integrity during supernatural events.

Cross-border incident response protocols reflected the new challenges of hybrid threats. Enhanced beings could traverse traditional boundaries through probability manipulation, requiring new approaches to territorial security. The Brazilian delegate presented case studies from the Amazon, where enhanced entities regularly crossed multiple jurisdictions.

FINAL RESOLUTION

As the emergency session concluded, Secretary-General Holmes called for a unified response to the enhancement crisis. "We must forge new paths of cooperation between traditional supernatural authorities, enhanced human organizations, and conventional government structures," she declared. "The future belongs to those who can adapt to this new reality."

The Assembly adopted a comprehensive framework for managing global enhancement evolution. Quantum-enhanced voting systems recorded both traditional and supernatural support for the measures. Reality anchors throughout the chamber stabilized as ancient powers and enhanced entities formalized their commitment to cooperative governance.

"This is not merely an emergency response," Holmes concluded as probability fields settled around the chamber. "We are establishing the foundation for a new world order - one that embraces both our super-natural heritage and our enhanced potential."

CHAPTER SEVENTY-SEVEN
NATURAL ORDER

Dr. Winters sat calmly in the quantum-shielded interrogation chamber; his transformed masculine form a testament to the artifacts' power. Through the observation window, Alice studied her former mentor as supernatural science experts gathered data on his stable hybrid state.

"The artifacts weren't meant to be contained," Winters spoke directly to Alice, ignoring the assembled officials. "They're remembering what reality allowed before the Great Sundering. My transformation is just the beginning."

"Your transformation was a choice," Alice countered, entering the chamber. "You forced it on three thousand others. The cascading effects are still spreading."

The Global Supernatural Sciences Committee had established emergency protocols in the wake of the Daybridge Evolution. Enhanced humans were being processed through specialized containment facilities, learning to control their hybrid abilities under joint supernatural-corporate supervision.

"We've identified seven major categories of hybrid transformations," Ethan reported, bringing up holographic data. "Physical metamorphosis, energy manipulation fusion, psychic-supernatural blending, quantum state shifting, multi-species manifestation, temporal ability merging, and reality perception enhancement."

Dr. Winters smiled at the classifications. "You're still trying to categorize the uncategorizable. Reality doesn't work in neat boxes anymore."

"No, but we need frameworks to help people understand their new abilities," Alice activated her quantum scanner. "The artifacts didn't just transform bodies - they rewrote the underlying rules of supernatural genetics."

The newly established Supernatural Sciences Division had authority over all enhancement research. Corporate labs were being retrofitted under joint supernatural-human oversight. The old barriers between scientific inquiry and supernatural knowledge had dissolved.

"Your containment protocols won't last," Winters observed. "Reality remembers. Each transformed individual becomes a catalyst for further change. The artifacts simply accelerated what was already happening."

"Which is why we're not trying to reverse it," Ethan brought up global monitoring data. "The new protocols focus on stabilization and integration. Training centers instead of containment facilities. Research partnerships instead of regulatory barriers."

Supernatural factions had assigned their most experienced members to help guide newly enhanced humans. Vampire elders taught energy control. Werewolf Alphas demonstrated physical transformation management. Fae courts shared centuries of knowledge about ability fusion.

"The natural order isn't what you thought," Alice confronted Winters. "It's not about unrestricted transformation. It's about understanding our potential while respecting individual choice."

"Choice?" Winters laughed. "You still don't see it. The artifacts didn't force transformation - they revealed what was always possible. Everyone at that summit had latent supernatural genetics. Reality just remembered how to express them."

The monitoring systems showed stabilizing patterns worldwide. Enhanced humans were learning control. Supernatural beings were adapting to hybrid abilities. Corporate research was yielding new insights into the quantum nature of transformation.

"The Supernatural Sciences Division will continue studying the artifacts," Alice declared. "But under strict ethical oversight. No more forced transformations. No more artificial limitations. We find the balance between potential and choice."

"You can't stop what's already begun," Winters remained confident despite his containment. "Reality is remembering. The artifacts were just catalysts. The true transformation is only beginning."

The global response networks activated as another wave of latent abilities manifested. But this time, protocols were in place. Training centers activated. Supernatural mentors deployed. Corporate resources mobilized to support stable integration.

"We're establishing a new natural order," Ethan observed, watching the coordinated response. "Not through forced evolution or corporate enhancement, but through understanding what reality allows when artificial barriers fall."

The Supernatural Sciences Division became the centerpiece of this new paradigm. Research facilities worldwide operated under joint oversight. Enhanced humans worked alongside supernatural beings to explore the quantum mechanics of transformation. Corporate innovation merged with ancient knowledge.

And in his quantum-shielded cell, Dr. Winters watched as his vision of unrestricted transformation gave way to something more sustainable - a world where reality's expanded possibilities were guided by choice, understanding, and respect for the natural order that had always existed beneath artificial limitations.

The age of forced enhancement was over. The age of guided transformation had begun. And as reality continued remembering what it used to allow, humanity and supernatural beings alike adapted to a world where the boundaries between possible and impossible had fundamentally shifted.

CHAPTER SEVENTY-EIGHT

CHOICE AND CONSEQUENCE - UNRAVELING THE DAYBRIDGE CATALYST

LOCATION: Maximum Security Quantum Containment Facility

Time: Six Months After Initial Enhancement Wave

The quantum containment field cast a pale blue light across Dr. Winters' features as Marcus Wong calibrated his enhanced perception settings. Reality stabilizers hummed along the reinforced walls, designed to prevent any probability manipulation by the facility's high-risk inmates. The interview chamber represented the pinnacle of hybrid containment technology - ancient ward magic merged with quantum stabilization fields.

"Dr. Winters," Marcus began, his enhanced senses tracking multiple probability streams of the conversation, "let's discuss your role in catalyzing global enhancement. The Daybridge Protocol wasn't just research, was it?"

Winters smiled, the expression carrying traces of the quantum resonance that had transformed him from brilliant researcher to worldwide catalyst. "You're asking the wrong question, Mr. Wong. The Protocol didn't create anything new - it simply revealed what was always possible. Every human carries supernatural potential in their quantum framework. We merely... accelerated the inevitable."

Marcus's quantum scanner recorded subtle fluctuations in the containment field as Winters spoke. Even imprisoned, his connection to probability fields remained detectable. "You triggered a worldwide transformation without consent," he pressed. "Billions of lives altered without warning or preparation."

"Consent?" Winters laughed, the sound carrying harmonic frequencies that made the containment field ripple. "Did humanity consent to evolution? Did we ask permission before developing consciousness? Some changes transcend individual choice."

"But your forced catalyzation created unprecedented chaos," Marcus countered, his enhanced perception detecting the weight of truth in his own words. "We've documented thousands of cases of unstable transformations, reality fractures in major population centers, complete collapse of traditional power structures."

"Necessary chaos," Winters replied, his eyes showing traces of quantum illumination despite the dampening field. "The old order was stagnant. Supernatural beings hoarding power while humanity remained ignorant of its true potential. We shattered those artificial boundaries."

Marcus accessed multiple probability streams, reviewing alternate timelines of natural enhancement evolution. "Natural integration would have been slower but more stable. Traditional supernatural communities could have guided the process, preventing the reality fractures we're still trying to contain."

"Stability is stagnation," Winters declared. "The quantum framework of reality itself demanded change. We simply provided the catalyst. Every transformed being, every new hybrid capability, represents potential that already existed. We didn't create - we revealed."

"At what cost?" Marcus challenged, projecting enhanced data streams showing global chaos in the wake of the Daybridge Event. "How many lives were destroyed by uncontrolled transformations? How many communities torn apart by sudden supernatural manifestations?"

Winters leaned forward, nearly touching the containment field. "Consider the alternative, Mr. Wong. Centuries more of supernatural suppression. Generations of humans denied their true potential. The cost of maintaining artificial limitations would have been far greater."

Marcus's enhanced abilities allowed him to process multiple aspects of the interview simultaneously:

"You speak of liberation," he noted, "but your actions removed choice from the equation. True liberation includes the right to remain unchanged."

"Choice is an illusion shaped by limited perception," Winters responded. "Reality remembers its potential. The transformations were always possible, always waiting. We simply aligned probability streams to manifest what was inevitable."

The interview continued as Marcus balanced his role as both journalist and enhanced being. His coverage helped shape public understanding through:

"The Daybridge Protocol wasn't just scientific research," he wrote in his global broadcast. "It was a deliberate attempt to force evolutionary change on a quantum level. The question remains: did the end justify the means?"

His balanced reporting acknowledged both the benefits and dangers of forced enhancement:

"While the Protocol unlocked unprecedented human potential, its uncontrolled implementation created global instability. The challenge now lies in managing these changes while preventing further reality fractures."

As the interview concluded, Marcus made one final observation: "You claimed to be liberating humanity's supernatural potential, but you imposed your vision of evolution without regard for consequences. True liberation would have allowed natural integration."

Winters' response echoed through quantum harmonics: "Nature isn't democratic, Mr. Wong. Evolution doesn't ask permission. The only choice that matters is how we adapt to inevitable change."

CHAPTER SEVENTY-NINE

NEW DAWN - GLOBAL TRANSFORMATION MANIFESTED

LOCATION: **Multiple Global Nexus Points**

Time: One Year After The Daybridge Event

TOKYO CONVERGENCE

In Shibuya's quantum processing center, kitsune-AI hybrids danced through digital landscapes, their ancient fox magic merging seamlessly with artificial intelligence networks. Enhanced technicians watched in awe as centuries of supernatural wisdom filtered through advanced neural networks, creating unprecedented synthesis of old and new.

Corporate shrines rose from Tokyo's steel canyons, their traditional architecture housing quantum servers where Shinto priests in business suits performed digital rituals. Data streams flowed through torii gates enhanced with probability field generators, blessing information packets with ancient protection protocols adapted for the modern age.

Salary workers accessing dragon memories during their morning commute became a common sight. Their enhanced consciousness touched centuries of accumulated wisdom while bullet trains traced ley lines beneath the city. Ancient dragons, having evolved beyond physical form, shared their knowledge through quantum networks, guiding humanity's enhanced evolution.

Reality barriers strengthened through careful application of traditional practices. Tea ceremonies incorporated quantum stabilization techniques, while martial arts dojos became centers for enhancement training. The careful balance of old and new created unique stability in Japanese probability fields.

LONDON TRANSFORMATION

The City's financial district shimmered with Fae energy as ancient courts established trading floors in quantum space. Enhanced brokers negotiated deals with sidhe lords, their probability calculations incorporating centuries of supernatural market manipulation experience. Glass towers reflected multiple realities as corporate and magical interests merged.

The London Underground evolved beyond physical transit, running probability trains through quantum tunnels that connected multiple versions of the city. Enhanced commuters could choose their preferred reality version, while station masters trained in both electrical engineering and reality manipulation maintained probability stability.

The Thames barrier hummed with new purpose, containing supernatural surge tides that threatened to reshape London's quantum landscape. Enhanced engineers worked alongside water spirits to maintain reality integrity along the river's course. Ancient London magic found new expression through modern enhancement protocols.

Corporate-magical hybrid zones spread through historic districts, old power merging with new purpose. The Tower of London became a quantum secure facility where enhanced guards maintained reality anchors protecting both physical and supernatural treasures. Westminster's ancient magic adapted to enhance modern governance.

DUBAI ASCENDANT

Djinn enterprises dominated quantum markets from glass towers rising from desert sands. Ancient spirits of fire and wind adapted their reality-bending abilities to modern finance, creating new forms of supernatural commerce. Enhanced traders accessed probability streams through traditional magical frameworks.

Desert ley lines powered smart city infrastructure; their ancient energy channeled through quantum conversion systems. Palm-shaped islands generated reality stabilization fields, while enhanced architects designed structures that existed simultaneously in multiple probability states. Traditional desert magic enhanced modern urban development.

Oil fields tapped deeper energy as enhanced extraction techniques accessed supernatural power sources. Ancient desert spirits negotiated with modern corporations, their combined influence reshaping regional power dynamics. Reality protocols adapted to incorporate both modern technology and ancient desert magic.

MOSCOW EVOLUTION

Enhanced oligarchs met with vampire councils in quantum-secured chambers, negotiating new power structures for the modern age. Centuries-old blood pacts evolved to accommodate corporate interests, while traditional supernatural authorities adapted to enhanced human capabilities. Ancient Russian magic found new expression through corporate enhancement programs.

The quantum weapons program operated under joint supernatural military oversight, combining traditional Russian magical practices with enhanced military capability. Ancient defensive spells merged with modern probability manipulation techniques, creating unique hybrid security measures.

Traditional power structures evolved as enhancement spread through both official and unofficial channels. The Kremlin's ancient magic adapted to quantum enhancement, while corporate-magical syndicates established new forms of influence. Enhanced bureaucrats processed probability streams through traditional supernatural frameworks.

GLOBAL SYNTHESIS

Each major city developed unique expressions of enhancement integration, creating a diverse global network of hybrid power centers. Traditional supernatural authorities adapted to enhanced human capability while corporate interests learned to navigate ancient magical protocols. The new dawn revealed a world transformed not through destruction of the old, but through unprecedented synthesis of ancient and modern power.

Reality itself settled into new patterns as enhancement evolution stabilized. Probability fields normalized around hybrid power structures that combined traditional supernatural authority with enhanced human capability. Corporate interests learned to navigate both modern markets and ancient magical obligations.

The world that emerged from the Daybridge Event demonstrated remarkable adaptability. Traditional power structures evolved rather than collapsed, finding new expression through enhancement capabilities. Ancient magic enhanced modern technology while corporate efficiency streamlined supernatural practices.

CHAPTER EIGHTY

TOMORROW'S REALITY - THE NEW NORMAL THROUGH ENHANCED EYES

Location: Daybridge Ground Zero

Time: Final Moments of Traditional Reality

Marcus Wong stood at the epicenter of transformation, his enhanced consciousness streaming directly into the global quantum network. Reality rippled around him like water disturbed by countless stones, each ripple representing another probability wave of change spreading outward from this focal point.

"This is Marcus Wong, reporting from where it all began," his voice carried quantum harmonics that enhanced viewers could perceive as colors beyond the visible spectrum. "The air here tastes like possibility, metallic and sharp, charged with potential that makes traditional sensors overload and fail."

His enhanced perception tracked multiple probability streams simultaneously, showing viewers the layered nature of their transforming world. Through his quantum-enhanced senses, the audience experienced:

The physical landscape shimmered with newfound depth - buildings existed in multiple probability states, their foundations anchored in traditional reality while their upper floors explored quantum variations. Streets pulsed with ley line energy that had laid dormant for centuries, now awakened by the Daybridge Event.

"We've moved beyond simple enhancement," Marcus explained, his consciousness extending through probability fields. "What we're witnessing isn't merely an expansion of human capability - it's a fundamental restructuring of reality's basic framework. The membrane between possible and impossible has become permeable, responsive to conscious intent."

His enhanced vision tracked probability waves rippling outward:

First wave: Individual enhancement manifestations, humans discovering supernatural potential encoded in their quantum framework.

Second wave: Reality framework adaptation, physical laws bending to accommodate enhanced consciousness.

Third wave: Synthesis of traditional and enhanced existence, creating new baseline normal.

"The transformation spreads in fractal patterns," he reported, his enhanced senses processing multiple information streams. "Each enhanced individual becomes a new probability nexus, catalyzing change in their immediate environment. Traditional reality frameworks adapt or dissolve, replaced by quantum-enhanced structures that can support our evolving existence."

Through his quantum-enhanced broadcast, viewers experienced the layered nature of their new reality:

Physical layer: Traditional matter and energy, now responsive to enhanced manipulation.

Probability layer: Quantum potential waiting to be shaped by conscious intent.

Enhancement layer: New capabilities emerging from human-supernatural synthesis.

Integration layer: Where all aspects merged into coherent new normal.

"Look there," Marcus directed viewers' attention to a group of children playing in a nearby park. Their natural enhancement capabilities manifested unconsciously, probability fields bending around them like light through crystal. "They don't distinguish between traditional and enhanced reality. For them, this is simply how the world works."

His enhanced perception tracked the children's casual reality manipulation:

A young girl reached through probability fields to catch a ball that existed in multiple states.

Two boys merged quantum signatures to create shared imaginative spaces.

A smaller child unconsciously stabilized local reality fields while drawing with chalk.

"This is the true significance of the Daybridge Event," Marcus explained, his consciousness expanding to encompass multiple probability streams. "Not just the enhancement of human capability, but the transformation of reality itself to accommodate our evolved potential. The question isn't whether we'll adapt to these changes - adaptation is already occurring on levels too fundamental to resist."

His enhanced senses detected the deeper patterns:

Reality frameworks restructuring to support enhanced consciousness.

Probability fields stabilizing around new patterns of existence.

Quantum potential becoming accessible to conscious manipulation.

"We stand at the threshold of tomorrow's reality," Marcus concluded, his enhanced broadcast carrying subtle harmonics that resonated with viewers' own evolving capabilities. "The membrane between what was and what could be has become permeable. We're not just observing change - we're becoming change itself."

As his final broadcast from Ground Zero concluded, Marcus experienced a moment of profound clarity through his enhanced perception: "The new normal isn't a destination we're approaching. It's a process we're becoming. Each enhanced consciousness contributes to the evolving framework of reality itself."

The quantum network hummed with response as viewers around the world processed his enhanced transmission. Through their own emerging capabilities, they recognized the truth in his words - reality itself had become responsive to conscious intent, and their collective evolution was reshaping the fundamental nature of existence.

$$\sim$$

EPILOGUE: LEGACY OF CHANGE

The quantum aurora painted Daybridge's transformed skyline in sheets of probability-warped light as Alice stood atop the Supernatural Sciences Division headquarters. Three hundred days had passed since the Evolution, each one bringing new manifestations of their changed reality. Her enhanced perception traced the city's quantum framework - a complex tapestry of old magic and new potential woven through every street and structure.

"Final numbers from the Integration Council," Ethan said, joining her at the observation deck. His tactical gear now incorporated both enhanced tech and traditional supernatural materials, reflecting their new hybrid world. "Over two thousand registered transformations worldwide this month alone. Slower than the initial wave, but steadier. Natural resonance instead of synthetic triggers."

Alice's scanner hummed, tracking the familiar patterns of the Shadow Market beneath the city's official channels. Enhanced executives moved through quantum-masked safe houses while underground networks helped newly transformed individuals stay off the grid. Each secured cache of synthetic formula seemed to spawn two more hidden labs, despite their best efforts at containment.

"They're adapting faster than our protocols," she noted, marking three major underground networks across the city map. "Hybrid abilities combining supernatural stealth with quantum manipulation. Traditional tracking methods can barely keep up."

The city below them pulsed with transformed life. Quantum resonance barriers shimmered between buildings, marking designated practice zones where newly enhanced humans trained under supernatural guidance. Fae-crafted containment fields had become permanent fixtures, while vampire-run blood banks expanded their services to accommodate hybrid metabolisms. Werewolf packs patrolled alongside enhanced security teams; their ancient instincts merged with modern tactical awareness.

"The Integration Center's first class graduates next week," Ethan said, his enhanced senses automatically harmonizing with Alice's familiar quantum signature. "Professor Luna Wolf says they're showing ability combinations we've never seen before. Reality itself seems to be evolving alongside us."

The Daybridge Evolution Festival preparations filled downtown with a vibrant mix of traditional supernatural culture and enhanced human potential. Food trucks offered everything from hemoglobin smoothies to moonlight-charged entrees while children with newly manifested powers played in quantum-stabilized adventure zones. Local businesses promoted "hybrid-friendly" services, adapting to their transformed customer base.

"I received Marcus Wong's latest documentary footage," Alice said, pulling up quantum-encrypted data streams. "He's tracking second-generation effects - natural ability fusion, spontaneous hybrid manifestation. The transformations are still spreading, but they're more controlled now. Reality adapting to its expanded possibilities."

In secure facilities worldwide, Dr. Winters and other key figures from the initial incident remained under observation. Their stable hybrid states provided crucial data for understanding long-term enhancement effects. The knowledge they had unleashed - synthetic formulas, quantum frameworks, hybrid catalysts - could be contained but never completely suppressed.

Sarah's quantum form shimmered into visibility beside them, her unique state bridging physical and energy-based existence. "Underground networks are calling it 'quantum liberation' now," she reported, her form solidifying enough to interact with their enhanced scanning equipment. "The idea that supernatural potential should flow freely, without corporate or government oversight."

The International Supernatural Integration Summit had established new frameworks for their transformed world - global enhancement monitoring systems, corporate-supernatural partnership guidelines, enhanced human rights accords. But the true changes happened at street level, where ancient magic and modern potential merged into countless unique expressions.

"We adapt," Ethan said simply, his hand finding Alice's as their enhanced energies synchronized automatically. "Keep official channels open, make registration attractive, maintain readiness for those who choose another path."

The sunset painted their transformed city in layers of quantum-shifted light. Below them, enhanced humans practiced their abilities under supernatural guidance while corporate executives attended hybrid integration seminars. Security teams patrolled dimensional boundaries as reality itself continued expanding to accommodate their evolved potential.

This was their new normal - a world where artificial limitations had fallen and the boundaries between human and supernatural grew increasingly fluid. The Daybridge Evolution had ended, but its effects continued rippling through every layer of existence. And somewhere in the quantum-masked shadows, unregistered enhanced humans pushed those boundaries even further, ensuring that their true transformation was far from complete.

Alice and Ethan watched their city shift through quantum possibilities, their enhanced perceptions tracking both registered and hidden signatures. Together they embodied this new paradigm - science and security, human and supernatural, order and potential. Partners in guiding their transformed world toward whatever reality might emerge, one enhanced individual at a time.

The age of unrestricted supernatural potential had begun. For better or worse, there was no going back. They could only move forward, adapting to each new expression of their expanded existence. And as the quantum aurora danced above them, Alice smiled, knowing that despite all their protocols and preparations, their greatest transformations likely still lay ahead.

ABOUT THE AUTHOR

Rae Stonehouse turned to fiction writing after establishing himself as a prolific author of self-development and professional growth books.

With over 50 published works helping readers navigate personal and professional challenges, he embarked on a new creative path with the Ethan Reeves Werewolf Detective Series.

When not weaving tales of supernatural sleuthing, Stonehouse continues to share his expertise in personal development through workshops and speaking engagements from his home in British Columbia.

The Ethan Reeves series marks his debut in fiction writing, blending his understanding of human nature with a newfound passion for urban fantasy.

~